*Is her perfect
match the husband
of her dreams…
or the lover
of her fantasies?*

D0207990

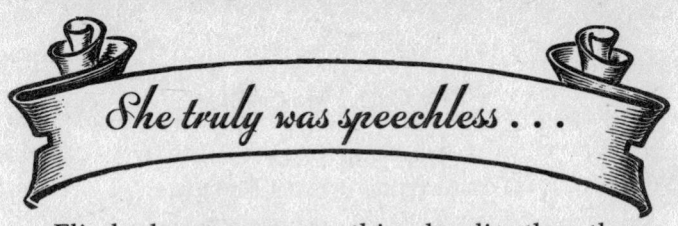
She truly was speechless . . .

Elin had never seen anything lovelier than these pearls. How could she have had doubts about this man? This marriage?

And she felt ashamed that she'd wasted her virginity on the wrong man. Tears filled her eyes.

"What have I done? Have I made you unhappy? You don't have to wear the necklace—" Gavin acted as if he would throw it back into the pouch.

Elin stayed his hand, catching him at the wrist. Her actions brought her closer to him. She could feel his body heat.

"The necklace is beautiful, Gavin. I'm just touched by your generosity. You honor me."

"You are to be my wife. I mean to honor you," he said. His gallant words went directly to her heart, even as his gaze shifted from her eyes down to her mouth.

She found her lips suddenly dry, too dry for a kiss, and she moistened them . . . an invitation.

"We are going to do very well together, Elin," he promised. He leaned toward her. Their closed lips met, brushed against each other, held sweetly for a second, then he drew back. Elin wanted to follow. Her breasts skimmed the material of his jacket, as her hand reached for his lapel for support.

That was not enough of a kiss. *More*, she wanted more. That tiny kiss did nothing save stir long-forgotten fires inside her . . .

By Cathy Maxwell

Marrying the Duke
THE MATCH OF THE CENTURY

The Brides of Wishmore
THE GROOM SAYS YES
THE BRIDE SAYS MAYBE
THE BRIDE SAYS NO

The Chattan Curse
THE DEVIL'S HEART
THE SCOTTISH WITCH
LYON'S BRIDE

THE SEDUCTION OF SCANDAL
HIS CHRISTMAS PLEASURE • THE MARRIAGE RING
THE EARL CLAIMS HIS WIFE
A SEDUCTION AT CHRISTMAS
IN THE HIGHLANDER'S BED • BEDDING THE HEIRESS
IN THE BED OF A DUKE
THE PRICE OF INDISCRETION
TEMPTATION OF A PROPER GOVERNESS
THE SEDUCTION OF AN ENGLISH LADY
ADVENTURES OF A SCOTTISH HEIRESS
THE LADY IS TEMPTED • THE WEDDING WAGER
THE MARRIAGE CONTRACT
A SCANDALOUS MARRIAGE • MARRIED IN HASTE
BECAUSE OF YOU • WHEN DREAMS COME TRUE
FALLING IN LOVE AGAIN • YOU AND NO OTHER
TREASURED VOWS • ALL THINGS BEAUTIFUL

CATHY MAXWELL

The Match of the Century

MARRYING THE DUKE

AVONBOOKS

An Imprint of HarperCollinsPublishers

AVON BOOKS
An Imprint of HarperCollins*Publishers*
195 Broadway
New York, New York 10007

First Avon Books mass market printing: December 2015

Avon Trademark Reg. U.S. Pat. Off. and in Other Countries, Marca Registrada, Hecho en U.S.A.
HarperCollins® is a registered trademark of HarperCollins Publishers.

Printed in the U.S.A.

10 9 8 7 6 5 4 3 2 1

For Pamela Jaffee
I've been waiting for the right book
to dedicate to you, and this is the one.
Although it doesn't have cats.
Should have thought to add cats.
Author note for next book!

The Match of the Century

In honor of

Miss Elin Morris

and her parents

Mr. and Mrs. Fyclan Morris

Gavin Whitridge,

the Duke of Baynton and Marcella,

The Dowager Duchess of Baynton

request your presence at a ball

Tuesday, 11 April, 1809.

Dances begin at 10 p.m.

An Announcement

of Great Importance

will be made before midnight.

A cold supper will be provided.

R.S.V.P. Menheim House

Chapter One

All of London, even down to the riffraff, already knew what the ball's special announcement would be. There was no mystery, although The Dowager Duchess of Baynton's guests would feign surprise when the moment for the announcement arrived.

They called it the Match of the Century.

Her son, the Duke of Baynton, London's richest and unarguably most handsome gentleman, would announce his betrothal to Miss Elin Morris, also known as the Morris Heiress, thereby uniting two great fortunes and two magnificent adjoining country estates in Leicestershire along the River Trent.

And the reason everyone anticipated the "announcement" was because it was a well-known fact that Elin had been promised to the duke almost since the day of her birth. Yes, she had been presented at Court and had gone through the motions of a First Season, but it had all been just a formality, a "show." The duke was hers. She had Baynton, the epitome of a lordly lord, the Nonpareil.

"And I am not *worthy* of him," Elin whispered, stopping the furious pacing she'd been at for the last ten minutes in an attempt to settle anxious nerves and a confused mind.

Her bedroom in her parent's London house was fit for a princess. The India carpet in hues of blue was thick and soft beneath her stockinged feet. Her furniture was gilded in the opulent manner her parents preferred.

Back in Heartwood, the Morris family estate, which adjoined the Baynton's family seat, the furniture in her room was simple and to her tastes. Here, her parents ruled. They were London creatures, darlings of society known for their generosity and deep, abiding love for each other.

And Elin? Well, their only child preferred the quieter life at Heartwood. Of course, all that would change when she became Baynton's duchess. He was too important to have his wife rusticate in the country.

She caught a glimpse of herself in her dressing-table mirror, a lone figure in finely woven petticoats, her face pale beneath a mop of overcurly brown hair. Her dark eyes reflected her agitation. They threatened to swallow her face.

"It's not that I don't want Baynton," she attempted to explain to her image. "It is that I *shouldn't* have him. Not without telling him—"

Her bedroom door flew open, interrupting her thoughts, and her mother, Jennifer Morris, sparkling in the famed Morris diamonds, swept into the room. Her dress was of Belgian lace dyed in her favorite shade of sapphire, a color that matched her eyes. Her honey blond hair betrayed barely a trace of gray. She glowed with eagerness for the evening ahead. She enjoyed crowds and being the center of attention. She had looked forward to this night for over twenty years, ever since the old duke of Baynton had suggested a match between their children.

Jenny shut the door and took in the situation in the room—Elin in her petticoats, her hair curling without a sense of order or style—and focused on the supper tray on the desk by the window overlooking the back garden.

"What is this? You haven't touched any of your food. Sarah said she encouraged you to eat, but I can see you haven't taken even a bite." Her mother approached her. Jenny was half a head taller than her daughter. She cupped Elin's face in warm, loving hands. The rose scent of her perfume swirled around them. "Elin, you must eat. This evening is all about you. You are going to be very busy tonight. So many people will beg your attention, you won't have time to sit, let alone enjoy a bit of supper. Cook prepared the chicken in that French cream sauce you like so much. And then, sweet bee, you need to finish dressing. In fact, while you are eating, let me call for Sarah to do your hair. We don't want to keep Baynton and his guests waiting—"

Elin caught her mother's hand before she could move away. "I can't do this. I thought I could, but I can't."

"*You can,*" her mother answered. "You were meant to do this. Born for it. Elin—" She paused, closed her eyes as if searching for the right words, or patience. When she raised her lashes, her expression was one of loving concern. "Elin, forgive yourself. You made a mistake. It shouldn't have happened, but it did. However, it was many years ago. What were you, fifteen?"

"I was to turn sixteen."

"So very young. How could you have known? You trusted Benedict. Your father and I trusted him."

"I was foolish." A hard lump formed in Elin's chest at the mention of Benedict Whitridge's name. Ben had been her closest friend, and he had taken what she should have protected—her virginity. He was also her betrothed's youngest brother.

Not only had the experience been painful and humiliating, he'd gone away the very next day. He'd left for a career in the military without a word of farewell. Or a warning that he was leaving, that he wouldn't be there to reassure her when she needed him most.

Her mother led Elin to her dressing table. She gently pushed Elin to sit on the bench, then knelt on the carpet in front of her, taking her hands and holding them.

"My daughter, we have discussed this. I thought you'd forgiven yourself. It was not a good incident in your life, but nothing terrible came of it."

"I have forgiven myself." Elin's voice sounded false to her own ears. "I just believe Baynton should know."

"That his *brother* took advantage of his betrothed? Is that what you want to tell him?"

"I wouldn't say who." Especially since Baynton and his brothers had shared a turbulent history.

There had been three Whitridge sons until Gavin's twin, Jack, had disappeared one night from Eton. Some claimed he had run off. Others believed foul play. No matter which, he was never seen or heard from again.

The disappearance had meant that the old duke had not wanted to let his third son meet the same end. Or have the same opportunity to escape. The old duke had been an exacting taskmaster.

He had high expectations for his heir. Ben often felt he was an afterthought. "A spare," Ben had always claimed, oftentimes bitterly. "Always kept at bay."

Because of Jack's disappearance, his father had kept him at Trenton, the family estate, and had him educated by a succession of tutors. Elin had been his sole companion.

As an only child of parents who were often in London, Elin had valued Ben's company. She'd trusted him and, to this day, could not believe he had taken her innocence to strike out at his oldest brother, as her mother had claimed. Then again, everyone knew the brothers were highly competitive. The old duke liked them that way.

However, to Elin, the loss of her purity was a small thing in the face of the betrayal of a trusted friend. She'd known he'd longed for independence. He'd yearned to buy his commission and set off into the world.

What she hadn't anticipated was that he would use her in such a deliberate way. That had seemed out of character. Her mother had assured her it was very much the nature of men and one of the reasons that, from now on, her parents would protect her more closely.

And so they had.

Elin was now three-and-twenty. Ben actually meant nothing to her save for a hard lesson learned.

She admitted to her mother, "Of the two brothers, I am marrying the best . . . but Baynton is known for his integrity. Is it wise to start a marriage with a deception?"

"And you could speak this honestly without telling the name of the man?" her mother repeated incredulously, then shook her head. "He would demand it or go mad with jealousy. Sweet bee, when a man's pride is on the line, he will move mountains to discover the truth. You know how single-minded your father can be."

Elin nodded. Fyclan Morris's story was well-known. He'd been an Irish nobody who had raised himself to the highest levels of society.

"Well, Baynton is even more so. Your honesty could destroy any chance you have at a happy marriage. He will not cry off. His honor won't let him. And this means so much to your father."

The marriage also meant a great deal to her mother as well. Jenny Tarleton had married beneath her.

Fyclan had been a man full of big dreams and confidence. He'd told her that his children were to someday be dukes and princes. His Romney grandmother had foretold it, and if Jenny ran away with him, if she eloped against her family's wishes, she would have no regrets.

And now, Fyclan was one of the most respected businessmen in London. Certainly, he was the wealthiest. Through Elin, the prophecy was about to be fulfilled.

"I know what this marriage means to you and Papa," Elin said as gently as she could. "However, I feel it only fair to tell Baynton of my indiscretion. I was foolish."

Her mother leaned forward. "My darling daughter, there isn't a woman alive who hasn't been foolish at one time or the other. You took it too far, but the simple truth is, you are not the first woman to go to her husband's bed after having lost her purity to another, and you will not be the last."

Elin knew this was true. She'd heard the other young women of her acquaintance whispering.

"Benedict is gone," her mother continued. "He is far away serving on some battlefield, plumping his vanity. He wanted to hurt his brother, and if you do tell Baynton what happened, then he will have succeeded."

For a moment, Elin sat silent. Then she pulled her hands from her mother's grip and turned on the bench to face her image in the mirror. Her expression had lost its haunted look. She lifted her chin with resolve. "Will you send for Sarah? I need to dress."

"Are you going to make a confession to Baynton?" Her mother rose to her feet.

"There isn't any sense to it, is there?"

Her mother kissed her on the top of her unruly curls. "Only the future matters, sweet bee. Baynton will make you a wonderful husband. Your son will be magnificent. Yes, I'll fetch Sarah, and don't forget to manage a bite or two."

She started for the door, but Elin had one last question, something she'd always wondered knowing how close her parents were. "Does Father know what happened between Ben and me?"

Her mother stopped at the door, one hand ready to turn the handle. "Men are not as wise about these matters as we women are. He would have called Benedict out. It would not do for a grown man to duel a seventeen-year-old boy."

She opened the door. "This is your night. Do not fear your destiny. Let this evening be one filled with the joy of an open heart. And when you walk into Menheim"—she referred to the Baynton's London home—"look toward the sitting room because someday soon, your portrait, the portrait of a young duchess, will grace the mantel there. The pictures of your children will line the walls around you. And Baynton will value you above all others." On those words, she left the room with perfumed grace.

Elin confronted herself in the looking glass. Since that fateful night, she'd lived a circumspect life. "My son will be a duke," she whispered, testing the words that filled her parents with confidence, and yet, she felt nothing.

However, when all was said and done, the least she could do was to please her parents, to make them happy. Baynton was a good man. She didn't know him well because he was so incredibly important, he was busy all the time, but she liked his mother. She respected Marcella and prayed she was half as dignified and good of heart as the Dowager.

A knock sounded on the door, and Sarah entered the room to help Elin dress.

Few women were as energetic as Marcella, The Dowager Duchess of Baynton. She was ten years Jennifer Morris's senior, but she appeared young enough to be her contemporary.

The Dowager's jewels of choice for the evening were her blood red garnets. They circled her throat, her wrists, and her fingers and stood out against silvery gray of her dress. In her white-blond hair, she wore a bandeau in garnet red. She appeared queenly and gracious, as was her welcome for her dearest friends in the upstairs sitting room reserved for family. They were not alone. The room was crowded with Baynton's relatives, some of whom Elin knew, but many she did not. The sound of the musicians tuning their instruments drifted up the stairs from the ballroom.

"Jenny, you are radiant," Her Grace said in greeting. "And, dear Fyclan, how handsome."

Elin's father did look good. He might not have been as tall as his wife, but there was a presence about him that made others take notice. Elin had gained the exotic shape of her brown eyes as well as her dark hair from him. His hair, once as black as a raven's wing, was now silver.

Surprisingly, the years had been unkind to him. He used a walking cane now and not just for effect. Elin and her mother both worried after him. He was a man who worked far too hard.

However, tonight was one for celebration. Fyclan offered the duchess the kiss of friendship. "You are stunning as well, Your Grace."

Marcella laughed, an expression that quickly took a dangerous turn toward tears. She pressed a gloved hand to her cheek. "I'm so sorry, Fyclan, it is nothing you said. My husband had so anticipated this evening and a wedding between our two families. You know how highly he thought of you?"

"I do, and I miss his friendship daily."

"Yes," the Dowager agreed and sent a sad smile in Elin's direction. "And here I haven't even told you how lovely you are, my Elin. You look like a young Helen of Troy," she declared. "The pale peach of that dress sets your skin off to perfection. Your mother and I knew it would when we saw it, and I so admire the bands of gold holding your curls."

Elin blushed with the compliment. But before she could respond, the duchess said quietly, "You and Gavin should have been married years ago. I feel so much regret over what happened."

Jenny rested a hand on her friend's shoulder. "My dear, it isn't your fault that your husband took ill. The marriage could wait until he was better."

"But he never became better." Again the duchess's eyes misted over the loss of her beloved husband. Elin and Gavin were to have been betrothed four years earlier, but the duke's illness and subsequent death, not to mention the challenges Gavin faced in assuming the duties of the title, had set back plans for a wedding.

"I'm sorry," Marcella apologized, taking a kerchief a footman offered and dabbing her cheeks, "for being a watering pot. I must stop this, or I will not make it through the night."

"We all understand how difficult it is," Elin's mother assured her.

"But John would have expected better of me." Marcella gathered herself with a sigh. "Here, I have not offered you anything in the way of refreshment—" she started but was interrupted by the appearance of her son in the doorway.

All the attention in the room went to *him*.

Gavin Whitridge, the Duke of Baynton, bounded into the room with his mother's energy. He was over six feet tall and had a smile that melted hearts. Dressed in his evening finest, he cut a figure that every dandy on the morrow would attempt to emulate and fail because the Duke of Baynton was truly that unique. That remarkable. That masculine.

He was known for his deep blue eyes, broad shoulders, square jaw, and the most perfect straight nose ever to grace a man's face. His thick hair was as black as night.

He was so completely an astonishing specimen of male beauty, Elin always felt a bit intimidated.

The crush of relatives moved forward, anxious to claim his attention, but then fell back when they realized he was searching for someone. His keen gaze fell on Elin.

He moved directly toward her. His gaze slid over her with appreciation, and he smiled. He liked her. He was pleased, and she was surprised at how his open admiration helped to settle her frayed nerves.

Gavin was nine years older than her and had thrown himself tirelessly into the duties of being a duke. Before his father's death, he'd been expected to deal with the minor responsibilities that had still kept him very busy. There had been times when he'd escorted her family to events, but the two of them had few opportunities to just talk or to relax around each other. There were expectations, just as there was now.

"You are beautiful," he said, his voice low. He held out his hand.

Elin found it hard to meet the intensity in his eyes. She offered him her gloved hand, but instead of bowing over it or even pressing a kiss to her fingers, he took her hand fully in his own. "Come." He started to cut through his relatives, pulling her toward the door

"Baynton," his mother said, "where do you believe you are going? We need to start the receiving line. And you haven't said a word of welcome to anyone else."

He laughed, the sound strong and sure. "Welcome," he announced with a wave as he continued guiding Elin to the door. "Go downstairs without us, Mother. We shall be there momentarily. I promise."

On those words, he hurried Elin across the hall to a wood-paneled library. The room was cozy and apparently also served as his office. The sounds of musicians beginning to play could not be heard here.

Baynton closed the door.

Self-conscious, Elin walked toward the desk. The walls were lined with overstuffed bookshelves. No wonder sound couldn't penetrate his sanctuary. There was a gilded clock on the mantel and a crystal-and-gilt inkpot and pen on the desk.

"Elin, face me."

She did as he requested.

Solemnly they studied each other. The anxiousness churning inside her began to slow.

He moved first, walking toward her, stopping when there was barely a foot between them. She had to tilt her head back to look at him. Seeing her do so, he sat on the edge of a leather upholstered chair, the sort men favored, to bring himself down more to her height.

"Are you ready for this, Elin?"

The question startled her. Did he have doubts? "I believe so, Your Grace—"

"Gavin. Call me Gavin." There was a beat of silence, filled only by the ticking of the mantel clock. Then, he said, "We are to be man and wife. I've waited for this time. I've longed for it."

She wanted to tell him that she'd waited for this moment as well, but shyness caught the words in her throat. Yes, shyness and also a bit of hope. What he was doing was good. Caring. She could love a caring man. She could love *him*.

And he wanted her.

Besides admiration there was an eagerness about him. An adorableness. She'd never seen this side of him or had ever imagined that he *wanted* to marry her. She had assumed his was nothing more than an obligation, an honorable one, but an obligation dictated by his father all the same.

Just as she'd been dictated to by her parents . . . however, now, her feelings shifted.

Elin kept such thoughts close. It was too soon for declarations of any sort.

Ben came to her mind . . . Ben and what she'd once believed was between them.

Gavin was not Ben, but let *him* be the vulnerable one, then she would know she was safe.

He didn't seem to be put off by her reserve. Instead, he gifted her with another of those smiles, this one making her almost sway with dizziness over how blinding it was. He pulled a velvet pouch from the inside of his black evening dress jacket.

"My father gave this necklace to my mother." He opened the pouch and poured into his hands a string of creamy pearls. "He said it had once belonged to Mary Stuart. His intent was that it be worn by the brides of Baynton. Would you honor me and my family by accepting this gift and wearing it this evening?" He stood, setting the pouch on the chair and holding the necklace out to place it around her throat. "May I?"

Now Elin truly was speechless. She had never

seen anything lovelier than these pearls. How could she have had doubts about this man? This marriage?

And she felt ashamed that she'd wasted her virginity, the only thing that had been truly hers to give to her husband, on the wrong man. Tears filled her eyes.

Even though she blinked them back, Gavin noticed immediately. "What have I done? Have I made you unhappy? You don't have to wear the necklace—" He acted as if he would throw it back in the pouch.

Elin stayed his hand, catching him at the wrist. Her actions brought her closer to him. Her skirts brushed his legs. She could feel his body heat. His shaving soap was spicy, masculine. She liked it.

"The necklace is beautiful, Gavin. I'm just touched by your generosity. You honor me. You honor my family." And the latter meant more to her than the former.

"You are to be my wife. I mean to honor you," he said. His gallant words went directly to her heart even as his gaze shifted from her eyes down to her mouth.

She found her lips suddenly dry, too dry for a kiss, and she moistened them . . . an invitation.

He smiled. This time, his smile was not blinding, but admiring. When he looked at her like this, she really did feel lovely. "We are going to do very well together, Elin," he promised. "I'm going to kiss you."

"I know." Her voice had gone low and husky.

"Good," he replied. He drew a breath and leaned toward her. Their closed lips met, brushed against each other, held sweetly for a second, then he drew back. Elin wanted to follow. Her breasts skimmed the material of his jacket, as her hand reached for his lapel for support. That was not enough of a kiss. *More*, she wanted more. That tiny kiss did nothing save stir long-forgotten fires inside her . . . *fires she had once discovered with Ben—*

The door to the library flew open and crashed against the wall.

The duke and Elin both jumped in surprise. Gavin placed himself between Elin and the door, the pearls still in his hands.

"Your Grace," Sawyer, the Menheim butler was babbling from the hallway, "I am sorry you are bothered. I tried to stop him. He refused to listen to me."

"Stop *me*?" the uninvited guest repeated. "From seeing my own *beloved* brother?" There was no love in that hard tone.

Brother? It couldn't be. Elin bent to see around Baynton.

It *was* him.

Benedict Whitridge, Lord Ben as he was known around Menheim, or Major Whitridge in his other life, stood in the doorway, his uniform disheveled by travel and his manner one of such anger, he appeared ready to launch himself at his brother.

But those were only surface changes.

Elin found herself shocked by the deeper changes. He was taller than his brother now and his shoulders as broad except that he had retained the lean physique and long muscular thighs of the horseman he'd once been. There were lines at the corners of his eyes as if he'd spent hours squinting into the sun or laughing. The smooth skin of his boyhood had given way to a day's growth of beard along the line of his hard jaw.

And his brows were thicker, more animated. Elin had always enjoyed Ben's brows because they said louder than words exactly what was going on in his mind. Right now, they punctuated the vivid intelligence in eyes that were a lighter hue than the duke's.

Of the two brothers, Gavin was definitely the more classically handsome. Still, each was the sort of man whose presence could fill a room.

However, while Baynton was known *for* his sterling character, Elin remembered how Ben had charmed her *with* his character, his humor, his witticisms over comings and goings of those around them. He'd made her laugh.

Until the day he didn't.

Until the day he'd broken her young, trusting heart.

Gavin tucked the pearls into his pocket. "It is all right, Sawyer. Please see to my guests. And as for you, *brother*, we will discuss anything you wish *later*. Right now, I am expected downstairs." He spoke with the cool dismissal of a man accustomed to being obeyed.

In answer, Ben slammed the door shut. "Your guests will wait, *brother*. We talk *now*."

Chapter Two

$\mathcal{L}$ord Benedict Whitridge—now Major Whitridge of his majesty's army—had never intended to cross Menheim's threshold again.

He'd been done with his family, content with his military career—until Gavin ruined it.

And he took great pleasure watching his brother's face shift from shock to outrage that anyone would dare to speak to him in such a manner.

Was it sane to attack Gavin? No, but Ben was beyond sanity. "You destroyed everything I'd built for myself. Everything I valued."

"I didn't—" Gavin started, but Ben was not ready for excuses and platitudes. He already suspected his brother's motives, and he hated them.

"I had a *career*, respect," Ben bit out. "I was a *warrior*."

"I know. I received reports. You are well thought of—"

"Then why did you order me home? Why did you end it?"

Gavin's gaze grew sharp, unyielding. His spine stiffened. He was the duke. Dukes did not explain themselves.

Ben had to step away, struggling with the urge to reach out and choke a reaction out of his brother. Gavin could not force him to accept his dictates—except he had.

"Undo it," Ben ordered. "Undo what you did. You had them remove me from my command, from the service, from everything that meant something to me. Now tell Whitehall, you made a mistake. You interfered where you shouldn't have. You want to have my dismissal overturned. You have that power, Baynton. Exercise it."

"I can't. This country is at war," Baynton answered, as if that should explain everything.

"We've been at war for most of the last fifty years. Father knew that when he sent me off."

"However, *I* will not have you in harm's way. I need you, Ben. The title needs you."

"The title? The *bloody* title?" Ben wanted to put his fist into the wall. "Is that all you think about? This is *my* life, Gavin." Ben hit his chest hard. *"Mine.* Not yours. I know you have the bloody power to do whatever you please. You and father are lions in the same den on that matter, but I have the right to be my own man."

"And I must protect the title." Gavin took a step toward him, which right now was not the wisest thing to do. "I need you, Ben," he said, his tone low, conciliatory. "If something happens to me, you must know what to do."

"Why?" Ben was genuinely confused, and that was when he noticed Elin.

For a moment, his mind reeled as he recognized her, as he realized what was happening.

From the moment he'd been ordered into his commander's tent and relieved of his men, Ben's whole being had been in turmoil. He'd been in charge of an infantry division and had been eagerly awaiting the return from London of his friend Lieutenant General Arthur Wellesley, who had recently been named the new commander of all British forces in Portugal.

Ben had been part of the drubbing the British had received at Corunna several months ago. He was not one who liked retreating. Having served with Wellesley in both India and on the Peninsula, he felt the right man was finally leading the battle against the French.

Furthermore, Wellesley had written Ben personally, informing him of his return and promising a promotion to lieutenant colonel as soon as the general set foot in Portugal. Since Ben had refused his family's help in purchasing his commissions and had to earn them on the battlefield, this was the opportunity for which he'd waited.

All of that was gone now. When he'd protested his being relieved, he'd been informed at headquarters that he was being ordered to resign because of national interest. They didn't explain what they meant, but Ben knew. Gavin wanted him home, and it didn't make sense.

Ben had walked out of headquarters that day and, without stopping, had marched for the nearest ship heading to London. There was actually the possibility that his ship and Wellesley's had passed each other on the Channel.

And all Ben wanted was to return to his men, to lead his troops, except here was Elin.

Elin.

He remembered her as a girl. He was shocked to see her a woman—although her impact on him had not changed. There had been a time when she'd been all he could think about. He'd had to work to erase her from his mind. He'd forced himself to let her go.

Now he realized he'd forgotten nothing.

He took a hesitant step toward the door. He'd been so intent in hunting Gavin down, many important details hadn't registered with him. They did now.

The duke was hosting a ball. Ben had rarely seen the house lit up the way it was this evening. It had been prepared for a truly memorable occasion. The foyer had been full of people dressed in their finest, and the musicians played with great vigor

And here was Elin. She, too, wore her best.

Maturity had added to her beauty. She had always reminded him of the wood sprites his Nan claimed inhabited the forests around Trenton. Elin was delicate, finely made, and yet full of spirit.

Her maid had attempted to tame the glorious curls of her hair to make her more acceptable to London society. They must have had a time of it. He remembered the way her curls would escape her braid and frame her face or her hair's heavenly mass when she'd worn it down.

However, the biggest change were her curves, the divine swelling of her breasts and the shadow through the gauzy material outlining her waist and legs.

Memory is a tricky thing. Yes, he could recall covering those breasts with eager hands. He also remembered his father horsewhipping him and, of course, the banishment . . .

Ben groped for his anger, surprised it could have dissipated so completely, diverted by Elin's presence. Why was he stunned to find her here?

He shouldn't have been. She was Gavin's. She'd always been meant for the duke. She'd told him often enough.

"I suppose the two of you are married."

He sounded harsh. He felt harsh.

"Tonight's the betrothal ball," Gavin answered. "We postponed the marriage when Father died. It took me a bit more time than anticipated to make the transition."

"Well, that explains all the nonsense downstairs."

Elin had not spoken. Ben was having difficulty keeping his gaze away from her. *Be angry. Stay angry.*

His brother came forward, blocking Ben's view of Elin's petite figure. "I'm glad you are here."

"I *don't* want to be here." There it was, his temper. He found his footing again. "And if you are marrying, what is this talk about needing me? Within the year, you will have begat a little duke with a host more to come. I'm *temporarily* your heir. You don't need me."

"No one knows what life holds," his brother answered. "After all, we didn't expect Father's death. He had been a healthy man, a strong one, yet he was gone before we knew it. I could meet my death on the morrow, or before Elin bears a child, then you will need to understand the demands of the title."

"You might meet your death right this minute,

brother, if you do not reverse what you did to me. I have no desire to be Baynton."

For a long second, the duke took his measure. He was known for his ability to read men. They said he was more skillful than even his father had been. Ben thought it pig swill.

"I can't," Gavin said at last. "Whether nothing happens to me before Elin bears my heir, or if she gives me a host of sons, someone I trust must be on hand to guide the next duke in my stead. That is you, Ben. You are the only one I can trust. If I could give you back your command, I would. However, you are needed here."

"To do what? Wait upon your death? I'm a man, Gavin, not a lapdog."

"I am aware I ask a high price," his brother answered, finally showing annoyance. "If Jack were here, this would be his role. But he is not, and so it falls to you."

"His role?" Ben echoed. "To wait in case I'm needed? To twiddle my thumbs at garden parties while you attend all the important meetings? To be a gentleman? To hop to your bloody orders? No wonder Jack ran."

"He didn't run. He wouldn't do that."

Ben gave a sharp bark of laughter. "Oh, yes, he would, Gavin. I remember the rows he had with Father. He didn't want what was planned for him any more than I do." He took a step forward. "You don't need me, Gavin. You are not going to die anytime soon."

A shadow crossed his brother's face. "You don't know any such thing."

"I'm fairly certain," Ben answered. "You look hale and hearty, and I see no reason for me to lose what I've built for myself because you have grown maudlin over Death."

That barb hit its mark.

"I'm not maudlin. I'm practical," Baynton said, his manner changing from brother to lord. "I accept you do not approve of my decision. However the matter has been settled. Prepare yourself, Ben. Your education is about to start."

"My brother, if you do not let me return to the war, then I'll be the one to teach you a thing or two. You are not Father, and I'm not some docile lad to be led by my nose. I'll *not* be the man *you* want me to be. You worry about the havoc of death on the title? You'd best start worrying about the devilment I can raise."

"The title is our family responsibility—" Gavin started, sounding like the bloody prig he was.

Ben cut him off. "*You are a damn fool.* And yet, I, of all people, understand why. Father molded you into the man he wanted you to be. You have no idea what it is like to live completely for yourself. You are full of shoulds and should nots. Be careful, the weight will crush the life out of you, but

I will not let it have me. Do you understand? I'm not a bloody sheep."

"Neither am I."

Gavin took a step forward. They were very much alike, Ben realized suddenly, both sons of their father. Neither would back down. Gavin proved him right by saying, "I have had your commission recalled. You have been dismissed from the military. I give you this evening to come to your senses and realize your responsibilities. We shall discuss this matter further on the morrow."

"There is *nothing* more to discuss," Ben returned, his fury with his brother's high-handedness simmering under every word.

"So be it." Gavin turned to Elin. "I'm sorry you were a witness to this, but it could not be avoided." He offered her his arm. "Shall we join our guests? It is past time."

"Yes, yes, please," Elin murmured. She placed a gloved hand on his offered arm. Gavin led her to the door as if she was a special prize—and she was.

At one time, she'd been everything to Ben.

But she hadn't been his. Except for one night.

Had his father been right? Had he wanted her for no other reason than to spite his brother?

Right now, Ben wasn't certain of the answer.

The door clicked behind them as they left the room.

Ben was alone. Alone and dressed in a uniform that was no longer his honor to wear.

His brother was bringing him back to where he did not want to be. And Elin was a symbol of all that. But she had changed. The woman he had just met was not the companion of his youth. That girl would have rallied to his cause. She would have dared him to stand up for what he believed right.

But she'd sold her soul to be a duchess. Baynton's duchess.

She hadn't even glanced at him as she'd left.

Ben walked over to several decanters on a table by the desk. He poured a very healthy glass and downed it.

This was going to be a long night.

Elin felt ready to collapse, and not from nerves over the evening ahead.

Her head reeled from Ben's sudden reappearance in her life, especially at this moment. She didn't know what to think, especially after witnessing the argument between the brothers. She felt she'd just witnessed a clash of Titans.

And the row didn't seem to bother Baynton at all. He'd returned to the eager man he'd been before Ben's intrusion. He even stopped at the top of the stairs and pulled the pearls from his pocket. "May I?" he asked.

Elin dutifully allowed him to fasten the strand around her throat.

"Beautiful," he murmured. He raised his gaze from the necklace to her face. "You are beautiful." He leaned forward as if to kiss her again, and Elin felt a moment of panic.

What if Ben came out into the hall? What would he think?

Why should she care?

"Ben is very angry," she heard herself say.

Gavin pulled back, concern crossing his face. "I'm sorry you witnessed the argument. My brother is headstrong."

"So are you."

Her comment appeared to startle him, then he laughed. "I was told you speak your mind. I don't mind that. Don't worry about Ben. He will come to his senses." He spoke with confidence.

Elin wasn't so certain.

"Your Grace, are you ever coming down?" a laughing male voice called. It was echoed by several others who were crushed into the front hall, waiting for their turn at the receiving line. Elin and the duke's presence at the top of the stairs had been detected.

Gavin knew who had called out. Taking Elin's arm and escorting her down, he said, "I can't believe you would begrudge a man a sweet moment when he has a lovely woman on his arm, Rovington." Lord Rovington was one of Baynton's closest friends.

Elin blushed at the compliment, yet felt ill at ease. She'd never been one who craved attention. Now, all eyes were on her as they reached the lower stairs. She could feel them evaluating the truth of his claim. Was she lovely? Even pretty? Elin could see the verdict in the side glances the women cast toward each other.

Baynton was immediately swamped by his guests, who included all the most important people in government and society. They came at him from all sides, wanting his attention.

Even during the receiving line, they pressed him with concerns, using this opportunity for their own purposes. He handled them effortlessly. He remembered names and graciously included Elin in conversations. Of course, sometimes, he used her as a foil to move certain people on their way.

She understood her role. She smiled and nodded. This was the part of Society she did not enjoy. It felt superficial. Her mother had chided her for expecting too much, and perhaps she did.

However, in truth, Elin had never minded the country dances in her parish back in Heartwood, but a London ballroom was different. She'd learned that during her first season. While her parents might thrive on the press of people in Town and the opportunities presented, Elin fought an urge to hide . . . especially this evening.

Many of the smiles directed at her were not sincere, especially those from marriageable young women who would have adored catching a prize like Baynton. Even the daughters of her cousin Robbie Morris, who served as her father's secretary, could not hide their envy.

It was a bit overwhelming.

Elin's smile began to feel plastered to her face. She couldn't relax because guests kept coming through the door.

Finally, thankfully, Marcella whispered in Gavin's ear. He excused himself from the receiving line. "We must start the dancing," he apologized to those who had not yet gone through the line. He took Elin's hand.

Her heart pounding, she followed him to the dance floor. Other couples quickly helped make up the pattern, and, at Baynton's signal, the musicians began playing.

Elin had practiced for this moment, months, weeks, *hours* of practice. Her dancing master had declared it would be nice if the duke could just once join them in their lessons. That had not been possible. Baynton was too busy for something as frivolous as a dance lesson.

However, he quickly demonstrated he didn't

need the lessons. He had the gift of athletic grace and did not seem rattled by having all eyes on them. Indeed, he'd spent most of his life being the one everyone watched.

Elin was not that certain of herself. Fortunately, she acquitted herself well enough although she was relieved when the music ended.

Gavin bowed over her hand and kissed her fingers, with everyone watching. A murmur of jealous approval ran through the female guests as fluttering fans were raised to hide any other comments they wished to make. Elin wanted to pretend she didn't notice. Her mother had always urged her not to be so sensitive to the moods of others, but then her mother was a social creature. Elin needed to contrive to be more like her.

"Let me take your to your parents," Gavin said, his voice low in his ear as he leaned toward her to be heard. His hand went to the small of her back to guide her. It was a small gesture, a surprisingly intimate one, and she found herself slipping her hand around his arm to break it—whether from shyness or embarrassment she could not say.

They had traveled only a few feet before Sir William Johnson, a gentleman who often came to her father for advice, begged for a moment of Gavin's time on a "delicate matter of state."

If Gavin was annoyed by the intrusion, he gave no sign.

"One moment," Gavin said as if he already knew what Sir William wanted. "Meet me in the library."

"I'll inform the prime minister."

"And the prince," Gavin said. He referred to the Prince of Wales, who was holding court by the punch bowls.

"I don't know if he will join us."

"He will. Tell him *I* wish him there," Gavin answered. "Come, Elin." Once more, he took her arm, but his attention was claimed several more times before they reached their mothers.

"The two of you are a remarkable couple," her mother answered.

"Miss Morris adds to my luster," the duke replied. "She is all I could wish for. Now, I'm terribly sorry, but you must excuse me. Mrs. Morris, Mother, Miss Morris." He said her name with just the right touch of heat before leaving them.

Elin watched him go, his tall figure standing out in the crowd. People called to him, begged his attention, wanted a moment with him. She overheard a woman not far from her mention to her companion, "Of course, theirs is the match of the century. Two very wealthy people becoming *more* wealthy. How can it be better?"

Had the woman meant for her voice to carry? Or was Elin too attuned to what people thought of her?

She looked to the Dowager, who appeared completely at ease. "Is it always like this?"

Marcella took in the press of people gathered around them. "Usually."

Her mother made a dismissive sound. "Elin, you have experienced this with your father. You understand that more work is done at events like this than in the hallways of government."

"I do," Elin answered, but she was lying.

Furthermore, she'd not been around Baynton often. During her Season, the most natural time for her to enjoy the duke's company at soirees and balls, the old duke had taken him traveling with him. They had been in Belgium, she remembered.

Shortly after the trip, his father had taken ill. Things like marriages had been postponed, then there was the period of mourning. Elin had actually been content to return to Heartwood and the country life she enjoyed.

Now, for the first time, she wondered what sort of marriage they would have. Her father was a busy man but devoted to his wife and made time for Jenny. His business dealings took second place and, however much he doted on Elin, she was the third in his sense of priorities.

Watching Baynton disappear into an adoring crowd, Elin wondered where she would rank with him?

A stray thought also asked if Ben had returned

to see his father before he passed? She'd not seen him at the funeral. Of course, there had been so many in attendance, it would have been difficult to lay eyes on every one of them.

But she would have noticed Ben . . . wouldn't she? Wouldn't he have been in the front, with the family? Or would he have hidden himself away?

Her father interrupted her worries by coming to her side. "You have made us very happy this night," he said. He gave her a fatherly kiss on the cheek and plunged into the conversations around them.

Very soon, their small group expanded. Her parents had many friends. Marcella was popular in her own right as well as being the hostess.

Elin understood why her mother had wanted her to eat. Everyone tried to include her in their conversations while they carefully watched her. Judged her. Many guests wanted the opportunity to claim on the morrow that they had met her, that they had danced with her or talked to her.

Elin began to feel like a garden statue on display. She understood now why Marcella valued her mother's friendship. In the world of London society, it was genuine.

The hour was approaching midnight. Gavin had not yet returned from wherever he was. The Dowager did not appear concerned. Elin was. She longed for a moment of respite and found the banalities she uttered or that were uttered to her boring. Gavin understood these people. He would shepherd her with his easy laugh and confident authority.

Even her parents were too busy to do other than smile indulgently at her as she was led to the dance floor by eager gentlemen wishing to impress her future husband or her wealthy father. She no longer tried to remember the names of Lady This or Lord That who were introduced to her. Her ability to feign interest was waning.

And then the evening turned.

Was it her imagination or had a hush settled over the ballroom? She glanced around and saw why—Lord Benedict Whitridge had arrived.

Since he was taller than his brother, he was easy to spot.

Since he was still in his travel-stained uniform, he stood out.

Since he hadn't had time to shave, he appeared grubby in the midst of such elegant company.

And he was heading directly for her.

"Is that my son?" Marcella asked. She moved to stand beside Elin. "I didn't know he was here."

Her statement, for an inexplicable reason, incensed Elin. Did Ben believe he could do whatever he pleased to anyone he wished? Was he just insensitive to everyone?

Apparently so, because when he stopped in

front of Elin and his mother, his breath was foul with whisky although he stood straight and tall. "My mother," he said with a stiff bow.

"I did not know you had returned," she answered, and took a step toward him as if wishing to wrap her arms around him.

Ben pulled back slightly, and Marcella's hands dropped to her side. "I'm surprised my brother didn't tell you to expect me."

He sounded cold, cruel even.

And then he shocked everyone by taking Elin's hand. "Come with me." He didn't wait for assent but pulled her after him through the crowd.

Shocked, Elin started to put up resistance but caught her mother's eye and saw her small shake of the head, a warning not to encourage a scene.

So Elin followed his lead, but she was furious. How dare he present himself this way? He was making a mockery of everything, including his mother.

And when she saw that he was not taking her to the dance floor but moved toward the portico door leading to the garden, she almost raced him for it.

For eight years she'd been waiting to tell him a thing or two. Her meager supply of goodwill toward him had been depleted by his callous, boorish behavior. Did he think Gavin had given him a set down?

He hadn't experienced anything yet.

In fact, the ballroom full of people, the importance of the evening, everything faded from her mind at the thought of finally having the confrontation she'd yearned for since he'd discarded her years ago as if she were used goods.

A footman standing by the door saw their approach and opened it. Elin flew into the garden. Ben was on her heels.

She marched across the stone terrace. Paper lanterns hung gaily around the terrace. Several couples were enjoying the evening air. Elin did not want witnesses to what was about to happen.

Now she understood why she'd been unsettled all evening. Ben's presence ruined everything. He'd been in the back of her mind whether she could have acknowledged that fact moments ago or not.

She would have her say, and when she was done, she was going to take herself back into the ballroom to stand beside her betrothed as the announcement was made. Gavin was a good and noble man; Ben was a scapegrace, a rascal, a no-good friend. The latter was the worst charge she could level against him. The *worst*.

Elin went down the terrace steps and out into the darkness of the garden. There was a rose arbor there, surrounded by tall shrubs that offered privacy. When she felt those staring after them on the terrace could not see their actions, she whirled on Ben so quickly, he almost ran into her.

And then she did something she'd longed to do for years. She slapped the side of his stubbled jaw with all the force in her small being.

There was a loud, satisfying sound of flesh hitting flesh. Then a pain, the likes of which she'd never known, shot through her hand to her shoulder.

Chapter Three

*B*en was drunk.

His father had always stocked the library with choice whisky, and his brother had apparently—thankfully—maintained the practice. The golden brown fluid in the decanter had been an elixir from the gods to a man who had traveled as far as Ben had, to a man whose goals, hopes, and dreams had been dashed and a bleak future lay ahead, to a man who had come face-to-face with the only woman who had ever mattered to him.

He'd thought he'd accepted that he couldn't have Elin. A man moved on, something that was vastly easier to do when oceans and countries were between them.

Ah, yes, and with the passage of time. Ben had counted on time being his strongest ally. He had been wrong.

Having his career terminated, finding himself summarily dismissed as if the sweat, the work, the sacrifices he had made for his country meant nothing—all of it had evaporated in Elin's presence, and he'd become a boy again. A boy who had been half-mad with lust for her.

And what struck him during his third glass of whisky was that she wasn't completely out of his grasp—not until the announcement was made.

Perhaps Fate was not being unkind. Perhaps the military dismissal was part of the plan of a benevolent God. Mayhap Ben was receiving a chance to make amends.

But Elin was obviously not happy with him.

She had just slapped him with all the passion in *her* being. He knew she'd given it her all because she grabbed her hand at the wrist in pain.

Uncertainty started to sober him.

The night came into focus and with it awareness. "Did you hurt yourself?" He moved toward her. "I'm sorry." He sounded boozy. He needed to gather himself.

She took a step back, warning him off, and helped his sobriety by announcing, "*You* stink."

"What?" Ben wasn't certain he heard her correctly.

Her hand still around her wrist, she clarified for him. "You *smell*."

He did. Now that she had brought it to his attention, he could smell his own person. There was the stench of travel, of the horses he'd ridden, of the salt in the sea air, of the rotting wood and foul fish, and just being a man. He was a reeking gallant charging forth to save her.

And perhaps that was not the wisest way to win his case.

He *should* have bathed before presenting himself to her, but Ben had never lived his life according to what he "should" do. Furthermore, strong drink had taken priority over sanity. Otherwise, he would have been in danger of throttling his brother, and it was never wise to throttle a duke. They had minions. He didn't.

However, it was unkind of her to make the remark. Her verdict stung already damaged pride.

Ben caught himself swaying slightly and squared his shoulders to stand erect. "Dear Elin, always saying exactly what is on her mind without a filter."

"*You* have a filter?" she countered coolly, releasing a hold on her hand, a sign she would survive striking him.

Touché. Had he truly forgotten how sharp her tongue could be?

He matched her tone. "You are too small to do any true damage to me with only your hand, if that was your intent. The next time you decide to slap me, may I suggest you use a book. A good heavy one."

"Let me go to the library then," she answered stoutly, and started for the house.

Ben hooked his hand in her arm and swung her around. The rose arbor gave them some privacy, and he wasn't ready to leave it.

"I must talk to you," he confessed.

She pulled away, but he felt her change, soften. Perhaps she was curious as to what he would say. Perhaps she cared more than she was allowing.

However, at that moment, they heard an intruder. "Elin," her father's low voice called.

She looked to the sound, then back at Ben. Her eyes shone in the moonlight but gave away none of her thoughts. "We are here, Father."

A beat later, Fyclan Morris came into the shadows of the arbor. He'd aged quite a bit since Ben had last seen him. Fyclan had been a witness as Ben had been marshaled toward a waiting coach and so had begun his military career. He had no complaint against Morris. If Ben had a beloved daughter of whom he expected great things, he would have done more than watch the randy bugger be hustled out of the country.

Morris did not glance at Ben. "Your mother requests your return to the ballroom. There are some people she desires you to meet. Baynton may also come looking for you."

Ben expected her to leave him. He stood, his arms at his side, feeling useless. Once again, his brother won the girl without even having to be present. It must be good to be a duke—

"Tell Mother I will return momentarily," Elin said, surprising Ben. "Lord Benedict and I are putting our heads together over a special treat for the duke. There is no other time to discuss our ideas."

"I don't believe you should be out here alone with him," her father answered.

"No, perhaps I shouldn't . . . but I am. Please, Father, I need this moment. Mother will understand."

Under the flickering light of a yellow paper lantern, Ben could see Morris's indecision. *Mother will understand.*

To Ben's surprise, Morris backed down. "I shall wait for you on the terrace."

"Thank you," she said.

Morris walked away, leaning heavily on his walking stick.

"Gout," Elin said, as if anticipating Ben's question. "He suffers terribly from it. Mother and I worry about him. He throws himself into his business interests with all of his being and doesn't take time for his health."

She'd moved so that now she stood in the lantern's light. Her father could see her from his vantage point. Actually, anyone could see her and possibly believe after the haste they had left the ballroom that there might be truth to her story of planning a "something special" for Baynton.

"Such a sweet bride thing to do," he murmured, his jealousy making his speak aloud.

"Is that it? Is that what you wished to say to me?" She shook her head as if he'd played her for a fool. "I *should* go inside—"

"Mouse, wait—"

She cut him off. "I detest that nickname."

He knew that and yet, she had never protested too hard when he'd used it. Sometimes she'd even referred to herself by the name.

And suddenly, what he wanted to say, rolled right out of him. "Don't marry Gavin."

Elin stiffened, then slowly faced him. Her expression was unreadable, and Ben found himself holding his breath, waiting for her reaction, knowing what it must be.

"I was always meant for him."

"Yes." Ben knew that.

There was a beat of silence.

If he said more, he would feel exposed, naked. He was now completely sober.

For the first time, he realized that the military had actually been a place for him to hide. It had provided a shelter from these things called feelings that he'd thought he'd mastered. He'd been fooling himself.

At just seventeen, he'd been a callow lad, awkwardly wanting to change what had been a friendship to something dangerously more. At four-and-twenty, he was learning that, when it came to Elin, he still didn't know how to proceed. And he wasn't such a fool as to believe they were the same people they had been eight years ago.

"Why should I not marry him?" she demanded.

Because I want you.

Such a statement was too bold, but he spoke the truth as he said, "Because you will always be second place. You will be an afterthought. He's like our father. He lives to be busy and important."

"He *is* important."

The strains of the music could be heard out here. It reminded him of how little time he had to plead his case. It reminded her that she was expected inside.

"Father is waiting for me," Elin said. "I must go."

Ben stepped into her path.

"Elin—?" He broke off, tightening his jaw as he realized he was no poet. Emotions were risky, especially when he wasn't certain of what he wanted to say.

"Do you hate your brother so much?"

"I don't hate him."

"No, you just want to see him humiliated on the night our betrothal is announced. Or is it *me* you despise? Do you believe I remained the same trusting, gullible girl you took advantage of? I understand you are disappointed about losing your place in the military but I will not let you use me to strike back at Gavin. Besides, he's right. Your place is here. You have a responsibility to your family. *Or must it always be your way?*"

Her distrust caught him unaware. "I did not bring you out here to discuss this."

"No, *I* brought you out here to say that." Her hands had balled into fists as if she wished to strike him again. "You and I made a mistake years ago. We were both young—but do you know, Ben, I believed you cared for me. I thought I mattered to you—"

"You do."

"So that is why you left?"

"Wait, it wasn't my choice. My father informed me I was leaving."

She dismissed his claim with a toss of her curls. "And so you didn't consider sending word to me?"

"I was seventeen—"

"Or write in *eight* years?"

"And say what?" he snapped back. " 'Don't marry my brother?' You can see how that has gone over here."

She made a small moue of fury. "What a fool I

was! I mourned your leaving. I was at a loss without your friendship, and I was afraid, Ben, afraid of what could happen—but it didn't. As mother said, it meant *nothing*."

"Elin—"

She held up a hand to ward him back. "*Don't*. Don't make excuses. Don't come near me. And don't believe for a second that I will allow you to be familiar with me. We will keep up pretenses. We'll proceed as if we mean nothing to each other beyond the superficial. I will be your brother's wife and a duchess, and all will be good. But I will *never* let you close to me again, so don't even try. And that is what I came out here to say."

Elin started to walk away. Ben reached for her. He needed for her to listen. He'd been drunk when he came out here. He'd squandered the opportunity to plead his case. He was a fool, but he *loved her.*

Ben dropped his arms, stunned by the direction of his thoughts.

Loved her?

That couldn't be possible. They hadn't seen each other in years. Yes, they had been friends, but love was something Ben had never imagined.

He couldn't love Elin. Why, he *shouldn't*. She acted as if she hated him—and she was well on her way back to the house and out of his life.

Nor did he want to live according to the terms

she had just described. He'd once treasured Elin's friendship. He couldn't let her believe that he'd brought her out here for no other reason than to hurt his brother.

Whether he loved her or not—and he needed to do a great deal of thinking before he accepted *that* idea—he did not want her to believe the worst of him.

He used his longer legs to fall into step behind her. She did not acknowledge him. Oh, yes, with that set of her shoulders, she would make a brilliant duchess.

"Listen to me," he said to those stiff shoulders. "You *must* listen. How long have you been out here? Has Gavin even noticed you are missing? Or is he surrounded by 'important' people who require all of his attention? Yes, he is a busy man, but is that what *you* want? A man who thinks his wife is just another task on his ducal list of 'expecteds.' Be careful, Elin. Gavin has been taught there is nothing more important that the legacy of Baynton. People don't matter. Certainly not his brother, and it stands to follow, not even his wife."

Elin whirled on him. "You are so bitter. Before you warn me about Gavin, you might be wise to see to yourself." Her words were like lashes. They stripped him bare.

"Yes, I am bitter. I'm the one who lost you."

He didn't know who was more surprised by what he admitted—Elin? Or himself?

"Ben, you never had me," she said sadly.

"Yes, I did," he answered, daring her to claim different. It was all there in front of him now. He'd not been able to understand back then because they had both been too young. He'd known Elin better than any other person in his life.

He loved her, and in the space of moments, the word no longer frightened him. In a way he could not understand, he believed she loved him in return. Or had.

Was this the whisky talking? Did it matter? It all made sense to him.

Of course, there was a strong possibility that the events of years ago might have destroyed any feeling she held for him, except she was out here. She was talking to him. That must mean she cared.

All Ben wanted was an opportunity, even a tiny one, to redeem himself. It was not too late to save both of them.

"Ben," she started, her voice gentle as if she wanted to deny him once more.

"No, Elin, listen to me. We have time. There is a chance—"

Before he could say more, he was interrupted by the sound of a man desperately shouting her name.

She turned, glancing at the terrace, her gaze searching. "Father?"

Fyclan Morris had said he would wait on the terrace, but it was another man who hurried toward them. In the light of paper lanterns, Ben had trouble recognizing him until he grew closer. When Elin said, "Robbie, is something wrong?" Ben remembered her cousin Robbie Morris, who served as her father's secretary.

He was a slender man of middling height with reddish blond hair and sharp features. He might even be referred to as handsome although right now, Ben could have wished him to the devil. He was not done with his conversation with Elin.

"*Your mother. She needs you. Come,*" Morris said as he took her hand and began pulling her to the house.

"What is it?" she asked, moving with him. "Where is Father?"

"He is already inside." Morris took her arm. "She collapsed, Elin. She fell to the floor."

"Is she all right?"

Morris lowered his voice to murmur something, and Elin's feet took flight. She reached the terrace and dashed to the door

Ben began walking quickly toward the house, toward *her*.

Years ago, his father had bullied him into leaving Elin. Fyclan had been there as well. They had known what the two of them had done—

Ben forbid the thought. He *hadn't done anything* to Elin that was not right and very much wanted between them. They had been young, *too* young, and naïve—but he now knew he'd loved her. He'd *always* loved her. What had happened between them, bumbling, silly, awkward—well, it had been the actions of youth.

He was wiser now and much older. However, his feelings were ever true. He needed to tell Elin, to set aside masculine pride and the wretched weight of family honor and be honest. He had to finish the conversation that had been interrupted.

Ben was running now, a premonition growing inside him with each step. "They" were going to separate them again. Whatever had happened to her mother would change everything. Elin would not come back to him, not unless he reached her before they did.

Years ago, he'd been wrong to have let them force him away from her. He would not allow it now.

He reached the door. The footman wasn't paying attention to his door duties. Instead, he craned his neck, trying to see what was happening on the far side of the room where everyone was gathered.

The musicians had stopped their playing. Women were crying. Men appeared grave as they comforted them.

As Ben flung open the door to charge past the startled footman, he heard Elin scream.

And he knew he was too late.

There were many questions and much confusion the night Elin's mother died.

The doctors told Elin and her father that Jenny had been gone before she'd hit the floor that night. "Her heart stopped," seemed to be the only explanation. Those who heard it would murmur that Jennifer Morris's time had come, and there was nothing to be done when God sent His angels.

Elin hated such talk. There were other condolences. Few people said simply they were sorry for her loss. *That* statement she could respect.

The thought that her mother was needed in heaven more than she'd been wanted on earth made Elin wanted to roar with rage. However, she didn't. She was too inconsolable.

As was her father.

From the moment Elin had come upon her mother's prone figure on the floor, she and her father stood side by side but were lost to each other. It was almost as if Jenny had been the bridge between them, and now that she was gone, they were both too shocked to lean on each other.

Elin also learned that Ben had been wrong in his accusations against his brother. In the days following her mother's death, Gavin was more than generous with his time. He had lost a parent. He understood. For the first week, he was always by Elin's side although she made for poor company. She was drowning in grief.

Jenny's death would delay the marriage once again. When her father apologized, Gavin assured him that if anyone understood, he did.

"We'll start again after this is past," he told Fyclan. "We will announce the betrothal then."

Of course, the duke couldn't stay with her all the time. After the first week, responsibilities took him away. He was an important man.

Her father, too, threw himself into his business dealings. He and Elin couldn't sit alone together for very long. It was too difficult for them both. They reminded each other of what they had lost.

Elin had seen Ben at the funeral, where her mother was buried with as much pomp as her father could buy for her. Ben had looked terrible. He appeared weighed down with concerns as if he had been the one to lose a loved one. He tried to talk to her, but Elin was not ready for him yet. If she had not been out in the rose arbor with him, she would have been by her mother's side, and who knows? Could she have prevented Jenny's death?

Guilt was a rogue emotion. Elin didn't really know why she felt guilty. She could form a list of all the times she had not been the most dutiful of daughters. She should have eaten more of the supper her mother had had Cook prepare for her that night. She should have been more excited about marrying the duke.

Indeed, the marriage was the one thing her mother had desired for her. Jenny wanted Elin's portrait hanging on walls of Baynton's estates. She had envisioned it, dreamed it, and made Elin see it.

Marrying Baynton was the sole fitting tribute to her mother's memory.

But Elin was in mourning. The wedding need wait at least a year out of respect to her mother's memory. She wished she could hear her mother call her "sweet bee" once more or feel her warm, loving touch.

Over time, Elin did learn that Gavin and Ben had argued. They said Ben seemed to have disappeared from London. "Run off without a word to anyone" is what they said and "tsked" their thoughts.

In truth, Ben had tried to see her before he quit the city. He'd left his card. He'd called several times, but Elin was not receiving visitors, especially him.

However, Ben was not one to be ignored. He had sent her a rose, a rare white one. A single bloom.

Peace, he had written on the card. An apology of sorts and one that had infuriated her and brought tears to her eyes at the same time. She'd been trying so hard to keep her emotions contained. Her mother would expect her to be strong. Jenny had not admired "weepy" women.

And once again, without *even being present*, Ben proved he could threaten Elin's fragile hold on herself.

Peace. Her whole world had been upended with her mother's death, and she didn't know if it would ever be right again.

Nor did she understand why, out of all the flowers that had been sent and all the cards, she took the rose and Ben's one, heartfelt wish and pressed them between the pages of her journal.

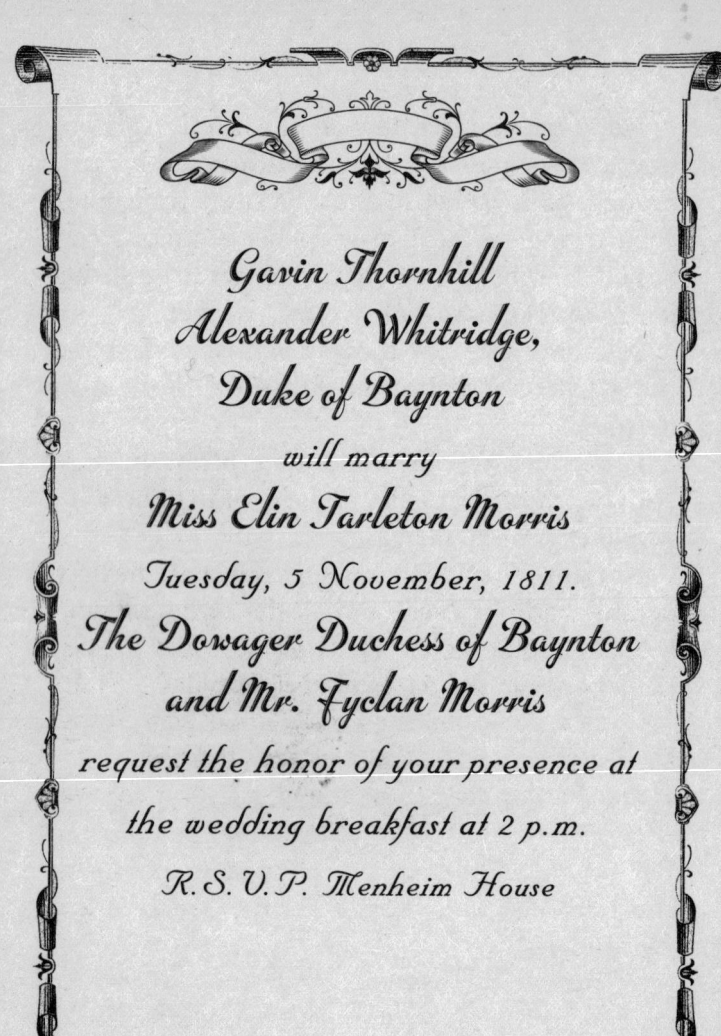

Gavin Thornhill
Alexander Whitridge,
Duke of Baynton

will marry

Miss Elin Tarleton Morris

Tuesday, 5 November, 1811.

The Dowager Duchess of Baynton
and Mr. Fyclan Morris

request the honor of your presence at

the wedding breakfast at 2 p.m.

R. S. V. P. Menheim House

Chapter Four

October 1811

Elin wasn't ready to return to London.

There were too many reminders of her mother there—her favorite amusements, the shops, the friends who met Elin with long faces and eyes melting with pity.

Her father sought out those people's company. Elin could not. Her grief was still too private. Too consuming.

In truth, in the past many months, she and her father had grown even more distant from each other. They had never been close—the way Elin had been with her mother—but this was something deeper. Perhaps Elin reminded him too much of the wife he'd lost. He'd given his wife a funeral the likes of which London had never seen. It had been a tribute for the love of his life, but now, he seemed adrift. He compensated by working more hours on his business interests than he ever had before and often took his meals at his club.

This had left Elin rambling around their large London home. In truth, she wasn't accustomed to talking to her father. She knew he cared for her; however, her mother had been the one to communicate between the two of them. She'd planned their outings and had encouraged their closeness. Without her, they acted like polite strangers.

As soon as Elin was able, she'd returned to Heartwood. The country was where she belonged. It was also easy to pretend her mother was still alive and living happily in London. Life could go on the way it had before the ill-fated betrothal ball.

Except that it was a lie.

At the end of the first year of mourning, Elin realized she couldn't hide from the truth. Her mother was gone and, in many ways, so was her father. He rarely wrote and had not come to Heartwood even for hunting, for while he no longer rode, in the past he'd often hosted large parties.

While she was in London, the Dowager Duchess and Baynton had called on Elin to see how she fared. Now that she was back home, Baynton had made a point of writing Elin at least once a week. His letters were brusque and far from newsy. He'd mention a piece of legislation he was trying to see passed or the name of someone he'd dined with, then close with just his signature. Elin suspected he dictated his letters to his secretary, and she could hear her mother's voice chiding her to be more patient with such an important, busy man.

And then, after months of silence, a week ago, Elin had received the invitation to the wedding breakfast and her father's letter ordering her back to the city. *The time has come, daughter,* he wrote, *to see to your obligation to marry Baynton. I would have it done before Christmas.*

The letters were delivered by the hand of a woman named Madame Odette. Madame said she was the daughter of an impoverished French émigré. Although she now was forced to oversee the creation of fine wardrobes, she made a point of telling Elin that her father had been a count before he'd been cruelly robbed of his estates and riches by the rabble during the revolution, a theme Madame harped on every evening over her wine.

She had arrived in Fyclan Morris's traveling coach followed by a wagon full of fabric, dress patterns, small clothes, and all of the embellishments. She was almost ten years older than Elin and as petite, except with blond hair and blue eyes . . . reminiscent of Jenny Morris.

"Your father wishes me to see you outfitted properly," she'd informed Elin in her accented English. "You must set aside your black, and the styles in London, they change, they change. Mademoiselle is to be a *duchesse*. She wants to be an asset to her husband, not an embarrassment."

So began an agonizing week for Elin of being poked, prodded, and continually criticized by Madame Odette. Or Madame *Odious* as Elin referred to her in her mind.

Elin did set aside her black. Not willingly, but she did it, and there was more than a little resentment in her doing so. It felt too soon, and sometimes she had the sense of being a sleepwalker. She went through the motions but only because she could not think of how to object, not if this was what her father wanted.

Meanwhile, the dressmaker took numerous liberties. One morning, Elin had come downstairs to seeing the woman mentally cataloging the furniture and art in Heartwood's front room. She gave orders with the authority of Elin's father. She talked to the other servants as if they were underlings and had even threatened Mrs. Varney's housekeeper position when the woman did something that displeased her.

It didn't make sense to Elin that her father would choose such a woman to escort her to London. She also didn't appreciate having the safe, predictable sameness of her days interrupted by Madame, and yet Elin did nothing to stop the Frenchwoman from setting her return in motion. Elin knew she must go. He was right when he wrote she had an obligation to Baynton, who had been patient long enough.

She remembered her mother's saying that the duke wasn't the sort of man who would cry off. He was honorable, and if she had any pangs of conscience about her not being honest about that "incident" in her past, she reminded herself that this marriage was the one thing her mother wanted. The only meaningful tribute to her. Perhaps she and Baynton would name a daughter after her. Jennifer Tarleton Whitridge. The dream of a daughter helped Elin out of her sadness.

Village girls were hired to finish what sewing needed to be done with the dresses. Heartwood became a hive of activity. The work was done quickly, and Madame announced that the wagon with Elin's trunks would leave that next morning, while they would depart on the day after tomorrow.

"Why not leave with the wagon?" Elin had asked.

"Because we must leave on Thursday," was the answer, as if it explained all. Perhaps it did. Madame Odette wore Elin down. She did as told. It was easier than arguing with a Frenchwoman.

And all probably would have been fine, except

for what Elin overheard Mrs. Varney whisper to Tillman, the butler, the morning of her departure.

Madame Odette was already in the coach. Elin was saying good-bye to the servants. "This is not farewell, really," Elin assured them or tried to convince herself. "When I return I will be Trenton's mistress, but I will see you often. I'll make a point of it."

She was going down the line of servants who had turned out to wish her well, offering them little reminders and pretending to be happy. Even Norman the stable master had come up, and he had brought several of his lads with him.

"Mademoiselle," Madame Odette barked in that imperial tone of hers. "*Vite!* We must be on the road."

"She's anxious to return to London," Elin overheard Tillman grumble.

"If the master had to choose a mistress, did he have to choose a French whore?" Mrs. Varney had answered.

The housekeeper was known for strong opinions. She had something to say about everyone in the parish.

But *this* suggestion that not only had her father taken a mistress but that the servants believed she was Madame Odette stunned Elin. It also explained everything—the woman's high-handedness, her disdain over what Elin thought, and the way she coveted all she saw at Heartwood, the way she acted as if she could own it.

Elin didn't want to go toward the coach. If the duke had not been expecting her, she would have refused.

However, she had no choice. The duke waited for her. If Heartwood had another traveling coach, she would have ordered that prepared, but there was only the one.

"Mademoiselle, we *must* leave," Madame Odious called. Elin faced the coach.

Old Jensen the coachman had come to the door. Elin had known him since childhood. "It would help if we leave, Miss Elin. You never know what we'll find on the road."

Her favorite footman, a young man named Craig, a Yorkshireman, held the coach door open. He smiled as he waited, always pleasant and accommodating.

Elin walked to the coach and climbed in, careful to keep her skirts from touching the Frenchwoman's.

Protecting the coach were two outriders, James and Toby, stable lads who were handy with their fists and could fire a shot. They were good-natured men who had been raised at Heartwood and were loyal to Fyclan Morris. They would keep Elin safe.

Mrs. Varney leaned into the coach. Had she meant for Elin to hear what she'd said? She gave no indication. "We'll keep you in our prayers, Miss Elin. Don't worry about Heartwood. I shall run matters as you would wish."

"Thank you," Elin heard herself murmur, then the door was shut. The coach swayed as Jensen and Craig climbed up into the box. There was a snap of a whip, and they were off.

They had a three-day trip to London ahead of them with nights spent at inns along the way. The first day's travel would be relatively short, but the next day would be long.

Too long, Elin reflected, to spend it trapped in such a small space with Madame. She attempted to shut her out with needlework and reading. She tried not to talk, just speaking when asked a direct question. Elin needed to do this as she processed the thought of her father with not only another woman, but *this* woman.

It defied her imagination.

The second day of travel was worse.

Madame knew Elin was ignoring her and took delight in taking little jabs at her.

"If you keep such a long face, you will create wrinkles that will make you appear a crone," Madame sang to Elin, as the coach bounced and rolled over a particularly difficult track of road. The movement was upsetting Elin's stomach, so she couldn't read or do handwork. The day was also dreary, one of those threatening rain without delivering it.

Elin ignored her by studying the passing scenery outside the coach window. Craig had told her this road was called Woods Road because it traveled through a thick and obviously lonely forest. Elin hadn't seen a soul for over two hours. A bridge was out on one of the other connecting roads, so Jensen had taken them this way to pick up the Post Road. He'd heard about the bridge the night before at the inn where they had spent the night.

"Is that what you want, Mademoiselle Morris, the wrinkles of a crone?"

No, what I wish is for you to disappear. Vanish. Begone.

Actually, what Elin really wanted was to return to Heartwood.

"You, English, so stoic."

Elin didn't respond but had a vision of giving Madame a push out of the coach.

"I know what you are doing," Madame said. "You choose to ignore me as if this is a problem. It is not. You may pout all you wish. Of course that is the problem with you Englishwomen. Never satisfied. From the expression on your face, one would think you were returning to London for your beheading instead of a wedding. Or that the duke was ancient or ugly." She gave a small, cynical half laugh filled with secret envy, and added, "Or poor."

There was a beat of blessed silence. "I know poor, and I shouldn't," Madame continued. "If my family had not been chased out of France and robbed of what was ours, I could have married a prince. And I would not be pouting, I tell you that." She punctuated her opinion with a condescending laugh and, after listening to more of this chatter than any person could tolerate, Elin had had enough.

She turned to the dressmaker and said, "Are you and my father lovers?"

Madame's brows lifted.

Elin held her breath, hoping for a denial.

Instead, a change crossed Madame's lovely face. A mask fell away, and Elin had the impression she was seeing the true woman. She smiled, the satisfied expression of a cat that had got into the cream, as if she knew something Elin could never imagine. "Do you think we are?"

Uncertain, Elin curled her gloved hands in her lap into fists. The day was chilly with a damp that seeped into the coach. She wore a good wool, dark blue cloak over her travel dress and a pair of warm socks with her sensible shoes, but still she felt a chill.

Or was the chill because she found herself in the presence of—what? Avarice? Smugness?

Elin kept her voice level. "If I knew the answer, I would not have asked. However, you seem very sure of your place and disrespectful of mine."

"One lesson I have learned is that roles can change quickly in life."

"What does that mean?"

"That you needn't worry about your future. There, do you feel better now? You will be free of him."

"What do you mean?"

Madame laughed silently. "You will find out."

The cramped quarters of the coach became suddenly too close. The woman's threatening confidence was unnerving. Elin didn't know how to react or what to think, so she acted. She reached up and knocked on the roof to signal the driver to halt.

Madame Odette grabbed her wrist and pulled her hand down to the tufted velvet seat between them. "What are you doing?" she demanded, but it was too late.

The door slid back, and Craig, who was riding in the box with the driver, said, "Yes, Miss?"

"I wish to stop," Elin said.

"*We will not stop*," Madame countermanded.

Crag closed the door and in seconds the coachman slowed the horses, saying, "Calm, calm now."

Elin fought the urge to give the dressmaker a triumphant look. The servants were hers, and they listened to her, not a dressmaker.

The battle between the two women wasn't over yet, but Elin had won a skirmish and given herself the opportunity for a little distance so she could think clearly.

"It is not safe for us to stop here," Madame Odette complained. "This road is lonely. There could be highwaymen."

"Highwaymen?" Elin almost laughed.

"*Yes*," the Frenchwoman insisted. "It is dangerous. Why else does your father have outriders?"

"He always has me travel with outriders," Elin answered. "There hasn't been a highwayman in these woods since the reign of the last king."

"Times change," Madame answered, an echo of her earlier words.

"So you have told me." Elin jerked her arm free and held up a hand to stave back any other attempt to grab her again. "Enough. Leave me alone."

Craig opened the door. "Is there a problem, Miss Elin?"

"No, and there won't be." Elin climbed out of the coach, taking her velvet cap with her. It was a smart thing with a pheasant feather pinned to it. "I need a moment of privacy."

"Yes, Miss."

Madame leaned out of the coach. "Do not dawdle. We have a distance to travel."

Elin didn't bother to answer. She pulled the cap over her curls, which she wore loose around her shoulders and down her back in defiance of the seamstress's desire for her to pin them up.

The outriders had been riding a bit ahead and now circled back to see why the coach had stopped. "For a bit of privacy," Elin said, almost through clenched teeth.

Her servants exchanged glances at her testiness. Elin didn't care. She started off the road, moving into the woods.

"Don't go too far," Toby called.

Elin waved a hand to show that she'd heard him but the truth was, she wished she could walk all the way back to Heartwood. She had no desire to climb back into the coach with Madame Odious. Perhaps Jensen would let her sit in the box and they could put Craig inside with the dressmaker. The footman would be pleased with the idea since he was showing signs that he was sweet on Madame.

It helped to breathe fresh air. As she walked, Elin was startled at how heated her cheeks were.

The Frenchwoman needled her. She'd been deliberately provocative, as if she did not care for Elin's good opinion. As if she was not worried if Elin reported her conduct to her father. She was very secure in her position. Too secure.

There was a mystery here, and Elin was determined to reason it out.

Her step faltered. She stopped. She was in the

center of a copse of trees. Ferns and damp leaves covered the forest floor, muffling sound. Even the birds had fallen silent here in the deep woods.

She took a step back, then another. Her shoulders hit the trunk of a giant oak, and she slowly sank down, resting her head on her knees, heedless of the damp ground.

There had been a time when she'd been certain of God's good grace, that He had blessed Fyclan Morris and his family. Those were the days when Elin had felt life had purpose.

Now, she wasn't certain.

The suddenness of her mother's death had rattled her confidence. Why suffer through the motions of living if Death was all that waited? The futility of life preyed on her mind. She struggled to fight off the blue devils. Right now, they seemed to surround her

And now, her father was making a mockery of his marriage to her mother by giving *carte blanche* to Madam Odious.

Hot tears threatened, but Elin was made of sterner stuff. She stood up. Her mother would not have let the Frenchwoman have the upper hand, and neither would Elin.

Furthermore, she would tell Baynton the truth about herself. That decision had come to her just in the moment. She was surprised that it still weighed on her mind. She would not tell him of

Ben's involvement but she must let him know she wasn't perfect. Indeed, she was far from it.

And she needed to be brave, to live as if life did mean something.

Perhaps if she went through the motions of acting as if it all made sense, then someday it might. Someday, she'd understand why she was on this earth and her mother ripped away. "I'm trying to have faith, Mother, but it is so, so difficult."

Elin began walking back to the coach with a new, forced resolve. She would tolerate Madame, but she would not give her one inch more than she must. When they arrived in London, Elin would make a decision on what to say or not say about the dressmaker to her father.

Chances were, she wouldn't say anything because she didn't know if she could stand hearing him profess to love another . . .

She stopped, puzzled.

She'd thought she had walked a straight line into the woods. To her surprise, she hadn't. The road was not where she had expected it.

For a second she was tempted to call out and see if anyone answered. However the vision of the smug look on Madame's face dissuaded her. The road was close. She'd keep walking.

To her relief, she had meandered only a bit, and the road was not that far from where she'd stopped. As she moved forward, she heard a horse whinny and an answering cry. There was the muffled sound of male voices and Madame's light laughter.

Elin caught sight of the coach through the trees. She was perhaps a hundred yards behind it. With a frustrated sigh, she decided to reach the road before closing the gap between herself and the vehicle.

However, once she had a good view of her coach, she was surprised to see a party of three men on horseback approach. The strangers appeared well traveled, with the brims of their hats pulled low over their eyes.

For some reason, Elin stepped back into the shadows of the trees.

Madame had climbed out of the coach and had apparently been flirting with Craig. She knew the footman found her attractive, and Elin had noticed that when she wasn't around, the dressmaker enjoyed testing her wiles on any available man. Her poor father. He should have chosen better.

James and Toby had been sitting on their horses, talking to Jensen but at the sight of the travelers, they straightened. The men stopped and nodded in greeting

Madame stepped forward and said something. Elin couldn't hear the words exchanged, but the servants relaxed.

All seemed fine, and Elin felt foolish lurking in the trees. She had been gone quite some time. They did need to be on their way.

She was about to step out of the tree line when all three of the travelers pulled pistols from their jackets and shot the Morris men.

Chapter Five

*E*lin stopped midstride and fell back in shock.

She didn't believe what she'd just witnessed, what she'd heard. The air still rang with the crack of the shots. Her father's men crumpled. James, falling off his horse; Toby grabbing his chest before dropping to the ground. The coach horses began to startle, but one of the strangers caught the lead horse and held them.

Craig began shouting. "What did you do? Why?" He moved toward Jensen, slumped over in his seat on the box.

The stranger closest to him whipped his arm forward, and Craig clutched his throat. Blood spurted from his neck where the knife was buried. Craig reeled toward Madame Odette. She stepped back in distaste, and he fell to the ground, his hand stretched out to her.

Elin doubled over with the pain of loss. Death had stuck again. Death was all around her.

The murders had happened in the blink of an eye. Minutes ago, these men, who had been part of the Heartwood's staff since she could remember, had been alive. Now, the only one left standing was Madame Odette, who did not appear frightened at all.

Instead, as the strangers began reloading their pistols, she took the men to task, her voice shrill and carrying, the French accent gone.

"Why did you do that without waiting for a signal from me? We were to meet farther up the road."

"We tired of waiting." The killer had a gravelly voice, a distinct one.

Madame sliced the air angrily with her hand. "More fool you. The girl is not here. If you had waited until I signaled you, then we'd have her."

Now she had his attention. "Where is she?"

"She's out there." She pointed in the direction that Elin had left. "If she heard the shots, even clumsy as she is, she's probably running to London by now."

He growled an oath. "Peters, Tucker, go after her."

"Bring her here?" one of them asked

"No, kill her," the leader ordered. "That is what were are being paid to do. And make it quick. I want to ride back to London within the hour.

There's an extra bit to the one of you who bags her."

His men set their heels to their horses and rode noisily into the forest. Elin's heart pounded in her throat. *They had come for her.* They were hunting her. She tried not to panic.

"An extra bit?" Madame questioned, disdain dripping from her words. "You were paid to do a job a certain way. There will be nothing in it for any of you if this does not look like a robbery. And don't think *he* is not going to hear about this. You fools have made it more difficult than what it needed to be. He should cut whatever he is paying you in half—"

A shot brought her scolding to a halt.

Elin craned her neck around the trees, trying to see what had happened. Madame took a step, and Elin saw the pistol the leader held leveled on the dressmaker.

Elin grabbed the silly velvet hat from her head and stuffed it in her mouth to keep from screaming.

Madame's body stiffened as if in surprise. "No." She shook her head. "This was not to be."

"It was. *He* just didn't tell you." The leader turned his horse to follow the others as Madame Odette sank to her knees.

"You, fool—" she spit out with her last energy, sinking to her knees, before slowly falling to the ground beside Craig.

Elin's heart was in danger of bursting in fear.

She couldn't breathe, let alone speak, and that might have been a saving grace. She curled into a ball as if she could disappear. She started to shake but stopped herself. There wasn't time to indulge herself. *Think.* She had to think what to do. She dared to peek once more at the road to see what was happening.

The leader was scanning the area as if divining her presence, yet he was unable to spot her. He frowned at the bodies, then directed his horse into the woods to join the search.

They would find her. This was a dense forest, but they were mounted and could move faster than she did.

Elin must escape. She had to tell the world what had happened here. She needed her father to know. It wasn't just that someone wanted her dead—they had murdered people she cared about.

She was also too frightened to move—then she thought of Ben.

She had completely pushed him out of her mind, or so she had thought. Last week, in the middle of the turmoil of trying on dresses, she had taken down the journal where she'd pressed the rose he'd sent. It was no longer white but brown and gray. The scent still lingered and reminded her of her mother.

Elin had closed the book and shoved it back onto the shelf. Even after all this time, Ben could disturb her composure.

But now in the forest, she remembered him in a different way. She recalled the games they had played as children, including one where she would hide and Ben look for her. She'd been good at outwitting him, and if she could outsmart Ben, then those murderers pretending to be highwaymen should be simple to fool.

Armed with new courage, Elin considered her options. She could steal a horse. James and Toby's horses stayed close to the coach horses, but the animals had started to realize the humans would not bother them. They wandered to the side of the road where they could graze.

But then she reconsidered. The horse she chose could make a sound that would alert her hunters to where she was. She was an excellent rider, but she didn't believe she could outrace three desperate men.

No, her best chance was on foot. It would also help if she crossed the road. They wouldn't expect her to be over there.

Determination replaced fear. Elin was not ready to die. Not this way. She even managed to whisper, "Thank you, Ben." Those childhood games might keep her alive.

Elin lifted the hem of her cloak and skirts and

scurried across the road as fast as she could, praying that she escaped notice. She plunged into the forest on the other side and flattened herself on the ground as she used to do as a girl.

No shout went up.

If she listened, she could hear the horses thrashing through the woods. She found it hard to tell, but she believed the riders sounded as if they were going in the other direction, and so she took off running away from them.

The silly velvet cap with its fashionable pheasant feather went flying from her head. It landed someplace on the forest floor on top of years, maybe decades worth of pine needles and leaves. She didn't stop to pick it up.

Elin didn't think about where she ran. She just moved. She clutched her cloak with one hand and concentrated on placing one foot in front of the other. Thorny hawthorns and needle-tipped hollies caught on her clothing. She yanked and traveled on.

Sometimes, she thought she heard voices. She could sense their presence in the woods around her, yet no shot rang out. No one called a warning. She began to imagine she was alone in the world, and as daytime passed, it grew dark under the tall pines and oaks with bare branches stretching to the sky.

Her pace slowed. She was hungry and thirsty.

She had no money and only the clothes she wore. She tried not to think about who the "he" who had paid for her murder was.

She had to reason things out. She must be clever. The coach had been traveling into Northamptonshire. They were supposed to have stayed the night in a place called Corby. Jensen had known the innkeeper.

Elin eyed the moss on the trees and thought she was moving west.

Night fell. Doubt about the direction she was traveling contributed to the fears she'd been doggedly trying to ignore.

Every sound made her jump. The dreary day had become a dreary night. There was no moon.

Her feet ached, and she stumbled over hidden roots. The forest was now more frightening than the men searching for her.

Every myth she'd ever heard, every story, every tale echoed in her mind. She knew wolves no longer roamed the land, but that didn't stop her from thinking about them—and then she saw a light through the trees.

She moved toward it and discovered herself approaching what looked to be a tavern. The light from the windows appeared welcoming . . . until she walked closer and realized how dirty those windows were.

Several horses were tied together in a lean-to at the side of the building. Muffled male laughter could be heard from inside. Hearty laughter, the sound of bold men.

"Please, God," Elin whispered. She needed help, but she was one to always err on the side of caution. Stealing a horse might create more problems than the men hunting her.

So, she approached a window and peered inside.

It took a moment for her eyes to adjust but what she noticed immediately confirmed her first impression—this was not the sort of place for a lady. There were no chairs but benches around rough tables. The floor looked like the windows, as if it had never been cleaned.

A group of four men were gathered around one end of a table. Their concentration was on the dice being tossed. The roll was not to the liking of most of them. They shouted their feelings and slammed the table while the winner laughingly raked their money toward the pile in front of him.

Something about the winner with his unshaven jaw and his long hair tied back in a messy queue appeared familiar to Elin; however, it was the scent of cooking food that claimed her attention.

A man with a rag around his portly waist was ladling out a bowl of stew by the hearth. He carried the bowl to the bar and began to eat his supper. Elin had no money and nothing to sell save for the cloak she wore. The innkeeper might advance her credit based upon her father's name. Mayhap they had heard of Fyclan Morris in these parts, or the Duke of Baynton—

Elin's jaw dropped.

She *did know* the man winning at dice.

Startled by the recognition, Elin forgot her hunger and leaned closer to the window, the better to see him, and realized she made no mistake. Ben Whitridge sat at the table.

Or were her eyes and mind playing tricks on her?

She blinked.

Yes, that was *Ben*. She was certain although he didn't look any better than the rest inside the tavern, and they were a disreputable lot—

A deep, male voice spoke behind her. "Little Miss, Little Miss, what have we here? Are you spying on the lads?"

Elin could have jumped out of her skin. The man stood so close she could feel his hot breath. She whirled, expecting to see pistols aimed for her heart.

Instead, the wan light on the window behind her fell on a huge bulbous nose, a grizzled jaw, and a mouth lacking a few teeth. He leered. "You are a sweet one. Come on in, lass, and join Big Roger—"

With a shout, Elin stuck that man in his big nose

and did the only sensible thing she could think of in that moment. She ran for Ben.

It had been quite awhile since the dice had rolled in Ben's favor. Tonight, it was almost as if he couldn't lose, and that was a heady feeling, especially among this lot.

His mates around the table were grim and grimy. They were adventurers and former soldiers with perhaps unsavory pasts, and Ben adored them.

There was Hooknosed John, Big Roger—he thought that name particularly clever—and Nate. "Just Nate," the man with a patch over his eye had growled at Ben when he'd wondered if he didn't have a more colorful name.

I'm Whit, Ben had told them, taking his cue from "Just Nate," and no one had asked for more. Every man served himself; every man kept to himself.

He had fallen into step with them while attending a fight in Sheffield. He'd been at loose ends for some time, and these mates appealed to him. They did odd jobs here and there, honest ones, to replenish the coin they lost to gaming. Hooknosed said they'd had enough of being afraid for their necks, but that could change. One never knew what to expect on the road ahead.

Ben had no doubt that each of his new companions had done unsavory things. He wasn't the only man in the room with a knife in his boot, but he wasn't uncomfortable with them. He'd rubbed shoulders with rough characters during his military days and preferred them to the entitled arrogance of his brother and his sort.

At least with these gents, Ben felt useful. He liked using his muscles and being so tired at the end of the day that he could think of nothing but sleep. The hot anger that had trailed after him since that night he'd severed ties with his brother had begun to fade, and he was finding a measure of peace.

Nor was it bad living hand to mouth. He had no responsibilities and answered to no one but himself.

And he rarely thought of Elin Morris.

He'd finally managed, once again, to tuck her away into a distant memory, a youthful foolishness. He no longer brooded over her as he'd last seen her. She'd been walking by his brother's side as she'd followed her mother's casket, so lost in grief she was oblivious to Ben's existence. It had been Gavin's hand she'd gripped for comfort.

Love was for poets, not men of the world like Ben. He didn't have a need for her or any other bit of muslin.

Oh, the ladies always fawned over Ben . . . but after a time, he grew tired of substituting what he didn't want for what he wanted.

Pulling the pile of coins on the table over to join

his other winnings, Ben called to the innkeeper, separating a small stack of coins from the others, "Osprey, we are all in need for another round of your good ale." That offer brought grins to the faces of his brothers of the spirit.

"Aye, the *good* ale," Nate instructed, "and not the piss water you've been serving us."

A heavyset man with a smattering of hair on his pate, Osprey left the bowl of stew he'd been eating and slid the coins from the table right into his pocket. "You'll take what I give you. Are you including them?" With a nod, he gestured to the local lads sharing a corner of the bar. One was tall and beefy, the other his exact opposite.

"Include them," Ben said, feeling generous.

"Thanks," the short man said.

"Speaking of piss," Hooknosed said with a grin, "if Roger doesn't come back, I'll be drinking his share of your largesse. I swear that man goes like horse—"

The tavern door flew open in a blast of chilled air that made the flames in the hearth dance. Ben looked up, expecting to see Big Roger lumber in through the door.

Instead, a young woman, her dark hair curly and wild, her dark blue cloak flying behind her, stood framed in the doorway for barely a second before she launched herself into his arms, practically flying into the room.

"Ben," she said in a voice that had haunted his dreams. "Help me. You *must* help me." Elin Morris then threw her arms around his neck, almost knocking him from his seat on the end of the bench, and burst into tears.

For a second, Ben couldn't breathe. He couldn't think. Had he conjured her? Or was he going mad and imagining her? Except she felt solid and real, and she smelled of flowers and the night air and a sweetness he had always identified with her.

His arms closed protectively. She filled them well. She wore a heavy wool cloak, but he noticed she felt light as if she hadn't been eating, as if she'd lost at least a stone.

Elin had always had a healthy appetite for all things in life—food, adventure, whatever. Her weight loss, her crying, this was not characteristic of her. Elin was made of sterner stuff.

And where was her retinue? She couldn't be alone. Neither Gavin nor her father would allow her to be traipsing around this lonely stretch of countryside alone. She was the Morris heiress, her father's sole heir. One carefully guarded any daughter, but when she was an heiress, a wise father was doubly careful.

Standing at the opposite end of the table, Big Roger roared his disapproval. "Here now, I saw her first. Caught her peeping in the window."

Peeping? Elin?

Her response was to tighten her hold around Ben's neck. "I'm sorry, mate, she chose me, " he answered. "And have you no manners, shut the door."

Big Roger kicked the door shut. "The only reason she is holding on to you is because she hasn't seen me in the light."

That response set everyone laughing, including the lads at the bar. The impossibility of any woman's choosing the luggish Big Roger over Ben was a good joke between them, one that had good-naturedly whiled away many an hour. Besides, Big Roger had a wife and six children he kept in Sussex.

At the sound of their laughter, Elin seemed to return to herself. She looked around, her nose adorably red from weeping. Her hold on Ben didn't loosen, but she asked, "Who are these men?"

"Friends," he answered almost defiantly. He knew what his brother would think of his companions.

How would the future duchess of Baynton react?

The future duchess? Hell, she might even already *be* the duchess. It had been weeks since Ben had heard any word from London. He had no idea what was happening in his family, and he liked it that way.

But Elin gave no opinion whatsoever on his friends. She didn't join the banter or dismiss them with a sniff.

Instead, her large eyes dark with fear, she said, "Someone wants me dead, Ben. Someone is trying to murder me."

Chapter Six

$\mathcal{B}$en set Elin on her feet, not believing he'd heard her correctly. "Someone is trying to kill you?"

For a second, she was in danger of blubbering again. Instead, she pulled herself together. She pushed away from him and he let her go.

Pressing the back of her hand against her mouth, she regained her composure. "It was terrible. They shot Craig and Jensen and the outriders—"

"Jensen, your coachman?" Ben had grown up with Old Jensen teasing him.

Her answer was a short nod. "They even shot Madame Odette, and she was talking to them as if she was one of them." Elin drew a shaky breath as if she was afraid she would come undone once more.

"Have her sit here," Hooknose said, giving up his spot next to Ben at the table.

"Yes, yes, Miss Morris, sit," Ben said, a bit annoyed with himself that he hadn't had her take a seat already. However, her story was incredible, and he hadn't minded having her in his lap.

Gratefully, she practically fell onto the bench.

"Have you eaten?" Ben asked.

"I'm starved. At the same time, I don't know if I could eat a bite."

"Let's try." Ben looked to Osprey. "Do you have brandy or even something stronger? And a plate of that stew you have been dishing out?"

"Aye, I do." The innkeeper walked over with a jug that could have had anything in it. Or anyone drinking from it. The Oak did not serve a picky clientele.

"A glass?" Ben prompted.

"A glass? Aye, yes." Osprey hurried back to his bar and returned with a somewhat clean glass he polished with the somewhat clean rag he wore at his waist.

Ben sniffed the bottle and was pleased to smell the fumes of what might be good brandy. "You surprise me, Osprey," he said, pouring a bit into the glass and handing it to Elin.

"I surprise most, Whit."

Elin's brows came together at the name. "Drink," Ben ordered before she could ask questions. She took a sip, then downed the rest.

"Gor," Nate breathed in admiration.

"Another?" Ben asked.

"Yes, please," Elin answered, primly.

He refilled the glass, and this one she sipped as Osprey set a bowl of his rabbit stew in front of her. Steam rolled off it. "The brandy is good," she said to him, earning a beaming smile from Osprey.

"So is his stew," Ben assured her.

Elin picked up her spoon and blew on the stew to cool it down. "I'm surprised to see you here . . . Whit."

"I'm surprised to find myself here and to meet you here, as well. Tell us your story."

"In front of them?"

"They are good listeners."

Elin frowned at Big Roger but didn't seem put off by the others. She began speaking.

"We were traveling to London. I'm to marry—" She paused, once again looked around at his companions, and said, "Your brother in a few weeks."

Well, that answered one question.

"Who is 'we?' " Ben wondered. "Was your father with you?"

"No. He is in London waiting for me. I traveled with servants and a dressmaker, Madame Odette."

"Why were you traveling through this area?" Ben had to ask. "Why weren't you on the Post Road?"

"There was a bridge out," Elin said. "Jensen felt

this way was as good as any. We were to pick up the Post Road on the morrow."

"So, you were traveling through here, and then what happened?"

Elin stared into her untouched bowl of stew. Ben could see her mind churning as if trying to make sense of events. She was in shock. He'd seen it more than once in men who had feared for their lives, then found themselves safe. He leaned toward her. "Elin?"

She jerked as if startled. He tapped her bowl. "Eat."

"I don't know if I can."

"A bite."

Her dark lashes swept her cheeks a moment, then she took the spoon. She still wore her kid gloves, and they gave the movement of her hands a ladylike fragility that was not lost on Ben or the men watching. Who could have known there were so many chivalrous souls in the room?

She chewed slowly as if not trusting the taste of the stew, then took another spoonful before setting it down. "It is good," she told Osprey. "I'm just too—"

Her voice broke off, and she closed her eyes a moment as if unable to describe exactly what she felt.

Visibly gathering herself, she began speaking. "Father sent this dressmaker to prepare me. Madame Odette. She was accompanying me to London, but we argued, and I was angry enough to stop the coach. I needed a break from her. I walked into the woods a ways, and that is what saved me."

"How do you know your father sent her?" Ben asked.

"Aye, it could have been a kidnapping," Big Roger agreed, reading Ben's mind.

"She had a letter from Father . . ." Elin stopped and frowned, as if questioning the letter had never dawned on her. "I don't know that it was from Father. I recognized Robbie's handwriting. You remember Robbie, my cousin who serves as his secretary?"

Ben nodded. "Are you certain he wrote the note?"

"I didn't see him write it," she answered with a touch of impatience, "but I've been reading letters from my father written by Robbie for years. I had no reason to doubt its authenticity. After all, it arrived with the invitation to the wedding breakfast. I knew I was expected to return."

"Or someone could have created a ruse to kidnap you," Ben answered. He didn't appreciate her testiness. He was trying to help.

His suggestion gave Elin pause. She frowned,

then shook her head. "They want to kill me. They were paid to see me dead. They said as much to Madame Odette."

Ben was certain Elin hadn't understood correctly. What good was a dead heiress? But one held for a ransom could make some desperate men wealthy, and he wondered about the dressmaker.

"Why would your father send Madame Odette instead of coming for you himself?"

"He is busy," she answered, looking away before seeming to decide it might be best to be honest with him. "He *is* busy," she insisted, this time in a gentler tone. "And he's been ill—his gout has been very bad. In the past, when they wanted me to return to London, Mother would come with the dresses. I thought it was a bit odd to send a seamstress to fetch me, but she said she was the daughter of a French count, and the letter didn't seem out of the ordinary, so I just supposed it was the signal to me that I was expected to do as bid. You know how it was," she reminded him.

He did. Whenever Mr. and Mrs. Morris wanted Elin in Town, they always outfitted her first. That way they signaled to their independent-minded, wild, romping girl that she was to act the part of a lady.

And Elin could play the lady well. She was doing so right now. She appeared fragile and yet resilient. It was apparent that Hooknose, Nate, and Big Roger were charmed by her need for their help.

As was Ben. Damn it all.

He'd always had a strong desire to protect her, and her story was playing to his every instinct.

"Why did you argue with the dressmaker?" he asked.

Her chin came up, and her mouth clamped shut. Obviously, he had touched a nerve, but before he could chide her, she said, "I asked if she was my father's lover."

"And she said?"

"She didn't. She was very coy, as if she had a secret and was extremely proud of herself for it." Elin leaned forward. "She was very much like my mother in coloring, so I thought perhaps he'd been tempted by her But my father worshipped my mother. He couldn't have taken a mistress so soon after her death, could he, Ben?"

"I don't know. Men don't mourn like women do," he had to say honestly.

Elin rocked back. "I never believed he would fall in love again so soon. My parents were devoted to each other. And I did not like Madame Odette. There was something about her that was distasteful. She was French, or said she was. Toward the end, she sounded as English as you and me. She could go on and on about her family in France but—have you ever sensed someone was trying too hard, so you wondered whether they were being honest? And she was always comparing herself to me. It became quite unsettling."

"I could see your not liking her just because she said she was French," Hooknose observed.

"I feel that way about French *men*," Nate countered. "But not the women."

The men laughed, but Elin's brows came together. "If you want her, she is lying in the road where they shot her."

That statement brought the men to their senses.

"So she wasn't part of a plot?" Ben said.

"That is what is so curious. I think she was. She didn't act surprised when those men murdered the servants. Instead, she chastised them for not waiting. Apparently, they were supposed to meet the coach farther down the road. But the leader said he'd grown tired of waiting."

"Your father had outriders with you?" Ben said. She nodded. "Then why didn't they see these men?"

She reached for the brandy. "Because of me." She took a sip, tears welling in her eyes. She forced them back. "When I stopped the coach to be let out, they circled back to check on me."

"They shouldn't have done that," Hooknosed observed.

"They were probably stable lads," Ben explained. "Not guards in the sense that you are thinking. They could shoot, and they would, but I can see them taking a moment to talk to the others."

"I took a good walk into the woods," Elin continued. "When I returned, I'd lost the direction of the coach so I ended on the road well behind it. The men approached, speaking to James, Toby, and the others. When I saw them, something warned me to step back into the tree line. A moment later, the three men shot Jensen, Toby, and James. One of the men, the leader, threw a knife at Craig and struck him right in the throat." She took another sip of brandy, before confessing, "You are right. It was my fault. *Mine.* If I hadn't been so angry at Madame, they would have been doing their duties."

A tremor had come to her voice. Ben took the glass from her. "It was their task to be aware at all times. You mustn't blame yourself, Elin."

She didn't agree. He could see that. "Don't focus on it," he ordered. "Tell us what happened next."

"Madame was very angry with the men for not obeying what had been planned."

"She said that?"

"Yes. Then she told them I was in the woods. Two of the men went after me. Tucker and Peters were their names. The leader stayed behind, and that is when he shot Madame."

"Shot the dressmaker? After she sounded as if she was an accomplice?"

"The leader said 'he' wanted her dead."

"The leader wanted her dead?"

Elin made an impatient sound. "No, whoever had sent them wanted her dead as well as me. And he just killed her as if her life *meant nothing.*" Ben knew she was just holding on.

"So there were only three men in the attack?" Nate asked.

"Attack?" Elin repeated, surprised at the word, and then said, "Yes, I suppose it was. Three. I heard two names. Peters and Tucker."

"Is one of them the leader?" Ben pushed.

"No." Her shoulders slumped. She had to be exhausted. She yawned, a sign the brandy was doing its work.

"Osprey, do you have a room?" Ben asked. "Some place private for Miss Morris?"

"She can have my room," he answered. "It is off the hall in the back."

Ben and the others expected to sleep out on the benches. Over the past year, Ben had slept on the ground or the floor. He'd been leading a rough-and-ready life, but Elin needed something better. Safer.

Ben had explored the area earlier when they had first arrived. The Oak was comprised of two rooms—the main taproom and another room that was large and empty. Perhaps it was used for gatherings, but considering how isolated the tavern was, Ben couldn't imagine much call for the space. Off the hall, several tiny rooms were used for supplies. One of these small rooms contained an unmade cot, which the innkeeper used.

The room had also had a window and a floor littered with shoes, a tap for a keg that was soaking in a bucket for some reason, some leather harnesses, and a number of other things of the sort men collected.

"Let me straighten it up a bit," Osprey said, rushing out of the taproom to do so.

"Try and eat a bit more of the stew," Ben advised Elin. "He may be awhile at it."

She attempted to comply and looked up in relief when Osprey came back into the room and nodded to Ben, a sign that he could take Elin back.

"Excuse me, lads," Ben said rising. He reached for Elin's arm. She was exhausted and had grown uncharacteristically quiet and docile. She allowed him to escort her to the back room.

Osprey had left a candle burning in his room. The yellow light was a beacon in the room's shadowy blackness.

The innkeeper's idea of clean and Ben's were two different things, but Elin didn't raise a fuss.

No, she had something else on her mind.

"What are you doing here?" she asked once

they had stepped inside the room. "Why are you with those men?"

Fooled again. He had completely misunderstood her silence.

"They are my friends," Ben answered.

"Perhaps, but they aren't the sort I would think the duke would admire."

Ben bristled. He tried to tamp it down, but the hour was late. "You may dance to my brother's tune, but I don't."

"I'm not criticizing—"

"You are not? Of course you are. And here, I thought you were glad to see me. At least, you expressed that an hour ago."

"I *am* happy to see you—" She caught herself and stopped, releasing a breath with great patience before saying, "I am *very* happy to see you. What is between you and Gavin is none of my business."

"Exactly."

"Then again, it is obvious you are not complying with what he wants you to do."

"Why do you say that?"

"The untamed hair, the clothes, the companions."

"Next you will be pointing out that 'I stink.'"

His accusation, softly spoken, was a direct reference to their last meeting and words he had never forgotten. They burned deep inside him.

She didn't pretend not to understand. A dull stain crept up her cheeks. Her jaw tightened.

And he could have kicked himself.

Why was nothing simple when it came to this woman?

Moments before he was completely sympathetic to her. But he always seemed to be waiting for her to say one thing wrong. To offer any criticism . . . and he didn't understand himself.

"That was crude of me," he murmured. "Ignore me."

Now she appeared genuinely confused. "Well, you do smell better than you did that night."

"I'd traveled a long way that day and the days before it," he admitted.

"And had drunk quite a bit."

"I bathed in whisky," he agreed, and surprised a laugh out of her.

She covered her mouth as if afraid she offended him again, and he waved her fears away with a motion of his hand.

"I wasn't good that night," he confessed.

There was beat of silence. "It was a terrible night."

"I know."

Now it was his turn to pause, to consider carefully what he wanted to say. A year and a half ago, he had attempted to make amends and had not heard one word from her until she'd run into the Oak's taproom this evening.

And what did he want to say? *She still isn't yours,* an inner voice reminded him. She'd announced in front of Hooknose and the others that she was bound for London to marry his brother and all of her own free will.

But she wasn't married yet.

It was amazing how insidious those little voices in his mind were. How they battled with each other, but only over this woman. Especially when she looked as vulnerable as she did now.

Her hair was a tangled mess and her face pale from worry and smudges of dirt from her ordeal. However, her dark eyes told him she was grateful to have found him.

Grateful. What a weak word. Too weak for what he wanted from her, and it was as if the years fell away, and he was once again under her spell. A spell she hadn't woven because she was oblivious to him.

Self-pity, anger, and heartache started to raise their ugly heads. He forced them back.

God damn it all. He was a bloody fool.

And the sooner he scooted her out of his life, the better he would be. He'd found peace without her twice now. He would find it again.

"So," he said, clapping his hands to punctuate

the word and return his mind to good sense. "You need your rest, and tomorrow, we'll take you to your father." He moved toward the doorway, and half-out of it, pulling the door shut when Elin took a step toward him—and that was all it took for him to pause.

"Thank you, Ben," she whispered. "Thank you for being here."

Elin had never had guile. She had always said exactly what she thought. It wasn't her fault that this defenseless side of her ripped all of his good intentions to shreds. He wanted nothing more than to fall on his knees in front of her and beg her to give him another chance.

But he was a man. Men didn't beg.

"Right," he said, sounding almost cheery. "Tomorrow." He shut the door and, at last, took a full breath.

"Ah, yes," he muttered to himself. "St. Benedict Whitridge, martyr to lost causes and defender of stray kittens." He balled his hand into a fist and pounded it into the wood of the wall across from her room.

The pain felt good.

It felt manly.

And suddenly he realized what was missing between them. The love he'd once hoped they shared—and it was strictly all his belief because she had never professed it—had died, lost to his adolescent fumbling and to his foul temper over a year ago.

And there was nothing he could do about the impression. In truth, Gavin was a better man than he was.

Never once in his life had Ben had such a thought, and now here it was, full-blown in his mind. His ducal brother was the better man—especially where Elin was concerned and perhaps everywhere else.

Ben walked back to the taproom, his hand smarting, as was his ego.

He'd prided himself on his honesty. He knew he resented his brother. He just didn't want to delve into why. It was enough that Gavin had effortlessly claimed Elin. And if there was more to his resentment, Ben wasn't certain he wished to examine it—

Three feet from the light flowing from the taproom door, Ben sensed something was wrong. There were no voices, no idle chatter, no rattling of the dice. Cautiously, he moved forward, and as he did so, Hooknose took up a post in the doorway, leaning against the frame.

Ben came up behind him. Hooknose was expecting him. "We have visitors," he murmured.

Leaning around his friend, Ben's gaze fell upon three hulking men who looked the worse for wear.

They stood at the bar gobbling down Osprey's stew. In their long canvas coats and worn boots, they would fit anyone's image of "murderers."

Ben wanted to return to Elin, to see her safe. However, the moment he prepared to back up, the tallest of the men caught sight of him in the doorway. For a long moment their gazes held, and if Ben had any doubts about Elin's story, they were dispelled.

The leader had removed his hat. Greasy dark hair stood this way and that. He would have appeared comical if not for the growth of beard on his jaw and the menace in his light brown eyes. Wolf's eyes.

His gaze shifted from Ben, scanning the room.

"You don't have any bread?" one of his men growled at Osprey, who was pouring more ale into their mugs.

"They ate it all," the innkeeper said, nodding to the table where Nate and Big Roger sat. They had started taking turns disinterestedly rolling the dice. Ben's winnings were still on the end of the table. That was too bad, because Ben had a feeling he wasn't going to be staying long enough to collect them. He just hoped the other lads would enjoy the bounty.

The Wolf took a moment to glare at the two young men who stood at the far corner of the bar. Ben hadn't paid much attention to them himself.

Osprey had said they were local lads who left their wives for a night out every chance they could. The heavy one's face was marred by spots. The other had a huge Adam's apple. Ben's thought was that their wives were probably happy to have them out of their way. They didn't look like the sort who were hard workers.

Feeling the Wolf's scrutiny, they hunkered down, not wanting trouble. He dismissed them with a curl of his lip and picked up his tankard.

Ben decided to take a step back and see what happened. He knew he could depend on Hook-nose, Nate, and Big Roger. He could feel them watching him, waiting for a signal of what he wanted to have happen. It should be easy to over-power the threesome—

The Wolf slammed his empty tankard upside down on the table and pulled a horse pistol from the inside of his coat. He cocked it.

Ben froze.

"We are looking for a woman," the Wolf said, his voice deep, gravelly, and surprisingly cultured. "She may be lost. We'd like to find her. Has anyone seen her?"

Osprey quickly said, "I've not seen any lost women wandering in here."

"Haven't either," said Hooknose. Nate was quiet, but Big Roger shrugged his agreement with his mates.

The Wolf's glance fell on Ben. "She left tracks. It's dark out there, but I'm a good tracker. She was coming this direction. I think she would have been attracted to the light. We were."

And then he turned to the two lads standing at the bar, the ones who had been trying to make themselves unnoticeable, and he smiled. It was a horrible expression to see because his teeth were sharp and jagged from having been broken. He aimed his pistol at them, and the lads were undone.

"There was a woman," Spot Face said, "and you can ask that man where she is." He pointed to Ben in the doorway.

"Ah," Ben said with mock sincerity, "you didn't need to tattle, lad." On those words, Big Roger and Nate picked up the table where they'd been sitting and threw it at the Wolf and his men.

Ben turned and ran for Elin.

Chapter Seven

Elin had heard Ben slam his fist into the wall and had even heard the small grunt of pain he'd tried to swallow afterward.

He had never been one to hide his feelings. In their youth, she had witnessed him giving vent to his temper with his fist against a wall and once into a tree trunk. But only when he was truly, *truly* angry.

Of course, in the past, his anger had been directed at his father.

Tonight, she knew it was directed at *her*.

Or was it that they were once more thrown together whether he liked it or not?

She raised a weary hand to her hair and pushed the weight of it back over her shoulder. "I don't like it any more than you do," she whispered.

And yet she was so blessedly grateful for his presence.

All would be right now. She knew it. Ben was a return to a reality she understood. What had happened on the road had shaken her, as it would anyone. Her servants didn't deserve to die, not even Madame Odious.

A part of Elin wanted to pretend the murders had never happened and that she was meant to be in this rabbit warren of a tavern. She could imagine her meeting with Ben had been planned . . . once again practically on the eve of her wedding to his brother.

That thought gave her pause and indicated just how exhausted she was. She unfastened the frog of her cloak. She was so tired, yet she feared sleep would be impossible and, in spite of her doubts, she wished Ben hadn't left her, that he'd stayed close or even in this room.

Of course, he was not far away, but right now, she felt very fragile. It had been good to have his strong arms around her and his quick mind to challenge hers.

Gingerly, she sat on the edge of the rickety bed where Osprey slept. It smelled of the onions and meat he used in his stew. She huddled under her cloak, pulling it around as if it were armor. Her nerves refused to settle. She glanced at the door. "Ben, come back," she whispered.

Then, maybe she could sleep in spite of the place smelling of turnips. In the morning, they would talk sensibly and kindly to each other. She might learn why he'd hit the wall, what she'd done or said.

And maybe he'd explain why he had left all those years ago, why he had betrayed *her* trust—?

A muted crashing sound came from the direction of the taproom. Elin leaped to her feet, her senses alert. A beat later, her door was thrown open, and Ben came barreling though.

"Are you dressed?" he demanded, answering the question himself with, "Good. You are. Shoes? Good." He opened the window. It was stuck, so he pounded it with his fists to knock it loose.

"What is happening?" she asked.

"Blow out the candle," he ordered, raising the sash.

Elin did as bid, throwing the room into blackness. He grabbed her shoulder. "Out the window," he commanded, practically picking her up and tossing her, with her cloak, out onto the ground.

Fortunately, the ground was soft albeit uneven. She wobbled, but before she could regain her balance, Ben landed beside her. "Run."

He didn't have to say that word twice. She understood the danger.

Clutching her still-unfastened cloak, Elin ran.

Ben was right behind her. His hand on her back guided her once again into the woods.

"What is happening?" she repeated at the first opportunity.

"Your friends."

Shots came from inside of the inn, confirming his words. Ben stopped; he turned. He would have gone back, but she found his arm and gripped it tight.

There was a beat of silence, of Ben's indecision, then the leader's unmistakable voice shouted, *"Find her."*

"Run," she whispered, and run they did. Ben's arm scooped around her and he half carried her forward. Behind them there was the sound of horses running and men shouting. Everything seemed to be happening at once, and the silent woods were a perfect foil for the confusion they heard at the tavern.

Elin's feet only touched the ground every other step—and then they were falling.

There was a drop-off that Ben had not seen in the darkness. He lost his footing, and they went flying, then rolling over and over again into what seemed to be the blackest pit, the dry bed of a brook that no longer existed. The ground was rocky, hard, and covered with damp leaves.

Elin didn't make a sound as they rolled. She

couldn't. Every time she thought to scream, his weight was on top of her, and yet, he seemed to be trying to bear the brunt of the force of their falling. She knew her suspicions were right when they finally came to a halt, and she was on top of him.

Panic threatened, but Ben rolled her on her back, his body covering hers. "Are you all right?" he whispered, running his hand over in the dark as if the check for himself.

"I think so."

"Wiggle your toes."

She frowned. Considering the circumstances, his order sounded silly. Still, she obeyed. She circled one foot and then the other. She would be covered with bruises, but her toes moved.

"Wiggle yours," she whispered back.

She sensed that mobile, irrepressible mouth of his stretching into a grin. "As you wish."

"I can't tell if you moved them," she only half-mockingly complained.

"You would have heard me groan if they were broken."

"So you are together?" she asked.

"I believe so."

"Good, because you may need to carry me—not because anything is broken," she quickly added lest he mistake her meaning.

His hand came up to cup the side of her face as if he were reassuring himself that she was well.

Or perhaps he wished to bolster her, which the gesture did. His hand was rough, masculine. He had calluses; then again, Ben had always been ready to work with his hands. Still, his hands were in stark contrast with those of most gentlemen she knew.

Nor was his body soft.

He was taller than his brother and leaner but as muscular. She preferred being with him right now. He had fought in war and experienced who knew what other adventures. He would see her through.

Ben started to rise, but then his body went rigid, and he came back down, gathering her to him.

A beat later, she heard what he had. "Over here," a man's voice carried in the night. "Darby, I heard something over here."

Elin stopped breathing. She inched even closer to Ben.

"Where?" the leader's unmistakable voice asked. A horse blew and stamped the ground. It sounded too close.

Darby was the leader. Tucker, Peters, Darby. These were the names of her attackers and Elin stored this information away.

"Along here." The light from a lamp flashed above them.

She inched closer to Ben, praying they were hidden in the shadows.

And then there was the sound in the distance of running hooves.

Darby swore. "They were at the horses."

"We looked there."

"They are riding away." Rocks, twigs, and leaves fell down into the dry bed as the men turned their horses and went riding toward the sound.

And then they were gone. Elin heard them go crashing through the woods after the riders.

Elin released her breath, as did Ben. He jumped to his feet. "Stay," he whispered, and scrambled up the bank to scout.

He jumped back into the dry bed, proving he was completely sound. "They are gone. For now. Let me help you up."

She needed his help. Her knees hurt, her ankles hurt, the left side of her hip hurt as he helped her up the bank. He took her hand, lacing his fingers in hers. "Can you walk?" he asked.

"Do I have a choice?"

"Possibly. Let's see what we can find out. Come."

Elin followed. It seemed the most natural thing to do at this moment. Follow Ben; be safe.

Of course, there had been a time when she'd followed him into all sorts of adventures. Being with him right now seemed natural to her. Peaceful, even, as if she'd found a part of her that had long been lost—until she realized he was leading her to the tavern.

She dug in her heels. "Shouldn't we be going *away* from here?"

"We will, but we need a few things first. If you wish, you may wait here."

"I'm not staying alone," she informed him, but he had already let go of her hand and was stealthily making his way to the front of the building. She followed.

Her night vision was very good right now. She noticed that the horses were gone.

Ben peered through a window, then opened the front door and walked right in. Elin came behind him. She blinked in the light from the hearth and a few candles, then she saw the bodies.

A beefy man lay on his back next to the door. He was Peters or Tucker. There was a trail of blood where they had dragged him from where he died.

The room itself was in a shambles. Tables had been overturned and chairs broken.

Osprey came in from the outer room. He held an ancient blunderbuss. He smiled with relief at the sight of Ben and raised the gun, nodding to the body beside the door. "Still works. I wondered, but now I know."

"So you returned," Big Roger's voice said as he stood up from where he'd been in hiding behind the bar. He, too, held a gun, a horse pistol like the one Darby and his men had been using.

"What happened?" Ben asked.

"You left in the ruckus, Whit," Big Roger said. "Those are dangerous men. They don't hesitate to kill."

"How did that one die?" Ben asked.

"I shot him," Osprey answered, waving his gun.

Big Roger placed the horse pistol on the bar and lifted a tankard he'd been using. "They didn't want us. They want your lass. They want her bad. After they saw you leave the room, they went after you, but I was right on them. I thought I was handy with my fives, but they are meaner." He lifted a hand to his jaw to show what he meant.

"Knocked him out," Osprey said, impressed. "So, I shot one of them. They didn't even stop for their companion. Roger is right. They want you," he said to Elin.

A coldness stole over Elin. A dread.

"Who rode off?" Ben asked Big Roger

"Who else? Nate and Hook Nose. They think to lead those bastards a merry chase, pardon my bluntness, Miss."

Elin waved away any offense. As she did so, she realized she still wore her gloves. After every-thing she had been through this day, she had the absurd notion to laugh at her properness.

Ben cast a worried glance at her and walked to the bar. "Any more of that brandy?"

"Nate bounced it off the head of that lad who pointed a finger at you," Osprey said. "That lad is a fool. Always thinking he is better than he should be. He won't be showing his face here again."

"Try this," Big Roger said, and pushed his tankard toward Ben, who carried it to Elin.

"Courage," he said as he handed it to her. The mug was full. She drank, then wanted to curl up and weep.

"Do you have any food we can take?" Ben asked the innkeeper.

"I have cheese and some dried apples. That's all you and your mates haven't eaten."

"We'll take that with your leave," Ben said. "I don't know where the money I won is now that the table is broken, but you can have it all."

"Don't worry," Osprey said, turning on his heel to fetch the food from someplace in the back.

Ben went to the dead body and knelt. "It is too bad we couldn't learn his secrets."

"Such as?" Big Roger said.

"Who hired him. I have no doubt he is being paid well for his services. The heels of his boots aren't even worn down." Ben started going through the man's pockets, something that gave Elin the chills.

"Already did that," Big Roger said. "He had nothing but this gun and a powder pouch." He placed the pistol and pouch on the bar. "Here, take it."

Ben felt something in the man's sleeve. He

rolled it back to reveal a hidden pocket. He pulled out a small pistol, the size of his palm. It was an ornate thing, with a gilded wheel lock and ivory carvings embedded in the grip.

Big Roger whistled. "It is too pretty to work."

"Why else would he have it?" Ben held the gun to the light and cocked it. "It's loaded."

"Tricky bastard, wasn't he?" Big Roger said. "He meant business."

"We already knew that." Ben stepped over the man's body. Uncocking the pistol, he offered it to Elin. "Are you still a good shot?"

"With a hunting gun."

"There isn't much difference," he assured her. "You cock it and fire."

She took the weapon. It was surprisingly heavy for its size. She dropped it into a pocket inside her cloak. Meanwhile, Ben went over to the hook where his wool coat, one from his military days, was hanging among the others. The length went down to the top of his boots.

He also collected the horse pistol and gunpowder Big Roger was generously giving him. "Thanks, mate."

Osprey returned with a sack of food for them. "Here you go, Whit. Good luck to you."

"Thank you, Osprey. Big Roger." He nodded to them. "Our paths will cross again. Come, Miss Morris."

But Elin had something to say. These men had risked their lives for her without even knowing who she was.

She stepped forward. "Thank you. I will remember this, and so will my father. You don't know, but the man you called Whit is the Duke of Baynton's brother." She felt impelled to share this. "Whit" had powerful connections.

The two men appeared unimpressed.

"You know who the Duke of Baynton is?" she prodded.

"Aye, we've heard of him," Big Roger said with a touch of distaste. "And we always knew there was more to Whit than meets the eye." He turned to Ben, and said, "Nate served under you. You wouldn't remember him, but he said you were a right one. Having spent my time marching for the king, I knew what he meant. Most officers are bloody fools. You're not. We helped you, Whit, because we like you. And," he added, a bit of mischief in his eye, "you don't win that often at dice. I hope your luck is better giving those bully lads a chase."

Ben moved forward and took Big Roger's hand in a strong grip.

"Safe travels," Big Roger said.

"Same to you," Ben answered. "Come, Miss Morris."

"We've heard of Fyclan Morris as well," Big

Roger called after her, as she went out the door, then he began laughing, a huge, hearty sound that followed them into the night.

Ben moved forward, but Elin held back. "Did I offend him?"

He had her by her cloak and gave it a yank, pulling her. "What? By letting him know what a service he'd done for the nation in helping to save the mighty duke of Baynton's future duchess? Hurry on now, will you." He moved ahead of her.

Elin grabbed her cloak and pulled back. She had no intention of being led through the forest all night as if she was a toddler. Nor did she understand his testiness.

"I never mentioned myself," she declared, careful to keep her voice low.

"No, you were too busy babbling about my brother."

"What does that mean? And will you slow down? Or are you so annoyed with me you wish to walk off?"

"I'm not annoyed with you," he threw out without easing his pace. Indeed, they had reached a path that even she could see in the forest. He turned, walking backward to remind her, "There are men who wish to kill you, or have you forgotten?"

"I hope you trip over a tree root."

Ben laughed, the sound almost bitter. "I don't

know why I try," he said to himself. He turned around and went striding off.

Elin took three quick skips to catch up to him. Walking right at his elbow, she said, "Try?" She shook her head. "This is you trying to do what? Leave me behind? Pretending innocence? I know you too well. When you are in a good mood, you match your step with mine. But when you are being testy with me, you seem to enjoy watching me run to keep up with you."

"I'm not testy," he answered testily, not breaking his stride.

He carried the sack Osprey had given them slung over one shoulder. She grabbed ahold of it, the same way he'd taken her cloak and pulled back.

Ben stopped. "*What?*" The sound was loud in the night woods. Too loud. They both knew it, and she could almost see his face flush at his silly mistake.

"What have I done wrong?" she whispered. "You are out of sorts with me. We're both tired. I'm exhausted. This day has been—" Her voice broke off as she searched for a word and had to settle on, "*Trying*. But I don't understand how *I* have annoyed you."

He did not want this conversation. The tension radiated off of him, the same way it had the night of her betrothal party.

"Very well," he said, the words curt as if she should already understand. "In London, it is good to be a duchess or related to the Duke of Baynton, but out here a person must prove himself. I proved myself to those men, and I believe I've proved myself to you, over and over again. Yet you focus on my sainted brother, the anointed one. The Chosen."

"Ben, I appreciate what you are doing for me. I saw those men respect you. They offered their lives to help us."

"But . . ." he prompted, as if anticipating what she would say.

"But?"

"There is always a 'but, Ben' with you."

"Stop that. You are being ridiculous. I meant no insult to you or to them. I am thankful you are here. I just thought . . ." Her voice trailed off as she realized she had wanted to impress the innkeeper and Big Roger.

"You just wanted them to know that you were important," he accurately finished for her. "As if being a mere person who was in trouble and needed help wasn't good enough. Well, Elin, they didn't care. It made no matter to them. But don't worry. I'll see you back to my brother. The two of you can talk about how important each of you are. You can even have dinner parties on the subject."

He began walking away, but after a few steps, he stopped. He looked over his shoulder at her. "Coming?"

"You are important, too, Ben."

"The devil I am." He came back to her in two strides. "I was important once, important of my own making. I was a good officer, Elin."

"I believe that." After all, he'd left her to become a good officer.

"And, yes, I have a *well* of resentment in me," he confessed. "I've never wanted to be second-best. And I believe I know why Jack ran away. He hated the competition. Father pitted him against Gavin all the time but not because he wanted Jack to excel. No, he just wanted Gavin to be better. The rest of us didn't matter."

Elin had thought she knew Ben well.

She now realized there were layers to him that she had never known.

"You believe Jack ran away?"

"And that it wasn't foul play? Or some other such nonsense?" Ben shrugged. "I don't know. But I learned what happens when I cross my father. Oh, yes, I learned indeed, and Jack had always been the more daring of all of us. Perhaps he learned that lesson as well and grew tired of it. Perhaps, he, too, didn't want to be the duke-in-waiting in case we were ever called upon. He wasn't that sort. He always bucked the rules."

"But the second son needs to be close at hand . . . if the title is to be handled correctly."

"*Think*, Elin. Look among the *ton*. What younger sons are doing anything of purpose that makes them happy?"

"Many are scholars. Some have been in the military."

"They are the ones who have other brothers than mine. If Jack were here, I'd be fighting the French right now, and he'd be the one expected to dance to Gavin's tune."

"Gavin is not that demanding."

"I am the judge of how he is. I've lived under him. I did try, Elin. I want you to know that. But Gavin expected me to wait on him every day. And I know it isn't his fault. He was just doing to me what Father did to him. How he stood it, I will not know. Then again, Father put his mark on Gavin at an early age."

"But not on you."

"Because there was Jack."

"Not always. Not after he disappeared."

"Right." He shifted his weight as if chewing on her observation, then dismissed it with a shrug. "It's all in the past. Father's dead. Jack is probably dead as well. Mother always claims that he is not. She says she has a mother's heart, and she would know if he had died. But none of it matters. My task now is to take you to Baynton, the man who has everything."

Again, she heard a touch of bitterness in his tone. He considered her a chore. His whole manner spoke of it, and maybe she was.

Of course, how would she feel if their roles had been reversed, if she were the one expected to take him to the woman who would be his wife?

Elin didn't like the idea, and she wasn't certain why. Something had happened between them years ago, something dark, and she sensed he held her accountable.

"It must be hard to live with such resentment, Ben. What is wrong? What happened to you?"

There was a beat of anger-laden silence, as if asking for understanding had also been the wrong thing to say.

Finally, he spoke. "Come, Elin, we have a long way to go."

Chapter Eight

What is wrong, Ben? What happened to you?

Elin's questions echoed in his mind as he traipsed through the woods. He wasn't certain exactly what she meant. He also didn't wish to explain himself to her.

He told himself to brush aside his annoyance with her. She wasn't the girl of his youth. She'd proven that by her behavior in London and her words at the Oak.

She wanted to be a duchess.

There was no middle ground there. There could be nothing between them. She was marrying the right brother. Huzzah! Let there be light and little dukes all around.

Ben thought he was taking them north. The earlier blanket of clouds passed and left a night sky full of stars. Cold weather always made the sky more vivid, or at least it seemed so in his mind.

He tried to keep his steps short, but he was too aware of Elin's presence. She'd been right—he did want to run . . . and she deserved better than that.

Ben appreciated the silence between them as they concentrated on placing one foot in front of the other. He walked ahead, feeling for thorny bushes, fallen logs, and dangerous ruts in their path. He wasn't worried about animals. Although they tried to be quiet, they made enough sound to warn away badgers, deer, and hedgehogs. Ben was more certain they would meet bats above all else.

No, his senses strained for sounds of Elin's pursuer, Darby. It helped keep his attention off of her, which is why he hadn't realized how tired she was. But when he turned to offer her a drink from the jug of cider Osprey had included in their sack he was shocked at how exhausted she appeared. He made her take a drink and offered some of the dried apple slices, but she waved them away.

"We need to keep going," she murmured.

"No, we are going to sleep," he decided.

"But—" she started, and he shut her off.

"Trust me, Elin. I know what I'm doing."

She pressed her lips shut then. He took her hand and led her off the path until he found what he deemed a suitable place for the night. There was a circle of five trees with the shelter of a good number of shrubs and bushes. The ground was dry and fairly level. "This will do."

Elin practically collapsed under one of the trees. Curling up with her heavy cloak around her, she rolled on her side, using her arms as a pillow. He sat next to her, leaning his back against the tree.

It felt good to rest.

"Here," he said, "you can rest your head on my leg."

She shook her head no, not even bothering to open her eyes. Her breathing became deep and regular.

What is wrong, Ben? What happened to you?

Almost with a will of its own, his ungloved hand went to her tangle of curls. She had rarely worn it loose like this. She used to tie it back, not having time to fuss with all the pins and irons of hairstyling. He remembered how she complained about her maid following her around.

Only when her parents came to Heartwood did she buckle down and become the debutante heiress of their expectations.

Their expectations. She was wrong when she said he'd always known she was Gavin's. In the beginning, he never thought about it.

"Do you remember the first time we really met?" he asked her sleeping form. "Not through our parents but when we knew we were kindred souls?" He rubbed one of her silky curls between his fingers before releasing it. "It was the day you rode your horse into the pond and disturbed my fishing. I was furious, and you laughed. You challenged me to a race. You were twelve, and you'd outdistanced your groom." He liked the memory. "We were waiting in the stables for him when he returned, flustered because he couldn't find you. We became inseparable on that day."

Because of Jack's disappearance, his father had refused to send Ben away to school. For a parent who had benignly ignored his younger children, his father had become a madman in his search for Jack. He'd had armies of men walking across the school grounds and using pikes to explore the bottom of ponds on the property. He'd hired a series of men to investigate and track what could have happened to Jack *if* his son had left the school, and they found nothing.

The disappearance became the talk of London. Ben didn't know very much except that the brother he admired was gone and that his father refused to let him go to school. Instead, the duke hired a number of tutors who saw to Ben's education.

Ben had been disappointed. He'd been anxious to go out in the world, as was done by every son of every other important family.

"You helped me through all that," he said to Elin. Funny, he'd grown so angry over the years, that he'd forgotten how much her friendship had meant. Elin had understood. Elin had listened.

Did he need any other reason to love her?

Ben stretched out beside her, remembering another night when they had slept side by side. The warmth of her body had felt good then as it did now.

He had the urge to lean closer, to drink in her scent.

That night was the first and only time they'd kissed. Of course, he remembered that kissing Elin had been as natural to him as breathing. She'd filled his senses . . . and they had been both so young.

Ben had a habit of writing out his last wishes on the eves before battle. He would let himself think of Elin then. He could recall every detail from the moment the storm had descended on them to their running for the shelter of an abandoned cottage, to their earnest fumbling.

"There had been no furniture in that cottage," he whispered to her sleeping form. "We were much as we are now."

They had huddled close, needing each other's body heat with their wet clothes. Elin had been shivering, and night was falling fast. Ben had been wearing an oilskin coat. He had taken it off and offered it to her. His jacket and his shirt were dry. She could be warm.

"And the next thing I knew, we were kissing." Ben lightly touched Elin's hair. Her back was against his side. He yearned to turn in to her, but that was tempting the devil too much.

Their lovemaking had been a miserable experience. For both of them. They had been two virgins without an inkling other that what they'd seen in the animal kingdom. He'd hurt her. He hadn't understood then. He'd been mortified at her reaction.

"It would be better now," he promised the sleeping Elin. A promise that he'd never have the opportunity to prove.

Elin was right. She wasn't his. His father had lashed that fact into his thick skull, a lesson never to be forgotten.

"Besides," he confided, "I do like Gavin. I care for him as a brother although I haven't ever said so. He's arrogant and single-minded and pursues all the wrong things, but he is the only brother I have left." He started to touch her hair again, then pulled his hand back.

Instead, he moved so there was some distance between them.

Tomorrow, in daylight, he'd work out where they were and how to see her to safety, to Gavin.

Until then, he needed to keep his hands and his mind off of her. Many things in his life had changed, but, surprisingly, Elin's spirit and her ability to move him was still the same.

Elin woke with her mouth open and drool running down her cheek.

She'd slept hard. Too hard. And her eyes were so crusted with sleep, she had no desire to open them.

Then she became aware that she was not in her comfortable feather bed or in her nightdress. She shifted, rubbed her eyes, and opened them.

For a second, she couldn't remember where she was. She was wearing her cloak and the lovely peacock blue day dress out of the softest wool imaginable that had quickly become her favorite out of the ones Madame Odette had made for her. She even wore her shoes.

Why would she sleep in her shoes—? A breeze curled around her, bringing her fully to her groggy senses and reminding her that she slept on the ground.

Ben.

All recollection returned with that one word. Madame Odette was dead, Elin was running for her life, Ben was helping her, and she must look horrid. Terrible.

Elin pushed herself to sit upright, combing her hair out of the way with her fingers. Her curls were going every which way with a will of their own.

The day was well advanced, or so she thought. Not only was the sky overcast, but she'd slept in the shadowy shelter of a copse of pines. Thickets surrounded her haven and, all things considered, the pine-needle floor had been comfortable.

But where was Ben? She thought about calling his name, then feared attracting any attention. Silence was better.

She stretched and rose to her feet. There was a cool heaviness in the air. Rain. She didn't want to think on it. Instead, she went in search of Ben. She found him not far from the pines.

He lay on his back, stretched out on the trunk of a huge fallen tree. The tree had snapped close to its roots and still had gray, withered leaves on its branches. He stared up at the sky, one foot on the ground, the other bent at the knee. She wondered what he was thinking, and in that moment, seeing him at ease, her heart ached for their lost friendship. She'd never trusted anyone as much as she had Ben.

He sensed her presence and in one fluid, graceful movement sat up. Last night, he'd been tense and sometimes angry with her. But now he smiled, and for a second, it was hard for Elin to think. She'd forgotten what a disarming smile he had. His was full of white teeth and the right hint of devilment.

"I trust you slept well," he said.

"Fair." Her voice sounded as if she were imitating a frog. She cleared her throat.

"Here have something to drink." He picked up the jug of cider they shared from the ground beside the log and offered it to her.

Elin came forward and took a sip. The cider was tart. "I'm feeling the exertion of yesterday. Especially that roll down the hill."

"Can you travel?"

"I don't have a choice, do I? Did you sleep?"

"I did," he answered, rising to his feet. "I had a good night."

"You should have wakened me instead of waiting. We should be moving on."

"Aye, but you also needed to rest. Yesterday was a hard day."

That was an understatement. "Will we reach some place civilized today?"

"I hope, if the rain doesn't stop us. But first, you need to eat. Breakfast will be more of Osprey's dried apples with a piece of the hardest cheese I've ever chewed on." His teeth flashed their agreement in his mobile, wonderful smile. He seemed so relaxed that her own anxiety eased a bit.

She handed the jug to him. "I need a moment."

He understood what she was saying. "There is a brook about forty feet in that direction. You'll hear it as you draw closer. If you need anything, call me."

Elin nodded her obedience and tried not to hobble in a way that he'd notice. She didn't think she succeeded.

All around her was the deep green of the pines and hollies dominated by the browns and grays of the other trees and plants. It was undisturbed and peaceful.

She heard the sound of the brook running over stones on its rushed way to wherever it needed to go. It had etched its way about five feet down a bank. After a few moments to herself, she carefully climbed down the steep bank and, keeping her cloak dry, tested the water. Nothing could be colder than this stream. She cupped her palm and drank a sip or two before splashing her face and removing the last traces of sleep from her eyes.

At last she began to feel ready for the tasks ahead. Even her sore muscles were easing. She might even manage to walk halfway decently again.

Her curls were loose and carefree. She ripped the lace trim off of her petticoat and used it as ribbon to tie her hair up so that it was away from her face.

But she didn't go back to Ben immediately. Instead, Elin savored this moment.

She wrapped her arms around her knees and rested her chin upon them, listening to the sound of the water. All was good right now. She prayed she had the courage to continue on without fear.

Across the steam from her, a rabbit stuck his head out of a burrow hidden by a clump of grass. He saw her and quickly retreated. Elin waited, knowing that for curiosity alone, the animal would return, and so he did. This time, he even took a step toward the water before deciding that taking a drink was a far-too-risky endeavor with her there.

Footsteps came up behind her. She wasn't concerned. She sensed it was Ben even before he said, "Elin, are you all right? You have been here for a while."

She tilted her head to look up at him. He stood about three feet up from her on the bank. If she squinted her eyes, she could imagine him as the Ben of her youth. He'd been lanky and broad-shouldered then, but now he had a man's presence. "I was woolgathering."

"You always did that," he said good-naturedly. "But we have a ways to go, and you haven't had anything to eat. Come along." He moved toward the top of the bank.

Elin stood, but instead of following, she asked,

"Are we ever going to talk about what happened between us?"

Ben stopped. "Between us? Yesterday? At your betrothal party?"

He knew what she meant. She knew it, and she was a bit stunned over her own audacity in mentioning the past openly.

This morning had brought a truce of sorts between them. She was now challenging what peace there was between them—and yet, she must.

"About the night we spent in that cottage together," she said, her voice calm in contrast to the tightening in her chest. "About your leaving the next day."

He crouched as if to bring himself to her eye level. The easiness had left his manner. Instead, a muscle worked in his jaw.

Yes, it was still between them. It would always be between them unless they confronted it now.

"I miss you," she dared to say. "I miss the"—she paused, searching for a word that could protect her—"friendship we had." She broke her gaze away from his, astonished at her honesty. She'd spoken up. She'd revealed more than she'd ever thought she would to him.

"Friendship?" he said. "Is that all we had?"

Her heart gave a start. "All?"

He dropped his arms to rest on his thighs. His gaze slid away from her to something in the distance that only he could see; and then he swung his attention back to her. "I loved you."

Elin didn't know what she had expected him to say, but it wasn't those words.

A jumble of emotions, including a senseless amount of anger, welled inside her. "*Love?*" The word didn't even taste good to her. It couldn't. "Then *why* did you *leave me*?" Naked pain etched every word. Pain that she'd pent up through the hours, days, months ruminating over how Ben could have abandoned her.

And he had the impudence to claim he'd *loved* her?

His idea of love and hers were obviously very different, and she knew because she'd loved him.

Oh, yes, *she had loved him*.

Elin might not have realized it at the time, but that was only because she'd been too young. Her mother had claimed her feelings for Ben had been nothing more than an infatuation, a silliness, really.

However, standing here, out in the open, Elin realized her mother had been wrong. Elin had depended upon Ben. She'd trusted him, in spite of a confusing, disappointing, and, yes, unsettling experience between them. She'd wanted to talk to him about it—but he'd left.

His leaving was more than saying he didn't care for her. It had been a betrayal of her trust.

For his part, the ever-mobile Ben had now gone very still, almost as if he'd turned to stone. As if he wasn't aware of the minutes stretching between them as she sorted out her mind, pulling them further and further away from each other.

"*Say something*," she demanded, angrily pulling on her gloves. "*Speak.*"

A glint came to his eye, a warning.

Elin didn't care if she went too far. She'd spent too much time not going far enough.

But in the end, he was the only one who could decide what came next, and he did.

"Yes. Well." He rose. "Come eat." He didn't wait for her response but began walking back to their haven of pine trees.

That was all he had to say?

Perhaps she should be glad for it. Perhaps, if he wasn't such a selfish, disrespectable blackguard, then that love she had once had for him might have flourished—and she didn't want that. Oh, no, *never* that.

In fact, in this moment, she was pleased, no, *thrilled* she was marrying Baynton.

And she was no fool. She knew Ben resented her betrothal along with everything else he claimed to dislike about his brother.

Well, he had now convinced her that her parents had been wise in choosing Gavin for her, and she would tell her father so when next she saw him. She would gratefully throw herself into his arms and beg him to keep Benedict Whitridge away from her.

Nor was she going to blithely follow him up the bank and munch on dried apples because he felt she needed it. She could take care of herself, thank you very much.

Elin lifted the hem of her cloak and dress. The stream was three feet across. If she wasn't lucky, she could land right in it.

But she wouldn't. She was too angry to fail.

She took a few steps back and then leaped for the other side. She almost lost her footing. The wet, soft bank threatened to give out beneath her, but she caught her balance and, with a few steps forward, righted herself by grabbing the thin trunk of a young tree. The rabbit poked his head out in surprise, saw her only inches away from his home, and scurried back to safety.

Elin wanted to roar in triumphant, pleased at what she'd done—until Ben appeared in search for her.

"Elin, stop brooding—" he was saying as he reached the top of the bank, then he broke off in surprise that she wasn't where he expected her to be, that she was on the opposite side of the stream.

With a wave of her hand, she bid him farewell,

scrambled up the other side of the bank, and dove into the dense brush of the forest.

Where the bloody hell did Elin believe she was going?

And was there a soul in the world who understood women?

If there was, Ben was certain it wasn't a male one.

He was also discovering that Elin had changed since their youth. Back then, he had thought them completely compatible.

Now, he realized there was absolutely *nothing* compatible between the two of them. He'd confessed that he had loved her. Those words had not been easy to say. And who, with any amount of reason, wouldn't believe it was true today?

Not Elin.

She'd behaved as if she hadn't heard a word he'd said. She had dismissed him and gone charging off in a female tiff. She thought she was putting him in his place.

Indeed, if he was smart, he would let her go. After all, no one wanted to kill him. No one was threatening him—but they were her . . . and even if she was being erratic and unpredictable, he didn't want harm to come to her—because he still did love her.

She was the woman by which he judged all others—and found them lacking—and it bit hard that she had been decidedly unimpressed with his confession.

Or was she too wrapped around the axle over *her* concerns? Too overwhelmed?

Then again, a man could only take so much. Elin had cost him his youthful pride, but it hadn't all been her fault. And he did have an obligation, and a desire, to keep her alive.

Ben didn't bother calling after her again. He knew she would ignore him. No, the only action he could take was to go after her. He'd have to chase her down, except he'd left the food sack and the cider jug by the tree trunk. He needed to fetch them first.

"But I'm coming after you, Elin. Oh, yes, I am," he promised as he started off the way he had come. "And when I catch you, then we'll have a discussion the likes of which you've never experienced before."

Chapter Nine

Stop brooding.

Elin couldn't believe Ben had said such to her.

However, after a good fifteen-minute trudge, the elation she felt at having outmaneuvered him and taken her fate into her own hands gave way to one overriding thought—she should have eaten something before she'd left.

Her stomach rumbled she was so hungry.

She could have stashed a few of Osprey's apples into the pocket of her cloak, nestling them next to the pistol; and then she wouldn't be so famished. Even the hard cheese sounded delicious. Placing one foot in front of the other, slapping overhanging branches out of her way, she walked with the determination of a woman too stubborn to admit defeat, her mind mulling over what sort of cheese Osprey had given them that had hardened.

From what little she knew of the tavern owner, it might have been a Leicester or a Swaledale, something relatively local. Why, he might even have made his own cheese, an idea she quickly rejected. Osprey's stew had been good and serviceable but she doubted he would expend the time for cheese making. Besides, he would need a cow or goat, and she hadn't noticed one around the tavern.

She herself was partial to Swaledale because it tasted richer, especially with apples. Those dried apples might taste very good with it.

Then again, Osprey may have given them a simple cheddar. One had to be careful with cheddar because it could have a bite. Elin never liked to eat anything where the taste was too sharp—

She heard the rustle of leaves, the footfalls of another presence.

She *knew* who was there. Ben had caught up with her.

Thoughts of cheese and hunger fled her mind. Her heart seemed to pick up its beat at the prospect of another confrontation. She'd acquitted herself well last time, and she expected to do the same during their next round of verbal sparring.

And yes, there would be another round because there was unfinished business between them.

Maybe there always would be.

Elin quickened her pace and found herself happier. It really hadn't been pleasant to be marching along alone, with killers on the loose.

But she was not going to acknowledge Ben's presence.

At least, not yet.

Of course, he didn't wait to let her know he'd arrived. He acted as if he'd always been there. So Ben.

"Do you have any idea where you are going?" he asked conversationally. He was closer behind her than she had thought, which made sense. His legs could eat up ground. He could take one step for her every two.

She debated pretending he wasn't there but couldn't. "South."

"Really?"

Elin drew her brows together. "Yes, really."

"Are you certain?"

Well, no, she wasn't.

She didn't slow her step, but she did glance around. She'd been using moss on tree trunks as her guide. It grew on the north side of trees, so she chose the opposite direction. And London was south. She was heading to London.

"Yes," she answered.

"Remember when my father's huntsman Herndon taught us that one could always tell which way was north by the way moss grew on the trees? It turns out that isn't always the case. Sometimes, if there is a great deal of moisture, like in a woods, such this one, well, moss can grow anywhere on a tree. Notice how it is growing all around the base of this beech right here? Fascinating."

Elin didn't find this information fascinating. It was dreadful news. She was tempted to change direction, to pause and consider where she was going . . . but that would be doing exactly what Ben wanted her to do.

He wanted her to doubt herself.

She could imagine how smug he'd feel if she even paused. He'd know he had the upper hand, and she was not about to let him have such satisfaction. She'd change her course, but slowly, so he wouldn't notice.

However, she was very relieved to have him with her.

They walked in silence for a good long way. Elin marched in the front with, she pictured, Ben sauntering behind her. He could have outdistanced her. He didn't. No, he shadowed her, obviously content to let her lead the way . . . wherever she was going.

The sky grew grayer, the clouds heavier, her hair curlier.

"Should we stop?" Ben asked.

Elin kept walking, feeling very noble that she was willing to plow on.

"I'm actually hungry," he complained.

Her stomach growled its assent. Her mind had been so preoccupied with him, she'd actually forgotten how starving she'd been. But she didn't stop. Her pride wouldn't let her, while another corner of her mind was a bit afraid of him.

He had once been her undoing. A principled woman should be cautious, and Elin wanted to be that woman. She'd failed once, but she'd been young, naïve. She was wiser now. She knew what was expected of her, what her mother would have wanted. Marrying Baynton would fulfill her parents' dream for her. So, instead of being so aware of Ben, she focused on his brother.

She began enumerating all of Gavin's good points: He was handsome. Certainly more handsome than Ben. Everyone agreed to that.

Although Ben had charm—when he wished to exercise it—and a definite presence.

Well, so did Gavin . . . but Ben's attention had always been focused on her. She'd never believed that he didn't see her for who she was.

He said he'd loved you.

It was a dangerous thing to think about that candid confession. Especially since, except for the night of her betrothal ball when Gavin had given her the pearls, Elin couldn't recall any meaningful conversations with the duke.

The thought unsettled Elin, and she wasn't certain why until Ben interrupted her thoughts by asking, "Do you still wear breeches when you ride?"

When she was a girl, Ben had convinced her to don a pair of boy's breeches under her riding habit. Her governess had objected strenuously and threatened to take away her riding privileges. A gentlewoman should never consider wearing breeches for any reason, she'd declared. However, since she never knew if Elin had breeches on under her habit or not, Elin did as she pleased.

Then, of course, the next step was to ride like a man. Elin had loved the freedom.

She'd continued the practice whenever she was in the country. The stable lads knew she rode astride every chance she could. But once she was married, she knew she'd have to give it up. Gavin wouldn't condone such a thing. He would side with the governess who had been horrified.

Ben began humming under his breath. The sound didn't carry any farther than to her. He hummed a jig, a silly sound, although she caught herself walking to its rhythm.

She tried to studiously ignore him, believing that would annoy him more than he was aggravating her.

After a few more minutes of winding their way through the forest, Ben proved her right.

"Elin, I cry quarter. Stop, will you? Look at me.

You didn't break your fast. You must be hungrier than I am. No wonder you are peevish."

"Peevish?" Elin whirled on Ben so abruptly, he had to take a step back or run into her. "I've never been peevish in my life."

"She said peevishly," he tacked on. Adding disclaimers to the end of their sentences had been a teasing game they had played years ago. A hallmark of their deep affection for each other.

"I'm not ready to stop," Elin murmured.

"Well go ahead then," he said, pulling the cider jug from the food sack and uncorking it. "I need a break. I'll catch up."

But she didn't move.

And when he tipped the cider jug offering it to her, she took it. Elin wiped the mouth of it with her gloved hand and drank. Her body needed the fluid.

When she lowered the jug, she found Ben holding a hunk of cheese he was prepared to slice with his knife. "Hungry?"

She was already reaching for a slice before he'd finished the word. Cheddar. But not a sharp one. She'd never tasted anything as good as that stale cheese.

"The apples are in the sack," he said, offering her the chance to help herself from the sack that he had set on the ground at his feet. She did so.

Pairing one of Osprey's apples with the cheese was divine, just as she'd imagined it would be. Ben kept cutting thin slices of the cheese, and she kept eating them.

"Feeling better?" he asked.

Elin nodded. "I'm never my best when I'm hungry."

"I know," Ben said. "I learned early on that you are a vastly happier woman when you are fed."

She pulled a face before drinking more cider. "It is almost empty."

"We'll fill it at the next brook or spring we come to." He took the jug from her and put a cork in it. He'd already wrapped what was left of the cheese and placed it back in the sack. As he did so, he said, almost casually, "I'm not your enemy, Elin."

"I know that."

He straightened. "Then can you let down your guard, even a little?"

She looked away. "You know I can't, and you know why."

"You're afraid I'll jump on you, rape you? Of all people, you should know better."

Yes, she did. "I need to keep a distance from you."

"*Why?*"

Oh, she did want to answer that question but couldn't. She wasn't certain yet what the truth was. It might not be wise to delve into matters best left in the past.

"It is wiser this way," she explained. "I belong to your brother—"

"*Enough* of that," he said, slicing the air with his hand to cut her off. "I believed this morning we were going to clear the air between us. Instead, you ran—"

"I didn't," Elin started, then stopped. She took a step away from him, unconsciously, then realizing what she was doing, she planted her feet. "I did. You caught me off guard when you . . ." She let her voice trail off.

"When I said I loved you?" he prompted.

"Or are you just trying to plant doubt in my mind about Gavin?"

Now it was his turn to inch away. He held up a hand as if letting her know she had hit upon something perhaps too touchy to pursue. "You hide behind that 'I'm his' very well, don't you?"

"What does that mean?"

"It means that you use your betrothal to my brother to keep a wall up between us—"

"That happens to be a very good boundary between us."

In two steps he was in front of her. "Really, Elin? Or is it just a way for you to punish me?"

"Punish—?" She did not like the word. "I don't punish you." The denial sounded false even to her own ears because she *did* want to punish him. She actually *liked* having a wall between them, a way to let him know he could not touch her . . . even while she longed for it.

And suddenly, she was tired of the game.

He'd been honest with her. By the stream, he had not told her anything she couldn't have reasoned out in her heart.

The excuses, the grudges she'd nursed against him since that ill-fated night began to lose their power.

She, too, missed her friend.

Tears threatened. But so did reason.

"I don't regret what happened that night," she said, carefully choosing her words. "What hurt, what makes me so angry with you, is that the next day you were gone. And there was no word from you—for years. You were a part of my life, then just left. What conclusion did you wish for me to draw? Because I'll tell you what I believe—I think you wanted to leave your mark on me. You knew you were leaving for the military, and you were so jealous of Gavin, you used me."

There, she said it, and quite well.

She looked at her gloved hands. "Dear God, I'm trembling. I've been *so* angry at you. I still am. You hurt me. I felt betrayed, I just want to—" She clenched her fists up in front of her.

And then it was gone. The anger left her. Years of pent-up resentment fell away because she'd finally spoken. "I feel better. I needed to tell you how deeply you'd hurt me. In fact, I actually feel lighter."

And almost dizzy. She took a deep breath, then another, and another before daring a glance at Ben to see how he'd accepted her outburst.

To her surprise, he wasn't angry. No, he appeared stunned, as if she had planted her fist in his face. "I didn't want to leave, Elin."

"So you say. You left. You didn't write."

Ben slowly sank to his knees on the ground in front of her. "Elin, you sent me away."

His words didn't make sense to her. "I didn't."

"Did you tell your parents what had happened?"

Elin released her breath slowly. "My mother, yes."

"Why? We had promised each other that we would keep it to ourselves."

There was much Elin had refused to remember about that time. Now, the shame, the fear, the shock—she recalled them clearly.

"I was upset," she said. "You knew I was."

"The moment I thought I hurt you, I stopped."

She nodded . . . still the damage had been done. The sharp pain had brought her not only to her senses but also to the exact nature of the damage being done.

"We were too young," he said. "We didn't understand the price."

The price, yes . . . and the guilt, the fear. She mutely shook her head.

There was also one more sin she needed to confess. "Mother blamed you, and I let her. I couldn't tolerate the guilt of misleading her. I didn't want my parents disappointed in me."

"I know. I understand."

But she was only beginning to do so.

I loved you, he'd said by the stream, almost as if it had been an accusation. As if he'd believed she'd betrayed him. Understanding dawned.

"My mother had a hand in your leaving?"

"Father knew what had happened. When he confronted me, I told him I loved you, that I wanted to marry you."

Elin's mind reeled at the implications of those words. "My mother would never have let you."

"Nor was my father about to let go of the Morris fortune. He had three men escort me from the estate. I did want to tell you I was leaving, Elin. They wouldn't let me see you."

There was something he wasn't saying. She knew it because she and Ben understood each other just that well. "What did he do to you?"

He pulled back as if not ready to share, but she came down on her knees in front of him. She reached for his hands. "Tell me," she ordered.

There was a beat of silence as he struggled with

his sense of honor. Elin brought his hands up to her lips. "Tell me," she whispered.

"Father had some men take me to a clearing, away from where anyone could see what he was doing. He horsewhipped me. It wasn't more than I deserved. And your father knew, Elin. He was there."

"He was? He never said and Mother always warned me not to tell him, to keep it secret." She shook her head, angry and confused. "You did not deserve whipping. I gave myself to you. I was as much a part of that night as you."

"Elin, if I had a daughter and some buck did to her what I did you to, then horsewhipping would be the kindest thing I would do."

"Our parents made you leave."

"*My* father sent me away," he corrected. "And in the end, Elin, it was the making of me. I thrived in the military. I was a good soldier. Since Jack disappeared, my parents had kept me tucked away. I wanted to be out in the world."

"But I lost you," she said.

He pulled his hand from hers and cupped her cheek. "You were never mine," he reminded her sadly.

"Yes, yes, I was." She leaned her head into his hand, relishing the warmth of his skin next to hers. How easy it would be to press a kiss in his palm. "My heart broke when I heard you had left. Mother made it sound as if you'd known all along that you were slated for a military career. Hearing that, I grew angry. I couldn't believe you would use me so ruthlessly."

"If I had planned to leave on my own, you would have been the one person who would have known. You knew all my secrets."

"I trusted you with mine as well. And I'm sorry, so very sorry, if I did anything that hurt you."

"They wanted to separate us, Elin. They were successful. We had no choice but to go our own ways, to be without each other."

But we are together now, she wanted to say, and yet, didn't.

Because she shouldn't. She was not his—

Elin caught herself. Ben was right. That statement had become a way of denying what existed between them. It might help to remind her of the promise *her parents* had made, but it did nothing to absolve her of the responsibility to her own heart.

To what she wanted. Whom she wanted.

And it was ironic, really, because her parents had eloped. They had defied her mother's family and all of society. However, they had wanted to choose whom she should marry.

He pulled his hand away and shifted as if he was ready to stand and end this moment of honesty between them.

Elin found she couldn't let that happen. Not until she did one thing. She reached for him, pulling his head down to her level, and kissed him.

But just as their lips met, a shot rang through the forest.

Chapter Ten

From the moment he'd seen Elin at his brother's ball, Ben had longed for a kiss whether he had admitted it to himself or not.

She had made him angry and frustrated and had frightened him with her crew of killers, but he'd always wanted a kiss.

And he'd always yearned for her to look at him the way she did now, as if he was the most important man in the world, as if she *understood* him . . . and then give him a kiss.

And now she was.

She'd initiated the action. She'd pulled his head down to hers. Her lips had been soft, yielding. He was transported back to his rash, seventeen-year-old self, who had done nothing but dream of being her lover.

Brother be damned. *Elin was his.*

And, of course, just as her lips were touching his, he heard the crack of a shot.

Damn killers.

Instinct took over. Ben threw her to the ground, covering her body with his. The ball whistled past his shoulder. They were still firing pistols. If they had used a musket or a rifle, either Elin or Ben would be dead.

Ben pulled the pistol from his jacket and cocked it. "Stay down," he ordered Elin. He scanned the forest in the direction of the shot. They had to be close. There had been some speed to the ball.

"Where are they?" Elin whispered, and would have raised her head except Ben anticipated it and, his fingers buried in her curls, pushed her down—and then he saw movement over by a big oak. Someone was behind it, taking aim.

"Move," Ben whispered, and for once in her life, Elin did exactly as he said. The two of them scurried toward the shelter of a clump of trees, Ben making certain they didn't travel a straight course.

Reaching safety, Ben took hold of her. "If you can escape, do so," he ordered.

"What are you going to do?" she asked, but he was already gone, using the forest for shelter and himself for bait as he ran away from Elin.

A shot came from the opposite direction from where he had anticipated. Ben dove for the ground. The bullet hit the tree. This was good. He was hoping they considered him a threat and would want to see him dead first, before they closed in on Elin.

He scrambled for cover behind a large tree trunk. There was a movement of an arm. He aimed, hoping the gun's sight was true, and fired.

The man yelped his pain. Ben fell back behind his tree and reloaded. Seconds were the same as minutes in a battlefield. Ben could load ball and powder with his eyes closed. However, his shot had alerted them to where he was. There was the sound of running footfalls, then a man's body seemed to jump out of a thicket of thorns and slammed into Ben.

Crashing to the ground, Ben caught a glimpse of a hand holding a knife coming down on him. He grabbed the man's wrist and found himself staring into Darby's ugly face. The man's breath was hot and foul. For that reason alone, Ben wasn't going to let him win. He'd not let vermin hurt Elin. Outrage gave him the strength of a hundred men.

He prayed Elin was taking advantage of this opportunity and bolting for safety.

However, she'd better not go far, he thought inanely. She also owed him a kiss.

The horse pistol was still in his hand. Using brute force, Ben held Darby's knife at bay while he lifted his other arm and brought the pistol down on the bastard's back as if it were a knife. He must have hit the right point because Darby jerked in pain.

Ben used his body as leverage to toss the villain onto his back. Darby hit the tree, but Ben was on him, holding him down and using the pistol to club him into submission with all the force in his arm, while twisting—a hand grabbed his hair and yanked him off balance.

Ben struck out with his elbow, hitting this new attacker in the jaw as he swung around, but this man was quick. He jumped on Ben, his pistol at the ready—

A shot rang out.

Elin had fired her pistol.

The man released his hold with a cry and tried to reach around his back. He stumbled, then, with the help of kick from Ben, fell flat on his face.

Ben spun around for Darby, but the man wasn't interested in Ben. No, he went for Elin, knife in hand, and Ben remembered her saying Darby had killed the footman with a knife. He'd thrown it and hit the man in the neck. Darby was that skilled.

Elin screamed and threw the gun, which was probably not her wisest course, but Ben understood.

However, he had this. He and Darby were now one-on-one.

Thankful that Elin was taking his advice and running, Ben pulled his knife from his boot and, with a flying leap, tackled Darby before he could stop her.

The two of them hit the ground hard. Darby managed to recover first and threw Ben off him.

However, as a penniless ensign, Ben had learned to fight. It had been a good way to earn money. He'd picked up a lesson or two from the ranks. He now used all his knowledge.

Shoving the heel of his hand upward, he broke Darby's nose. It made a sickening crunch.

Darby almost dropped the knife in his pain. Ben helped him finish the process by grabbing his wrist and forcing the blade toward him. "Who hired you?" he demanded. "Who is paying you to kill her—?"

The bastard struck Ben with his fist. He had a meaty hand and used it well. But this was life and death, and Ben kept his hold of the knife, burying it in Darby's thigh.

The man's shriek of pain was a frightening sound. So, for all his size and foul nature, the man was soft.

Ben gave the knife a twist, and Darby scrambled as quickly as he could off his body. He stood, his nose bleeding as he stared down at the knife in his thigh—and both he and Ben knew that Darby was in trouble.

By chance, Ben had hit his artery. If Darby pulled the knife out, his blood would flow right out of his body.

For a moment, Darby acted confused. He took a step toward Elin, who'd had the foresight to fetch her weapon. She held it, ready to fire although Ben doubted the gun was loaded. She was reacting now, her eyes wide and her gloveless hands shaking.

And then Darby stumbled backward.

"Give it up, man," Ben said, rising to one knee. "Tell us who hired you."

But there would be no remorse in Darby. Nor would he cry quarter. Instead, he tried to save himself. His pursuit of Elin forgotten, he held the knife in his leg and ran as fast as he could manage for the horses tied a hundred feet away.

The animals were prancing. They could smell the blood. One of them broke the branch holding the reins, and they both took off at a gallop, leather flying.

Darby was trapped.

Ben charged him, marveling that the man could still move as fast as he did. He tackled him to the ground. Grabbing his coat, Ben gave him a shake. *"Who sent you?"*

The answer was deep, guttural laughter, the sound the devil must make in hell.

Darby pulled the knife from his leg, sealing his fate.

Fury consumed Ben. He could not let the man die without an answer. *"Who sent you?"*

However, the light was already fading from Darby's eyes. He sneered, an expression frozen on his face as he died.

Ben released his hold. Darby's body dropped to ground. "The bloody bastard."

He rose and stepped away from the body before he unleashed his anger on it. He heard steps.

Elin. Precious, precious Elin.

She had both her hands still clasped around the small pistol. Her eyes were wide with concern. "Is he dead?"

"Bled to death."

"From the knife in his thigh? So quickly?"

Her voice had tightened. He heard her panic. "Elin, don't think on it. It was us or them."

"But I shot one. I shot him." She dropped the gun and sank to the ground.

Ben rushed to her side. He knelt. "Elin, you saved my life. If you hadn't fired, it would have been the end of me."

"But it was too easy," she whispered. "I don't understand. I don't understand at all."

"Understand what?"

"What is the *meaning* of *all* this?" Her arms moved to encompass the forest before she crossed them to hug herself tightly. "Of life? It doesn't make sense to me. We just die? One moment a person is *here*, and in the next *gone*?" She acted as if she wished to curl up into a ball, as if she could hide.

But Ben understood. He took her arms, forced her to rise. He didn't release his hold on her.

He'd heard this question many a time during battle. He'd lost friends, good ones, to Death. There had been incidents where he'd been standing right next to the man who died, and there was no reason why the bullet had claimed that man and not him.

"It is too much." She pressed her forehead against his chest. "I thought Mother's death was senseless. This is worse. First, servants that I've known most of my life, murdered for no reason. They were all good people, Ben."

"The men who murdered them are now answering to their Maker."

"Yes," she agreed quietly. "The same Maker who took my mother when she was far too young and let Darby and the others take the lives of innocent people. It doesn't make sense to me, Ben. It doesn't."

"And I have no answer for you." He framed her face with his hands and tilted it up to him. Her dark eyes were shiny with unshed tears. She tried to avoid his gaze, but he'd not have it.

"No one can be brave all the time, Elin. You are stronger than most. And if men of God, philosophers, and poets have attempted to make sense of Death and failed, I don't know that we will. But I do know this, our purpose is to live the very best life we can while we are here."

"How does one do that when it all seems useless?"

A tear had escaped, and he wiped from her cheek with the pad of his thumb. She was so precious to him. So perfect and precious.

"By making it matter," he answered. "And by believing that in this journey called life, we are moving in the direction we should."

"Is that enough?"

He looked down into her eyes and realized it wasn't. There was more. There had to be more, and he knew he was in the presence of it.

"And we can love," he said.

"But love hurts when Death takes someone dear to us. It's painful. It would be better to have never cared for anyone." She had stopped trembling. Her spirit was returning.

"Ah, to never care, Elin? Would that be better? What would life be like if we were forced to hold ourselves apart so that we could never care? Never love? What meaning would there be to living? We'd be no different than Darby and his ilk, men who sell their souls for murder."

Elin's lips parted in thoughtful surprise. She pulled back, and he let her go. "I was doing that," she confessed. "For the past year and more, I've been holding myself apart. I felt empty."

"Where was your father?" Ben knew that Fyclan doted on his daughter.

"He's been in London. Perhaps feeling the same." Her gaze dropped to her lap, where she still held his hands. "We haven't seen very much of each other. Mother was his life. His heart is broken."

"He has you."

Her lips grew rueful. "First and foremost, my parents' love was for each other. And, he prefers London, where he is important. He likes rubbing shoulders with people who listen to him. I don't enjoy London."

"What are you going to do when you are a duchess?"

"Do what is expected . . . I suppose."

Ben hated the thought of his wild Elin tamed by society and her docile acceptance of it.

Perhaps life was meaningless.

"You are right," he murmured.

"About what?" she asked.

"Your marriage to my brother does make a good boundary."

"I didn't realize we were discussing my marriage." She sounded annoyed.

Good. That could be a boundary also.

Ben turned away. "I need to do something with the bodies." He didn't wait for her response but moved forward to do what was right.

Elin watched Ben treat the murderers with far more respect than they would have ever given them. She remembered the smirk on Darby's face as he'd shot Madame Odette. He'd done this many times. Perhaps Ben had performed a service for the world by killing him.

It was impossible to bury the bodies. They did not have any tools. Ben carried branches the size of logs over and built a structure around the men that would keep out animals. He spent a good two hours working.

And she spent that time helping him when she could and watching him and thinking when she couldn't. Her thoughts mulled over what he'd said about life and death . . . and love.

She'd missed Ben all those years apart. Their friendship had been special.

That her confession to her mother had caused him pain and estrangement from his family troubled her. She was humbled to realize that instead of being the one betrayed, she'd been the betrayer. She would never have hurt Ben and yet, looking back with some maturity, what had she anticipated would happen? She'd also been foolish to accept her mother's words that she hadn't told her father. Her parents had shared everything.

Just as Ben finished sheltering the bodies, the rain clouds that had been threatening all day decided the time had come. The rain started as a mist, but Elin knew that could change quickly. So did Ben. With a shout, he came running over to her. "Let's find shelter."

She had already gathered the food sack and reloaded their weapons. He grabbed her hand, and they dashed through the woods in search of cover in any form.

The rain came down harder. Her wet cloak grew heavy. Ben's hair was plastered to his head, and she was certain she didn't appear any better. She found herself concentrating on each step her feet took and the strength in his hand holding hers.

He gave a glad shout. She looked up and realized they had come upon the ruins of an abbey. There were a few rooms standing and a long, vine-covered wall. The countryside was dotted with these reminders of the dissolution of the monasteries years ago. Locals would often carry away the stones for their own buildings, but there was enough left here to provide shelter.

But the ruins were not what had made Ben happy.

What had caught his eye was the saddled horse

grazing in the grassy center of the abbey. The animal was one of Darby's.

He left Elin where it was dry and tried to catch the horse to hobble him with a sling made by tearing off his shirtsleeves and tying them together. The animal was not appreciative of Ben's sacrifice. He proved uncooperative and for the next half hour, Elin was entertained by Ben's attempt to lure the animal's front hooves into each of the hobbles.

The animal was a wise one. He would wait, his nose to the ground grazing, until Ben was almost up on him. Then he would trot off, his ears pinned back.

Ben played the buffoon for Elin. He would stand in the rain, spreading his arms as if wondering how he would accomplish this, and Elin couldn't help giggling.

And in this way, the horrors of what she'd just experienced, the fear and the doubts, faded from her mind.

She knew Ben could catch the horse. He was doing this for her—and at last, without regret or resentment, she accepted how deeply she loved him.

He was part of the best memories from her childhood. And it had been love that had led her to kissing him when they'd been caught together in the storm all those years ago.

She'd understood her parents' expectations. For them, she'd tried to convince herself that Ben had only been a dear, close friend, someone she had trusted and shouldn't have. She'd believed her mother when she'd said what Elin felt for Ben could never be the same emotion the poets praised. They spoke of love everlasting and strong. How could Elin know anything of such matters?

But in this wink of time, Elin realized that what she felt for Ben was wrapped around the core of her being. She'd not made a mistake that night in the storm. Her body had known something that her head and heart had not yet understood—*Ben Whitridge was her love*. Her only love. The man she cherished.

She also knew her love for him would grow over time. What she felt now would be this and more on the morrow because love wasn't just one emotion but layers upon layers built through affection and respect and desire.

The duke was an admirable man. But she would never feel for him this whirlwind of passion, trust, and respect she held for Ben.

He caught the horse, hobbled it, and removed the bridle.

Triumphantly, he came walking toward her, holding the bridle like a trophy. He was a tall, lean figure with several days' growth on his face and thick hair that unfashionably reached his collar, and she had never thought he looked handsomer.

The rain started to come down harder. It would be a torrent shortly, exactly matching the intensity of the new feelings she felt for Ben. He was her protector, her champion, her knight.

"I won," he said. He unsaddled the horse. "There is a kit on the saddle. I don't know which man it belonged to, but we might find a clue as to who hired them."

Elin nodded. She watched Ben with a sense of pride in not only him, but also herself—because she was wise enough to be in love with such an amazing man.

"There, that should do the trick," Ben said. "Go on now, you beast. Eat and be lazy." The horse did as he recommended, dropping to the ground, rolling in spite of the cloth hobbles, then rising muddy to munch away the storm.

Ben laughed. "They all do the same thing. Happy they are as long as they have something to eat." He set the saddle, kit, and the bridle in a heap in a corner of their dry space. He wiped off his hands. "What do you think? We are good, yes? Well, we'll need a fire. Let me search for some dry wood—"

But Elin had been building her own fire inside her.

She cut him off by throwing her arms around him and blessed him with the biggest, most intense kiss she could muster.

There was a moment of surprise from him, then he gathered her up so that she was only standing on her toes, and kissed her back.

Chapter Eleven

$\mathcal{B}$en didn't know what he'd done to earn this gift from Elin, but he was not going to question it, especially since he liked kissing her so much.

And he was charmed that Elin kissed him with her lips closed, just as she'd done years ago. Of course, back then, he'd not known how to kiss either.

But he'd learned a thing or two over the years and was eager to teach her.

The kiss broke. Their lips barely left each other. Elin whispered, "The horse is running away." The truth of her words could be heard in the pounding of hooves on the ground. The hobble had apparently been too loose.

"I don't care," he answered.

"I don't either."

They found each other again . . . only this time,

Ben encouraged her lips to part. He tickled her with his tongue, stroked her. She started to laugh, and he took full advantage.

With a soft sigh, she was willing to follow his lead, and that was his undoing. Ben leaned her against the stone wall, wanting to cover every inch of her body with his, wanting to be in her body, wanting, wanting her.

And Elin was answering with a woman's desire.

His kisses moved to her cheek, her throat, her ear. She gave a small start and actually hummed her desire, the sound low in her throat and enough to send Ben over the edge.

The rain pounded around them. It hit the ground with enough force to splash against Ben's boots. It ran in rivulets down the wall, tickling the back of her neck. Elin laughed at the feeling of it, but Ben was not about to let anything, including Nature, intrude on this moment for them. He swept her up in his arms to carry into the main part of the abbey. Only two and a half walls stood, but the space was more protected and should keep them dry.

"Wait." Elin pointed to the ground. "The food bag."

He dipped her low enough to pick up the canvas bag. She cradled it in her lap as he carried her to shelter.

Under the shelter of an overhang, Ben placed

Elin on the ground and would have resumed kissing her except that her attention was on something else.

"Look," she said, pointing to the first room.

The horse was back. The beast had followed them through the door. Apparently, he didn't like the rain either. He took a look at them, then wandered over to the other side of the long, narrow chamber that was open to the sky.

"All that work trying to lure him in," Ben observed, "and he is smart enough to stay close to us."

"He likes you. I like you." She ran the back of her fingers against his jaw. "Even if you are scratchy."

"I didn't hurt you, did I?" He would pull his whiskers out one at time with his bare hands if it would please her.

She shook her head, her eyes loving. Her hand slid around to the nape of his neck. "Your hair is curling," she observed. "I never knew you had curls as well."

"You've never seen me with hair this long."

She made a small sound of assent, then, to his everlasting joy, she kissed him.

And, her free hand came to his chest to rest its palm right over his heart. Could she tell how fast it was beating? Or realize how much he wanted her? His every sense was alert, tense, and aching for her.

She swept her hand under his jacket and pushed his coat down his shoulder.

Ben had very little control left. In the back of his mind, he heard a reminder that he was a gentleman. He was no longer a lad at seventeen unable to control himself. Elin didn't know what invitation she offered. She was too inexperienced.

But when she tugged on his shirt, pulling it from his waistband, the gentleman was in danger of losing the struggle. He reached for her hand. "Elin, we need to think this through."

"That is what you said years ago."

"And you have made it very clear you wished that we hadn't."

Her eyes searched his face. "We were young."

"We were."

"But we know more now, don't we?"

"Do we? Because if we don't, I need to stop now."

Her chin lifted. "Mother said that when the right man came into my life, then there wouldn't be any pain."

Ben was certain there would not be pain. That had been seen to years ago, and now there would only be pleasure. He'd never wanted anything as much as he wanted to make love to her, to right the wrong he did her—still, he didn't wish to force her. He needed Elin to consider this through clearly. "Your mother was thinking of my brother as the right man."

"I'm thinking of you." She gave his shirt another tug.

"*Elin,*" he said with more force, "this is not a game."

"I've never been more serious in my life." She freed her hand from his hold and rested it on his shoulder. "Ben, I love you."

She searched his face as if afraid he would not accept her.

Such a silly notion.

He answered her with a crushing kiss because this was one of those times when words were not enough—and she replied in kind, offering all the boldness of her being.

This time her lips opened on their own, and Ben drank deeply. She could barely stand when he was done but leaned in the haven of his arms.

"Another?" she managed to suggest, and he was happy to oblige.

"I want to kiss every inch of you," he whispered. "I want to kiss your eyes—" He demonstrated, kissing her left, then her right eye. "Your nose—" She had such a perfect, straight nose. "Your chin—"

Elin delighted him by holding her chin up to him.

"Your throat—" he whispered hoarsely, knowing he was losing any control he held over himself. Her skin was smooth and warm. He adored the taste of her. He kissed a line from under her jaw down to her shoulder.

She reached up and unhooked the fastening of her cloak so that it fell to her feet. "What are you going to kiss next?" she asked, sounding slightly breathless.

He made himself place his hands on her arms. His grip light, he held her slightly away. "One more chance, Elin. This is not a game. I'll stop. It will be damned hard, but I'll stop. I'm not as noble as my brother."

"And I don't want you to be." She leaned forward and kissed him, and this time he was the one whose knees went weak.

She had always been a quick learner.

Furthermore, having worn men's breeches, Elin knew her way around the buttons. She unfastened one, then another.

He felt himself rise to her. She was his north star. His sole purpose in life had become loving her. He wanted her. Needed her—*and yet she was his brother's.*

The thought was an unwelcome intrusion. *Not now. He didn't want to think on this now.*

And yet he was no longer seventeen and ruled by his own selfish desires. He was a man, one who had battled for a sense of himself.

Elin slid her hands under the waist of his breeches and along the line of his hip as if she marveled at the feel of his skin. She was innocent in her seduction and remarkably effective.

He'd already unlaced her dress. All he had to do was slip the shoulder down her arm. He knew what waited for him. He'd spent hours imagining her. Her body was perfectly formed in her femininity.

Ben also had a debt to repay. The first time between them, he'd left her confused. He understood that now. He'd had little control over himself. In truth, he'd scared her more than loved her.

But now he had the chance to make amends. He'd botched her initiation, but he knew better now. He could love her the way she deserved to be loved.

For what? For his brother?

Having a conscience was a heavy burden. It was also sobering.

Elin kissed the very sensitive skin beneath his jaw. However, Ben realized he loved her too much to carry on with this.

With a power of will he'd never claimed to posses, he gently, but firmly, pushed her back.

Dear God, his breeches were around his hips. His desire was in evidence for all the world to see. He'd never been this hard, or this hungry for a woman.

Elin's eyes were dark with the daze of her own yearning. She tried to return to him, her arms reaching for him—

"No," he said hoarsely. "We can't."

"We can," she countered, and her gaze dropped to his impudent head, the bane of every male because it had a mind of its own. Her lips parted as if she was surprised. Their first time, they had been so anxious, so carried away, there had been no undressing. No chance to explore.

Elin looked up at him. Her lips curved into a smile. "It's a bit darling."

"It is *not* darling." That was an affront to his manhood.

Her response was to reach out and touch.

Oh, he liked that. He grew straighter and harder if that was possible, while Elin said, in a marveling voice, "Why, it's soft."

Ben's response came out in a low, shuddering groan as she dared to touch him again. Another second of this, and he'd show her there was nothing "soft" about him. Another second of this, he'd take her—and he could see everything clearly now. They stood almost naked in the woods with hard dirt for a bed. If he did this, he'd be nothing more than a rutting beast.

And a betrayer to his brother . . . and to her. Because she merited more than just him.

He saw himself even more clearly now. He had nothing to offer Elin except himself, and his self was a sorry thing. He'd allowed his own arrogance to lead him to this life, where he had nothing, *absolutely* nothing to offer her other than to tumble her as if she were a milkmaid.

Now, he walked away. He walked straight out into the rain in his sleeveless shirt, shoving that bit of himself back where he should be, and buttoning his breeches. The rain quickly soaked his shirt to the skin.

"Ben? Ben, why are you out there? What did I say, Ben? I'm sorry. Did you think I laughed? I didn't," she promised, frantic. "I was admiring. I love you, Ben. I *love* you."

He turned, held up his hands to beg for a bit of space. She stood where he'd left her—her hair a riot of curls, her cheeks flushed. With a shrug of her shoulders, her dress would slide down to her feet, leaving her in what he was certain was the sheerest of petticoats. The image sparked havoc between his sense of honor and his very virile lust.

But if he walked back to her right now, then he wasn't the man he had once thought himself to be.

Ben didn't trust his voice to speak. He wasn't ready for that, but he did know he'd have to answer for his sudden change of heart.

And he was not looking forward to the conversation.

Elin was confused.

He'd walked away.

She wanted to follow him, to demand an explanation, but something about the dogged set of his shoulders and the swiftness of his step told her he wished to be alone.

The rain picked up its pace, as if warning her to keep her distance from him, to let him be.

Elin reached behind her back and tightened her lacings. Her body still hummed with his kisses, but a new emotion was becoming prevalent. Deep within her was a tension, a dissatisfaction. Primal, demanding stirrings for what only he could give her were now replaced with an itchy, confused frustration.

She started pacing. Movement helped. She didn't have a great amount of space to explore. Their shelter from the storm was barely larger than a horse stall. The ground was cold and damp, offering her few variations to her pacing.

Picking her cloak up off the ground, she wrapped it around herself. It had been covering Ben's jacket, which lay in a heap where she'd pushed it off his shoulders. She folded it. He'd been so anxious for her to remove it.

He'd *seemed* to be willing to have her rip off all his clothing.

Frustration gave way to anger. *Had he meant to do this? It was almost as if he teased her.*

And there was no answer. Until he returned, she would just have to ruminate in silence, something Elin hated to do. She liked taking action. If there was a problem, she fixed it. If there was a concern, she poked and prodded until she had an answer.

However, this question lay in another person's inexplicable and rude behavior. A person who had abandoned her once before, except *this time*, she would not be meek.

Of course, until he returned, there wasn't anything she could do but wait.

When he did come back, which he would—she had a few things she wanted to tell him.

She'd wandered over to the other side of the wall. Her eye fell on the saddle kit. Wrapped in her cloak, she knelt, then sat on the ground by the saddle as she went through it.

There wasn't much of interest. She wanted to find a clue as to who had hired the men. Then, she would hold it up to Ben to show that while he was prancing around, she was doing good work.

But there wasn't anything like a clue in the leather bag. She found a money pouch with a few shillings. There was also a tinderbox, a comb, and a bottle of oil of clove—apparently her killer suffered from a toothache. She also found a pouch. When she opened it, a locket fell into her hand. She opened the clasp, and inside was a painted miniature of a young woman.

The picture made her sad. The girl was little older than she was. Elin couldn't fathom how a man could carry a keepsake like this around with him and murder people.

The idea was disturbing enough that she put the locket back its pouch and into the kit. Darkness was falling. The rain had let up a bit, but there was now a gloomy fog setting in, and the air grew colder.

The horse was eating away, oblivious to what was going around him.

Elin searched the woods around the ruins for Ben and didn't see a sign of him.

"*Ben,*" she called.

The rain dampened the sound of her voice.

"He'll return. He always does." And when he did . . . "No more running, Ben," she promised herself. "No more running."

She ate half of what was left of the dried apples and drank almost all of what was left of the cider. They would refill the jug with water. Fortunately, the sky was making plenty of it.

Curling up into a ball, she rested her head on the seat of the saddle. She watched, waiting for him to return . . . and must have fallen asleep.

When she opened her eyes, she wasn't alone any longer. Her mother sat on the other side of the saddle, resting her arm on it.

Elin pushed herself up, frowning. She was not alarmed to see her mother, just accepting. She thought she dreamed and yet, her mother was whole and breathing and surrounded by a soft glowing light. Elin even caught a whiff of the rose scent her mother adored wearing.

Her mother leaned across the saddle and offered Elin the bit of the petticoat lace she'd been using to tie her hair back. Elin took it. She could feel the texture of the lace and the warmth from her mother's fingers.

For a long moment, all she could do was smile at her mother, then she said, "I've missed you."

Jenny gifted her with her famous smile, which had won Fyclan's heart and captured the attention of the ton. *Life had been effortless for her. "I miss you as well."*

She laid a loving hand against Elin's cheek. "But I'm with you and also with your father. I'm always with you."

"Oh, Mother, everything is confusing." The words burst out of Elin. "I don't want to marry Baynton. I never have."

"You must. It's planned." Her mother picked up a plate from the service in the London house and nibbled on what was left of Osprey's dried apples. She held the plate out to Elin. "Here, eat something. You don't want to appear hungry later. Everyone will be watching."

Elin didn't want to eat. She needed to talk, to make

her mother understand. "I love Ben. You told me that in time my feelings for Ben would change, but they haven't. If I go through with the marriage to Gavin, it will be wrong."

"Elin, your son will be a duke. It is your destiny. If you don't marry Baynton, how can that happen? Do you want Gavin to die? Do you want someone to try to kill him the way they tried to murder you?"

"You saw all of that?"

"I told you, I'm always with you."

"Then you know how I feel about Ben."

"He won't make you a duchess," was her whispered response.

"I don't care—"

But her mother was already fading. She was changing from something solid and real into a memory. Right before disappeared completely, Elin heard her whisper, "You can't change what is to be . . . but you must live your heart—"

Elin came awake with a start. She blinked, expecting to see her mother there. She could swear she caught the scent of her perfume.

But the space on the other side of the saddle was empty, and the smells that filled the air were those of burning wood and roasting meat.

Rubbing her eyes, Elin rose and walked through the doorway to the other side of the wall. It had stopped raining, and Ben had returned.

He sat before a good-sized fire roasting what appeared to be a hare on the end of stick. His hair was curling as it dried, and she didn't think he'd ever looked so good to her.

The lecture she had intended to give him evaporated. Instead, she moved to sit by his side. She placed her hand upon his thigh.

"Did you enjoy your nap?" he asked. He was shirtless and wore only the jacket that she had folded what seemed moments ago. More time had passed than she had imagined. Night had fallen. She'd been asleep for a while.

"When did you return?"

"An hour ago."

"Why didn't you wake me?"

"That would have been a shame. You needed the rest, Elin. And you would have laughed at my attempt to light the fire with damp wood."

She looked up at him. *You must live your heart.* Her mother's advice, even as she'd chastised Elin for not marrying her parents' choice. She said, "I'm happy you returned."

He nodded, the gesture absent any emotion. "I won't leave you, Elin. I can't."

She understood.

He straightened his shoulders, cleared his throat, and began talking about what he'd been doing while she slept as if to fill a void.

"It took longer than I expected to find wood

that was even half-dry. Then I had a devil of a time striking a spark."

"A spark? There was a tinderbox in the saddle kit."

"I found it." He offered the sizzling meat on the stick to her. "Fancy a bit of rabbit?"

"You have been busy," she observed.

"Well, having a few productive tasks helps the perspective. Go on, have a bite. It should be good."

It smelled heavenly. Her stomach urged her to eat as well, so she pulled off a piece. "It is heavenly," she said with happy sigh. The meat was chewy, but Elin didn't mind. She even licked her fingers.

For his part, he seemed to studiously avoid meeting her eye.

Another time and another place, she would have been offended. She understood him better now. She believed she was beginning to understand them all better now.

"The cider jug was empty," he said. "I found a brook over yonder and filled it with water."

"You've taken good care of me."

He didn't answer. Instead, he put his attention on the fire. He stirred it with his stick, then, as the flames rose, he added more wood. The fire hissed and smoked from the dampness of the branches, but they quickly dried and burned nicely.

"I dreamed of my mother."

"Did you now?" He sounded disinterested.

She knew he wasn't. He was as attuned to everything about her as she was to him.

"It was one of those dreams where everything is so vivid it seems real," she continued. "She *was* real. I felt her touch. And I told her I wasn't going to marry Baynton."

The stick stirring the fire went still.

"She informed me I must. But she is wrong. You see, years ago, she married my father for love. She did so against everyone's wishes. They all told her she was making a mistake. Her parents disowned her, her sisters shunned her because they felt she was ruining the family's reputation, and many of her friends deserted her. Of course, now, these same people would do anything to gain my father's favor, but that isn't what is important. What I realized was that they took a risk. They defied their parents."

Ben looked at her now, his eyes solemn.

"I love you, Benedict Whitridge. My feelings have been constant ever since those days years ago when we rode together and explored the world side by side. I can't imagine being with anyone else. Indeed, I blamed the duke and your father's death, and then my mother for the reason we haven't married yet, but the truth is, I've been avoiding it. I left London as soon as I could, and not because I was mourning . . . but because I was running. Heartwood was a convenient hiding place. At no time did I want to encourage or force the idea of marriage. That I was in mourning made it easy to avoid the subject. Certainly there are those who believe I have been the most patient of women, but that isn't true."

She leaned closer to him. "I was waiting for you. I kept hoping I would see you again. I waited, Ben. I put them off as long as I could. And now, I want you to make love to me. Years ago, we tried, and I don't believe we did a good job of it. I panicked—"

"I didn't know what I was doing."

He looked so earnest, she couldn't help but smile. "I've heard some women whisper it is terrible the first time. But around Heartwood, the lasses like their lads, so there must be something to it."

"There is." Ben tossed his stick into the fire. "I think of my brother, Elin."

"I thought you were angry with him."

"No, jealous. He had you."

"That wasn't the argument the night of the ball."

"It was the undercurrent. Gavin can be clueless. He doesn't see nuances. He had no idea of what he has taken from me."

"I'm not going to let him take you from me."

He twisted toward her. "Are you certain, Elin?

I warn you, I'm not the man my brother is. I don't have a title or even a house to call my own. I don't have a living."

"But do you love me?"

"With all my heart."

"Then we'll sort out the details, Ben. But for this moment, let's trust our love."

His response was in his kiss.

Chapter Twelve

Elin grabbed ahold of Ben's jacket.

She wasn't going to let him run away. Not any longer.

They were also becoming very good at kissing.

And the doubts and fears she'd once had about the act of joining didn't even cross her mind. She wanted to be as close to this man as she possibly could be. She would do anything for him—endure any pain, face any humiliation, whatever it took to always have him close.

For his part, Ben didn't act as if he were going to let her go either.

The kiss between them deepened and changed in ways she could never have imagined. He teased her, tickled her, and made good on his promise to kiss every inch of her as he eased her back.

"I wish I had something more than just the ground for you," he said, his lips close to her ear.

Elin undid the fancy frog to her cape. "I don't care where we are. I'm just happy *we* are." She caught his face in her hands, his growth of beard rough against her palms. "Ben, don't ever doubt us. Please."

"I won't," he answered, and sealed that promise with a kiss in the center of her hand.

They began undressing each other in earnest. She stroked the hard, muscular planes of his chest. He was so perfect. Strong, long-limbed, vital, and alive. She would never tire of touching him, but it was what he was doing to her that threatened to rob her of all sanity.

"I don't care how *it* feels," she informed him. "I want you to be happy."

"How *it* feels?"

She swallowed. She tried not to be tense.

As if reading her mind, he said, "Elin, it won't hurt this time. I promise. Will you trust me?"

"I already do trust you."

"And if I do anything that causes you the slightest amount of discomfort, I want you to tell me to stop. Do you understand? I don't want you to be stoic on my account."

She would be. She would endure anything for him. However, she nodded. Ben looked hard into her eyes, then shook his head. "I have much to atone for, love. Let me see what I can do."

He kissed her then, and she threw her arms around his neck, savoring the taste of his kiss. He'd already atoned for everything, she wanted to shout. He'd called her "love."

Such a wonderful word. Such an amazing title.

Ben slid her dress down over her shoulders. She was busy kissing the line of his whiskers beneath his jaw, the place that seemed to both please and excite him.

The warmth of his hand felt good on her skin. Her breasts swelled and filled his palms when he cupped them. Her nipples puckered as if demanding a kiss.

When his lips gave them what they wanted, Elin almost swooned. She arched her back as he lowered her to the ground. Her fingers buried themselves in his hair, teasing the curls, loving them. She was never going to let him cut his hair. Never. She needed those curls to hold on to and keep her grounded when he drew tight on her breasts as he did now.

Once again, deep within, she experienced a growing need for something more.

She knew what he needed. She promised herself she would not flinch when he entered her. She'd not cry out the way she had years ago, something that had frightened both of them. The pain had been sharper than any needle, and she hadn't liked the bleeding.

But she certainly didn't want Ben to stop what he was doing now. She pushed his jacket off his shoulders, wanting to feel his skin against hers.

His lips left her. She started to protest until she realized he had stopped to finish undressing.

She watched wide-eyed as he pulled off his boots, set them aside, and stood to unbutton his breeches. He peeled them off. His manhood had a life of its own. He was definitely ready for her.

Firelight gilded his skin, and Elin could believe him a young god.

Ben knelt and pulled her dress down over her legs. She was naked except for her stockings and shoes. He removed those. She helped by lifting one leg, then the other.

He ran a finger across the bottom of her foot. She laughed and squirmed, unashamed to be so open with him. In fact, she liked the freedom of not having clothing. She'd never considered herself bold, but she was comfortable with Ben. She trusted him.

Her stockings had been the bane of her existence ever since she'd left the coach. The ribbons had come untied, and they'd fallen around her ankles. She almost celebrated when Ben tossed them aside. Instead, she reached up and pulled him down to her.

"You are so beautiful, Elin," he whispered. "So perfect and lovely."

She ran her hand over the curve of his hips. "You are perfect and lovely, too."

He laughed before kissing her forehead, her lips, her chin, and her new favorite place for kisses, her breasts.

In turn, her hand went unerringly to explore and marvel at his manhood. He liked it when she touched him.

He reacted by touching her.

His hand slid over her belly. His fingers dipped into secret places. He opened her world.

They had not done any of this that first time. They'd kissed and desired, but had been too elementary. They'd had an urge, but they had never investigated, never savored.

She'd not known how silky his skin could feel over his hard muscles or how circling that hard shaft could make him gasp her name. He covered her hand with his and showed her what he liked. He then mimicked the same movement on her own tender flesh.

Elin could barely breathe. His name became a litany, begging him for what she didn't yet know but was willing to discover.

And he liked that. She could feel his confidence.

He kissed her ear, as he said, "I don't want either of us to ever forget this night."

She answered by plastering her mouth on his and kissing him in a way she'd never thought possible, her hips moving against him, knowing there must be more.

Ben settled himself between her legs. She cradled his hips with her thighs.

And then he was at the portal.

The sharp pain she had once endured was a distant memory—and nothing, absolutely nothing in this world, felt as good as the sensation of his slowly sliding into her.

There was a tightness. She was aware of the proud length and breadth of him, but there was no pain.

"All you all right?" he asked. He sounded as if he was holding himself in check, as if it took all of his will to do so.

Elin arched and stretched beneath him. Her movements sent him deeper, and she liked that. "I've never been better," she practically purred.

"Then you like this?"

She let her smile speak.

"I believe you will enjoy this even more," he managed and, lifting her hips, began moving inside her.

He was right.

Elin looked up into the sky, her whole being

centered on where they were joined. He knew what she wanted better than she did. All she had to do was enjoy.

The rain clouds had given way to a sky full of stars, and Elin imagined herself as one with them . . . as one with Ben.

She reached for him, kissing him. His thrusts grew deeper, more meaningful. Her body answered in its own way, moving and meeting him. Together, they seemed to be striving for something—and then suddenly, for one blessed second, he touched the core of her, and Elin knew she would never be the same.

Her breath came out in a cry, a plea, then a sighing gasp of complete and utter satisfaction.

If she could have, she would have slipped beneath Ben's skin. She felt that close to him.

He buried himself deep as if riding the sweeping intensity of her release. He held his breath. She held hers. She never wanted to let him go. She wanted him to remain right where he was forever and ever.

Had she thought the stars bright only moments ago?

She'd been wrong. She was the one who glowed and pulsated with the fire of life. She was exactly where she'd always been meant to be.

Elin clung to his body . . . and then slowly, purposefully they returned to reality.

"I'm changed," Elin whispered to the heavens. "I will not be the same."

Ben lifted his weight on his arms as if worried that he was too heavy for her. She ran her hand over the desirable curve of his buttock, not wanting him to leave her.

"We are both changed," he answered.

She smiled, pleased and experiencing a growing drowsiness—as if she'd done something miraculous and now needed to rest after all the good work.

"Could it have been like this years ago?" she wondered. "If so, I fear we've wasted a good deal of time."

He laughed at her comment, and she felt the sound go through him to where they were both still joined, their legs intertwined.

But then he sobered. "I love you, Elin Morris. I will always love and adore you."

His hair had fallen over his forehead. She brushed it back, thinking he was the most handsome man in the world. She ran her thumbs over his expressible eyebrows. "Mine," she murmured.

He lowered his mouth to hers but right before their lips touched, he answered, "Yours. Always yours."

She felt him grow strong in her again.

His hips moved. His smile said it all, and Elin

opened herself once more to unspeakable pleasure.

Neither one of them was ready to leave the haven the abbey had become.

Ben caught another rabbit the next morning, and they feasted on it before once again feasting on each other.

The sense of loss that had dogged Elin from the night her mother died dissipated. Life took on meaning. Love was the answer, she realized now. Love always had been the purpose to life. She'd just not understood because she'd never given herself over completely to another.

She nestled her body against Ben's, resting her head on his shoulder, and the two of them shared their innermost thoughts. He talked to her about his complicated feelings toward his father and, consequently, his brother.

"I will cry off," she assured Ben. "Gavin is an honorable man. He will understand once I tell him that we love each other."

"Or he may be furious with me," Ben answered, combing her curls with his finger. "Either way, I don't care. I won't let you go."

"And what shall you do with me?" she wondered.

He was happy to show her.

It was late on the afternoon of the second day,

when the peace of their own private Eden was disturbed by a passerby.

A tinker was making his way through the forest.

Fortunately, both Elin and Ben were dressed. They had decided to search together for more firewood before nightfall.

The horse nickered a warning. A man's voice called a cheerful, "Halloooo? Is someone here?"

Ben and Elin had been about to leave. Ben pulled her behind him. "Right here."

The man's head appeared above the far stonewall. "I say, I don't usually meet many out here."

Ben shrugged his answer.

Their visitor took his gesture as an invitation and walked into the clearing. He had to be at least sixty years old, with long, straggly gray hair beneath a misshapen hat. He eyed their horse and pulled the hat off his head to nod to Elin. "My name's Robert Ingalls. I'm from around these parts. Where are you traveling?"

"Wherever we wish," Ben answered.

Mr. Ingalls was no fool. He caught the lack of invitation in Ben's tone. "Aye, well, you might want to be careful," he said. "There has been some bad doin's."

"What do you mean?" Ben asked.

"Murder," Mr. Ingalls answered. He obviously had a feeling for the dramatic. "There was robbery about seven miles from here on the main road. Of course you might be safe. There is a sizeable party of men searching for those who did do them. Shot right in the heart they were. Several men and *a lady*."

"That is bad news," Ben answered.

"Aye. They say there may be highwaymen, but I ask why?" Mr. Ingalls punctuated his words by spreading his hands. "Who travels in these parts who has money? A smart highwayman should do his work down around Londontown."

"If I take up robbery, I shall remember your advice," Ben said.

"Well, they will be caught soon enough. There is a duke involved in the search. He's offered a reward that would pop a man's eyes out of his head."

"For word of the highwaymen?" Ben wondered.

"There is a lass missing. She was with the coach. He's searching for her."

"How far away is he?" Ben asked quietly.

"One can wander these woods for days and not see a soul. But I would say he is a few hours behind me."

"Thank you for the warning," Ben said.

"We all have to look out after each other around here," Mr. Ingalls answered, and, with one last nod of his head, he replaced his hat and continued his walk.

Elin came out from behind Ben. "I'm not ready to leave." She didn't want the world to intrude on what had become an idyllic life. She'd woken that morning in Ben's arms, to Ben's kisses. Her thought had been she could live the rest of her life right here. She didn't need anything but him.

He nodded, watching Mr. Ingalls disappear into the forest, his expression pensive. Then he said, "Gavin himself has come."

A note in his voice made her uneasy. She reached for his hand. "I shall talk to him before we return to London."

He glanced down at their joined hands and frowned, as if something bothered him.

"What?" she asked. "Don't you believe I'll tell him?"

"I just have a bad sense of things." He shook his head as if shrugging it off. "Come, let us prepare to meet Gavin."

He leaned down and gave her a kiss, but he was distracted, and she knew he was already thinking ahead to the meeting with his brother.

Chapter Thirteen

*T*hey heard the men searching for Elin long before they saw them. Ben kicked the horse forward.

A line of men were beating their way through the woods. There must have been fifty of them. Gavin never did anything halfway.

"Hello there," he said to the man nearest him, startling the man. "Where is the duke?"

"Here now, what do you want with His Grace?" a man's voice said. Ben recognized Talbert, his brother's man of business. Talbert was dressed in country attire as if he was ready for some shooting. He was a short man of middling years. He had also served Ben's father.

At the same time, Talbert recognized Ben, although he wasn't certain. "Lord Benedict?"

"Yes, it is I," Ben said, a heaviness weighing on

his conscience. He was returning. Only for Elin would he go back.

"With all that hair, my lord, I couldn't tell."

"Talbert, have you met Miss Morris?"

If Ben had revealed he'd discovered the Holy Grail, Talbert's reaction would have been no different. The man hopped from one foot to the other. "Hold her here, hold her here," he repeated before pulling his hat off his head. "It is an honor to meet you, Miss Morris. *Bailey*," he shouted to one of his men, barely pausing to take a breath. "Sound the horn, man! We have found *her*."

Bailey obeyed the command, sounding an alarm on a huge hunting horn. The horse beneath Ben shied. He reached back to be certain that Elin, who was demurely riding sidesaddle, stayed on. She had her hands around his waist and tightened her hold.

Dear God, he never wanted her to let go.

His brother had mounted a major endeavor to find Elin. The search party seemed to stretch out forever.

"What of me?" the searcher Ben had first approached said to Talbert. "Fifty quid to the first man who discovers something, that is what you've said. I've earned the fifty quid. It's *mine*."

"Actually," Talbert started, ready to argue the point with him, "Lord Benedict found her."

"Pay him the fifty," Ben said. "Where is my brother?"

"Over yonder," a distracted Talbert answered.

"I'll find him." Ben kicked the horse forward.

"Wait," Talbert said, running along side them as fast as his pudgy legs could carry him. "I want to be there when His Grace first sees his bride. We've been worried for your safety, Miss Morris," he said between huffs and puffs. "Very concerned when we saw the bodies at the coach."

But before Talbert could say more, a snowy white horse with a flowing mane and tail came cantering through the woods.

Gavin has arrived.

Ben frowned. He wondered if his brother had purchased the horse so he could look particularly ducal.

That was an unkind thought. An unwarranted one. Still, Ben could not repress it.

Worse, his brother did cut a remarkable figure on the horse in his gray greatcoat and a wide-brimmed hat worn low over his eyes.

Gavin was one of those men who had been endowed by his Maker with every advantage. He'd been born the first of twins to a wealthy title and gifted with high intelligence, strong morals, and the face and form to make women fall at his feet panting. What had some love-struck woman said of him once? "That he had pierced her heart with his ice blue gaze?"

What rot.

Ben wanted to turn around the nag he rode and charge away as fast as he could with Elin.

However, that would not be right. Out of love, he tried to force the issue once. Now, out of love, he would trust Elin when she said she'd chosen him.

Him! The one dependent upon his brother for an income. The one who had merely average intelligence although he'd put his morals up against his brother's—with some caveats, of course. Him—a man with two eyes, a nose, and a mouth like a thousand others.

But his heart was *hers*.

Gavin spied them and slowed his horse to a walk, staring as if he wasn't certain he faced his brother.

Well, in truth, Ben did look rough. His hair was much longer than when Gavin complained about it last, and he had almost four days' growth of beard.

Harsh words had passed between them a year ago. Ben regretted nothing. He'd wager Gavin would not recall anything he said as well. Ben wondered how Gavin would take the news Elin intended to tell him.

"Brother," Gavin said, acknowledging Ben first. "Your Grace."

Gavin swung his "piercing gaze" to Elin, seemingly taking in everything from the wildness of her hair to her rumpled, travel-worn clothing. "Miss Morris, we are overjoyed to find you safe."

"As am I, Your Grace," Elin answered. Her arm around Ben's waist tightened as she spoke, as if to reassure him of her intentions.

He wasn't reassured. She was in an untenable position. He now realized that promises made beyond the manners and expectations of society were easy. Living them would be difficult.

"Is my father here?" she asked.

A cloud seemed to cross over Gavin's perfect features. "He is not. I'm—" he started, then stopped, as if he thought better of it. "I'm representing him as well."

But Elin had heard the hesitation. "What is the matter? What is wrong?"

Gavin frowned as if he regretted having alarmed her. "He is waiting for you in London."

"But why is he not here?"

"And how did you hear about the coach attack?" Ben asked, deciding silence would not serve his purpose. Besides, he wanted answers about the murder for hire. Someone had gone to great lengths to do Elin in.

"Word reached me the day before yesterday," Gavin said, answering Ben first, which meant he was too politic to address Elin's concerns. "Someone had discovered the coach belonged to Fyclan, and riders had been dispatched. You are lucky to be alive, Miss Morris."

"Yes," Elin agreed, her voice quiet.

"Have you seen the coach?" Ben asked. "Is there any evidence of who could be behind this?"

"I had the coach hauled to London. We did come upon a group of scoundrels at an inn several miles from here," the duke answered. "They told a story of a band of men whom they claimed were the murderers. They said they killed one of them. I'm having them held in custody until we can verify their story."

"Probably hanging by the thumbs until you approve," Ben couldn't help but mutter, and for that he earned another, well-deserved glare from his brother.

It was Elin who sensibly intervened. "They are Lord Benedict's friends, and they did help us escape."

"What were you doing in a rathole like that tavern?" Gavin asked Ben.

"With the 'scoundrels?' Playing cards. What else does one do in a rathole?"

"And you have been with Elin all this time?"

This question surprised Ben.

Gavin's welcome had definitely been a bit chilly, which Ben expected and had earned considering the nature of their parting. But there was an edge to his words as well. He was not pleased Ben had spent so much time with his betrothed.

His brother might be a duke, but he was no fool.

Elin chimed in. "I wouldn't have survived without Lord Benedict. Your Grace, this has been a terrible ordeal. I was fortunate I was not with the coach when those men attacked. But I saw them murder my family's servants. They made it very clear they had come for me. I escaped, but they attempted to hunt me down. Lord Benedict and his friends saved my life. Big Roger killed one of them and Hooknose and Nate drew them away from us. Lord Ben killed the last two of them. It was terrifying."

"You shot one," Ben said, wanting to give Elin credit.

"And I pray never to shoot another person again," she answered.

A muscle worked in Gavin's jaw. Ben imagined that Gavin had thought that he would be Elin's savior, and he wasn't. He could almost feel a bit sorry for his brother. Gavin had so much . . . but Ben had Elin, and that made him the richer of the two of the brothers.

Gavin seemed to take hold of himself. "What am I thinking? We need to take care of Miss Morris. The road is about an hour's ride yonder. My personal coach is waiting. Miss Morris, I wasn't certain what your favorite foods were, but

I had a hamper prepared with a little of everything."

Well played, brother. Ben could almost hear Elin licking her lips.

And there was a smile in her voice as she said, "I'm certain that after a diet of hare and dried apples, whatever has been prepared will be excellent."

Gavin smiled, pleased. "Let's find you a decent mount."

"Here," a man said. Ben had not noted his approach but he swung easily down from the saddle of a pretty bay. "Cousin Elin, ride my horse."

"Robbie," she said in greeting. "I'm so happy to see you."

"I'm relieved to find you well."

Gavin had dismounted with ducal grace, something Ben couldn't do easily with Elin behind him. He could have lowered her to the ground but, in truth, he didn't want her off his horse at all.

So, it was Gavin who escorted her over to her cousin's bay. She said something to Robbie that Ben couldn't hear. He kicked his nag forward in time to catch him saying they would talk about her father at a more opportune time.

Elin looked back at Ben with a worried glance. She was not pleased to be put off.

Gavin helped her mount, letting his gloved hand linger at her waist. Ben wanted to jump off his horse, jerk Gavin's hand off of Elin, and maybe land a facer right on his perfect nose. But he wouldn't. Such rash behavior was beneath his dignity, for now.

Fortunately, Elin kicked the horse forward so that Gavin's hand slipped away from her. "What shall you ride, cousin?" she asked.

"I'll take your place behind Lord Benedict," Robbie said easily.

Ben was really not happy with that arrangement, especially when Elin went trotting off alongside Gavin's mighty steed. However, Ben was trying not to appear churlish. Elin would not approve.

However, he was tempted to toss Robbie Morris to the ground when the man, after stepping on a log to climb on the back of Ben's horse, gave him a look of disdain, and said, "Obviously, you've been out here in the rough for some time, my lord." He rubbed his own cheek to indicate he spoke of Ben's beard and overall disreputable appearance.

Ben kicked his horse into a canter, almost, but not quite, toppling Robbie Morris off his seat.

"I'm not understanding what you mean by killers?" Gavin was saying as Ben brought his horse up alongside theirs. "The attack wasn't a robbery?"

"No, they wanted to murder me," she answered.

"Elin, tell him your story," Ben commanded quietly. "Start at the beginning."

And so she did. Ben listened carefully. Each time she told the story, he heard something different.

Gavin asked questions and so did her cousin. She answered as best she could.

Ben even let her tell them about the battle with Darby and his henchman, including how he'd protected the bodies since they couldn't be buried. Elin was generous with her praise of Ben.

"Do you remember where the bodies are?" the duke asked.

"Yes," Ben answered.

"Good," his brother said. He called over to a compact man riding a small chestnut. "Perkins, come here."

"Yes, Your Grace?" Ben had never met Perkins before. He was not a servant.

But he was also not the sort who would stand out in anyone's mind. He had brown hair and brown eyes and the most average of features.

"Perkins, this is my betrothed, Miss Morris."

"It is my pleasure, Miss Morris." Even Perkins's voice didn't command notice.

"This is my brother, Lord Ben. I want you to take some men and follow him to where he left the bodies of two men he says were trying to do Miss Morris harm."

"What do you want done with the bodies, Your Grace?"

"Whatever Lord Ben decides," Gavin said easily, and his eyes met Ben.

He might not know everything that had happened between Ben and Elin in the woods, but he was determined to remove Ben from being close to her. It was there in his eyes and set of his chin.

In that moment, he reminded Ben of no one more than their father, a man who prided himself in always gaining his way.

As for Elin, she smiled at him, her face pale. Ben knew her mind was on her father. She proved him right when she said to her cousin, "If you are here, who is with my father?"

"Theresa is with him," he answered, swinging his leg around and sliding off the horse.

"Theresa?" Ben questioned.

"My wife. In fact, her personal maid is waiting in His Grace's coach. We don't want it to be said that my cousin was not properly chaperoned."

"Absolutely," Baynton agreed.

"Pity those lads are dead," Robbie said. "I'd like to hear what they have to say. You didn't manage to learn why they were on such a murderous rage, did you?"

"No." Ben knew he was being terse but he was in that kind of mood. He was not pleased to be sent away like an errand boy even though at another time he would believe returning to those bodies was the wisest course of action. After all, he could have missed something.

"Miss Morris and I will see you in London," the duke said decisively.

Elin held up a hand. "Wait."

Ben's spirit lifted. Was she going to announce to Gavin now that her feelings had changed? Would she dare to cry off publicly?

"Before you go, do you need something to eat, Ben?" she asked.

In Greek times, the young Icarus dared to fly too close to the sun and plunged to his death.

Masking his disappointment that Elin was more preoccupied with fears for her father than this love they professed to each other, Ben felt very much akin to the foolish Icarus.

Then again, what did he expect her to do? Did he doubt her profession of love?

No. And whether he liked it or not, he knew he must trust Elin to see her way out of her entanglement with Gavin one way or the other.

In the meantime, he needed to find out who and why someone had hired killers to murder her.

"I'm fine, Miss Morris. I'm not hungry." Ben looked to his brother. "See that my friends are released, and you may want to give them a reward. After all, Miss Morris is alive because of them. Let's go, Perkins."

Ben rode off.

Chapter Fourteen

Elin knew Ben was not pleased. Tension, disappointment, annoyance—all the Ben emotions—had radiated from him.

She knew he had not been pleased that Gavin had taken control of the situation and her.

But what did he expect? For her to announce in front of all the men the duke had hired to search for her what she wanted to do with him?

How would such a display help? The whole matter of asking Gavin to release her from her promise to him was delicate. If she handled this in the wrong way, well, life would be impossible.

Of course, Ben would claim he didn't care whether they were outsiders to society or not. She could imagine him telling her that they could live in the woods forever.

But that was unrealistic.

And she had no intention of causing anyone, including the duke or her father, harm if she could avoid it.

She had been shocked when she discovered her father wasn't among the forces Gavin had marshaled to search for her. She could barely wait to climb in the haven of Baynton's well-appointed coach and ask for a moment alone with Robbie to discover why he was absent.

"First, let me pour you a glass of wine," the duke said. "Molly, a nibble of cheese and some bread for Miss Morris."

Theresa's maid was like most ladies' maids, an extension of her mistress. Robbie's wife was known for her excellent taste. She set a lovely table, and her home was to be admired. She understood the nuances of society, and there had been a time or two when Jenny Morris had openly wished Elin had a bit of Theresa's respect and affinity for the *ton*.

Elin took the food the maid offered. She sipped the wine from the glass Baynton pressed in her hand. They did not taste better to her than Osprey's cider and apples, especially when she was so worried about her father.

"May I have a private moment with Robbie, please?" she begged the duke. "And have you had the opportunity to clear the name of Lord Ben's friends?"

"I have not, but I shall give the word now." He reached for her hand. He wore gloves, and Elin found herself wondering exactly where she'd lost hers, then remembered taking them off so that she could fire the little pistol still in the pocket of her cloak.

"All will be well. I promise," he said.

"Thank you," she murmured.

"Come, Molly." The duke and maid climbed out of the coach, leaving Elin with Robbie.

She didn't mince words. "What is wrong with Father and why haven't I been told?"

"He didn't want you to know."

"To know what?" Elin demanded.

"It's age, Elin. Your father is up there in years, and you know he didn't take your mother's death well. He's been heartbroken."

"Why didn't he send for me sooner?"

"Why didn't you just come?"

Elin frowned at Robbie. "I'm not fond of the city. And," she had to concede, "Father and I needed time to mourn. He buries himself in his business concerns. There isn't much I can do in London."

"The museums, the theater, the soirees," Robbie said as if she was being silly.

"I was in *mourning*. Those attractions hold no amusement for me."

"Actually, I thought about writing to you of my concerns, but it seemed disloyal. Your father was adamant about keeping his difficulties from you. You know how he can be. Your mother was the only one who could bend him to a will other than his own."

"So you say it is just age?" Fyclan Morris had been years older than his wife, but Elin never thought of him as being aged.

"That is what the doctors are saying. He tires easily, and sometimes he forgets details. He's never done that before."

"No, never."

"Occasionally, he had pain in his abdomen, but he carries on. He's a stoic. There are times Theresa and I believe he is uncomfortable, but he doesn't complain."

"Who is his doctor?"

"He was refusing to talk to anyone until His Grace insisted he see the Dowager's personal physician, a Mr. Bartland."

"What does he say?"

"Age." Robbie shrugged. "Man does not live forever."

Elin fell back into the cushioned seat. Once again, Death was calling, and she felt a coldness steal through her. Had she just started to believe all was happy and right? More fool she!

There was a knock on the door right before it opened. "May I come in?" the duke asked.

"Please," Elin said. She looked down at her hands in her lap. They were trembling.

The men exchanged a glance. She caught them and was annoyed that they were trying to be so solicitous of her.

Something inside her seemed in danger of exploding. Nothing made sense. She wished Ben were here. Ben wouldn't be solicitous. He'd assure her that there was definitely something uncommon going on.

"I'll ride outside," Robbie said, and left—or rather he ran. Elin knew her strained silence made him nervous.

"Molly," the duke said, standing on the coach step. "We are leaving. Ambrose?" he continued, addressing his driver. "With all haste."

"Do you wish to stop for the night, Your Grace?"

"Not if we can help it," Elin answered.

"Did you hear?" the duke asked Ambrose.

"Aye, Your Grace."

Gavin gracefully swung into the coach. Molly hurried in on the other side, squeezing herself in the corner opposite Elin as if to make herself unnoticeable.

The duke sat in the bench seat across from them. He knocked on the roof, a signal to Ambrose that they were settled in and ready to go.

As the coach began the trip home, he leaned forward and reached for Elin's hands. She let him have them. He'd removed his gloves. For a long moment, her fingers rested on his. He had good hands. Swordsman's hands, her mother would say. Long, tapered fingers and a good grip.

Ben had the same sort of hands. She could close her eyes and recall his fingers teasing in all the secret places.

There was another difference—Ben's hands had calluses. He'd done work.

What could Gavin possibly offer her?

The thought almost moved her to tears. She wanted to pull her hands away from him and tighten up in a ball of self-pity.

Instead, she said, "Robbie informed me my father is very ill and didn't want to send for me."

The words were painful to speak.

"One of the reasons my mother pushed for us to move ahead with the wedding is because she knew that this was one way he'd let you come to London."

She glanced at the maid, who sat in the corner, silent and immobile, pretending she wasn't there. Her presence didn't seem to disturb Baynton. Then again, he was accustomed to having servants all around him. At official dinners at Menheim House, footmen were assigned to stand behind each guest's chair, ready to fulfill any need. If the maid didn't bother him, well, Elin would not give her another thought. Frustration and worry could not be held at bay.

"It seems odd," Elin said, "that a daughter must push a wedding to see her father."

"I don't know that he has any animosity if that is what you are suggesting," Gavin answered. "He has said nothing of the sort to me, and I've taken the liberty of calling on him almost every day. The days I miss, Mother visits."

"Did he not want me with him?" She frowned at her hands held in Gavin's as if they might reveal an answer.

"I know he has missed you," the duke quickly assured her. "But, pardon me for saying this, he is a stubborn man. He adored your mother, and his grief is very deep."

"Then why would he not reach out to me? Does he believe I don't care as deeply?"

"Elin, I don't know, but I'm glad you are returning to London. Perhaps you can renew his will to live."

"This doesn't make sense," Elin said, freeing her hands from his. "My father is a fighter. The idea of his being weak is hard to imagine."

"He hasn't been well."

She shook her head. "No, something is happening. I don't understand, but this is not the way things are supposed to be."

Then again, nothing had been the way things were supposed to be since her mother died.

Her glance fell on Molly, reminding her of Madame Odette.

"Father sent a dressmaker to fetch me back to London. You can't imagine the quality of the materials she had," Elin remembered. "I wasn't impressed," she confessed. "I mean, the dresses and workmanship were lovely, but I knew Madame had been sent to pry me out of my grief. I'd never considered that Father needed me. I feel so selfish—"

"*Don't*," Gavin said. "You are being too hard on yourself."

"Or perhaps not hard enough."

"Elin, stop."

His tone was calm, reasoned. He said exactly what Ben would have told her . . . but with less passion.

"You and your brother are very much alike," she told him.

"Truly?" Baynton laughed, the sound bitter. "I don't see it. And if what you say is true, I don't believe Ben would appreciate the comparison."

"He might appreciate it more than you believe."

His gaze shifted from her, a mannerism completely shared by Ben and, louder than words, denoting them to be of the same family. "I can only hope." He forced a smile.

The Whitridge brothers also shared the trait of stubbornness. But their brotherly relationship was not her concern. She had her own life to attend to. She needed to see her father.

And she needed to speak her truth to Gavin, to tell him that she loved Ben.

It was obviously not going to be easy.

Elin was not a coward. She was certain of her feelings. What she had to say to him was intensely private. She hadn't even formed the right words in her mind. She didn't want to insult Baynton, and she was well aware that gossips in London would see it exactly that way. Like all men with power, he had his enemies. They would enjoy seeing her jilt him. Her decision could fuel the gossips for months.

To make matters worse, Gavin might be heavy-handed in the manner in which he dealt with people, especially his brother, but he was a good man. A very good man.

He even sensed the conflict inside her although he might not understand its reasons, because he said, "I can see you are tired. Sleep, Elin, rest your eyes and be at peace. You are safe now."

"Thank you," she murmured, gratefully taking his advice and closing her eyes and escaping hard decisions. She did feel a bit of a traitor. She could see no way of being true to herself and sparing Baynton humiliation.

Her father, she must see her father, and once she reassured herself he was well, she would lay this whole story out in front of him. He would help her find her way clear in all of this. He must. She didn't want to live her life without Ben, especially since she could already be carrying his child.

"So exactly who are you, Perkins?" Ben asked. They rode through the woods followed by about four other men Perkins had pulled out of the search party. They were dressed like him, in hunting clothes, and had a sense of purpose that belied their being locals Gavin had hired for this task.

The nondescript man smiled. "I carry out tasks for His Grace when he needs me."

"A very private man, eh?" Ben suggested.

Perkins didn't answer, and Ben hadn't expected him to give one. He'd met Perkins's like before. His father had had several he used when he wished to acquire information.

And it bothered him that here, too, Gavin was following in their father's steps. It seemed distrustful.

He also wondered if Perkins had ever been asked to snoop around about Ben.

They found the ruins handily enough. Ben remembered that he and Elin had approached them from the long side of the wall.

However, he'd hidden the bodies well. The

small burial mounds looked like the landscape around them, especially after the rain had done its job. It took a good hour before Ben was certain they'd found the right place. He recognized it by the clump of trees he'd hidden Elin behind.

Perkins's men removed the logs from the bodies. Perkins motioned his men back so that he could study the killers' faces.

"Recognize them?" Ben asked.

Instead of answering, Perkins said, "What do you know about them?"

"The big one is Darby. He was the leader. Miss Morris heard him refer to the other two as Peters and Tucker, but we are not certain if this is Peters or Tucker."

"He's Tucker."

"Ah, so you do know them?" Ben tamped down a surge of temper even as his suspicions about Perkins were reinforced.

"One doesn't linger in unsavory places without eventually learning the names of some of the locals," Perkins answered, kneeling beside Darby and starting to search his clothing.

"I take it that you've met them in London," Ben suggested.

"Down by the wharves. Tucker is a petty thief. I wouldn't have thought murder his game. He surprised me."

"Surprised me as well."

Perkins raised a brow at the barbed comment. Ben smiled back. Perkins was Gavin's man. That he knew one of those who tried to kill Elin linked the murders to the duke.

Ben was not happy about this at all. He knew Gavin did not orchestrate the attack on Elin's coach. There was no reason to do so save to cry off from the marriage—but murder was a drastic method.

And the Gavin Ben had just spent time with appeared unwilling to let go of his betrothed.

"Have you found anything?" Ben asked.

Perkins looked up from pulling off Darby's boot and shaking it out. "Nothing."

"I'm thorough as well," Ben had to point out.

"I have no doubt of that, my lord."

"Then why don't we stop pretending, Perkins, and you tell me what you know?"

"I know very little."

"I beg to differ. You seem to know quite a bit. Who do you think attempted to murder Miss Morris and make it appear a robbery?"

"It could be anyone," Perkins answered. He motioned to his men. "Bury them." Two of the men climbed off their horses. Ben hadn't noticed that they'd brought shovels with them, but there they were. They set to work.

"We don't need to stay, my lord," Perkins said. "We can start for London."

"Good, we'll catch up with my brother's coach."

"Actually, that might not be possible," Perkins said.

"And why not, Perkins?"

The man didn't answer immediately but kicked his horse forward. Ben fell in with him. When the others were out of sight, Perkins said, "You understand how it looks, your being alone with Miss Morris for a long period of time?"

"I happened to be saving her life," Ben pointed out.

"Of course. You were successful. There is no doubt that without you, she would not be with us."

"Thank you," Ben said, meaning anything but a courtesy. "However, I sense we are discussing Miss Morris for a reason. Or do you enjoy speaking in riddles?"

"Actually, I do enjoy riddles."

"Good. You seem to have a talent for them."

Perkins actually smiled.

Ben did not smile back. He was thinking he'd like to plant his fist in the middle of the man's nondescript face.

Sensing his mood, Perkins came to the point. "It will be best if you and Miss Morris kept a distance from each other for a period of time. There will be those who speculate and talk; however, if the two of you are cordial but distant, the gossip will die."

Ben had no intention of being "distant" from Elin. "Did my brother put you up to this?"

"To what?" Perkins answered with a touch mild amusement.

Ben reined in his horse. "You aren't clever, Perkins. Furthermore, my father enjoyed playing these games with his sons. He called it keeping us on our toes. You can tell my brother he'll have to do better if he expects to bamboozle me into staying where he wishes me to stay or behaving in the manner he deems proper. I will not keep a distance from Miss Morris, and I don't care what the gossips say." Indeed, Elin might even now be telling Gavin that she can't marry him—which was another compelling reason for Ben to be with her.

"Clever? Oh no, Lord Ben, I'm not being clever. I'm direct. Stay away from her."

Ben's response was to put his heels to his horse, determined to ride as fast as he could to reach Elin.

Of course, a beat later, Ben heard the sound of horses following. Perkins was on his tail. He would stop Ben if he caught him.

Ben was determined that would not happen, and the race was on.

Chapter Fifteen

Elin woke as Baynton's coach rolled into London to find herself hunched in the corner and wrapped in his wool greatcoat, a still-warm brick at her feet. Molly snored quietly beside her.

She sat up, frowning. The duke sat opposite her and appeared to be sleeping, his hat pulled down over his face so he could rest his head, his long legs at an awkward angle.

Lifting the curtain, Elin glanced outside, surprised to see buildings.

"We are here," the duke said. Sitting up, he pushed back his hat and smiled at Elin.

"I slept the whole time?"

"Through two changes of horses," he confirmed.

"I'm surprised. I must have been exhausted." Her muscles felt tight, and she had a need to stretch. As she did so, she noticed Gavin's gaze drifting to her breasts. She quickly brought her arms down, troubled. "Is your brother with us?"

"He might be. He hasn't made himself known if he is."

"I was certain he would join us as quickly as he could." Elin tried to see all she could out the window. Several riders rode alongside, including her cousin. "They must be exhausted."

Gavin nodded agreement. "I'm certain many of them attempted to sleep. It isn't comfortable in a saddle."

"Will you take me directly to my father?"

"Absolutely."

"Thank you." She settled back. It would not be long before she would be home. Dawn was breaking, and she was beginning to recognize some of the area. She was certain she appeared a fright. It had been a long, terrible ordeal.

"Perhaps Ben found a clue or something on the bodies," she said, wondering at why he wasn't here in the coach with her. She missed him. After years of being apart, being gone from him for several hours seemed unbearable. They were a team. She was important to him; he was important to her.

And then she remembered she needed to speak to Baynton. However, Molly was coming to her senses, and perhaps now would not be the best time.

It might be best if she spoke to her father first.

A half hour later, the duke's coach stopped in front of her father's house. Henry, the Morris butler, opened the coach door.

"Miss Elin, welcome home."

She smiled at the man who had known her all her life. He did not appear his usual serene self. He acted relieved at her presence.

"I'm happy to be here." She knew her hair was wildly tangled, but she didn't care. She could have thrown herself into his arms. He was not a tall man, not like the footmen of most of the area homes. However, he was efficient and thoughtful. Her father trusted him as he did few others.

Henry held out a gloved hand. "Let's hurry into the house."

Elin gave Baynton his coat. She still wore her cloak. She climbed out of the coach. The duke followed, having to unfold himself.

"Tell me, Henry, how is Father?"

"Anxious for your safe arrival, Miss Elin," was the answer. He turned and began walking down the hall. Elin assumed he was heading to the small dining room where the family usually took most meals. Instead, he walked past it, moving toward the library. He opened the door. "She has arrived, Mr. Morris."

Elin couldn't wait for the formalities. She pushed Henry aside. "Papa." She hadn't called him that for years. She was halfway into the room when she stopped, stunned by the change in her father's appearance.

His face was so white, it seemed to blend with his hair, which had once been as black as Elin's, and his shoulders stooped. The change was startling.

He sat in his leather, high-backed chair in front of the fire, a blanket over his lap as if he were ancient, and he seemed to be. A steaming cup of tea was on the table beside his chair.

"Elin," he said, his voice rough with either emotion, or pain. "I was so afraid I'd lost you."

"I'm fine. It was terrible. Jensen, Toby, James, and Craig are dead, but I survived. Fortunately. Lord Benedict came across me running for my life and helped protect me until the duke arrived."

"Lord Ben?" Fyclan frowned as if he couldn't quite place him.

She knelt on the floor beside him. Deep lines etched his face. "What has happened to you?" she whispered. "Why did you not tell me you were not well?"

"It is a bit of gout or some bad food. Yesterday, I began feeling worse."

"I'm so glad I'm here," Elin said. "And I am the worst sort of daughter. I *should* have been here for you."

"It has been a bad time," her father admitted. "We've done the best we could." He smiled then, his eyes watering. "I see pieces of your mother in you. I've missed that."

"Everyone says I am the image of you."

"Not hardly. You are too lovely."

Elin felt herself blush. Her father had never spoken to her this way. If anything, he'd often seemed a distant and stern figure. His love had focused on her mother.

And the idea that he was being sentimental alarmed her more than anything else.

She reached for both of his hands. "I'm here now, and I am going to take over the care of you. Your doctor shall be answering to me if anything untoward happens. Do you understand? I won't let you go without a fight, and *I can fight*. Perhaps in that way I'm more like you than in any other."

He smiled at that statement. "What would make me happiest is to see you married to Baynton. I am looking forward to seeing you as his bride. I need to know that you will be cared for in the proper manner."

This was not what Elin wanted to hear.

In fact, she needed to tell her father the truth. She should do it now before she found herself wrapped in The Dowager Duchess of Baynton's plans. She knew Marcella couldn't wait to take control of the details of her wedding. Perhaps even her marriage.

Furthermore, if she was going to cry off—and

she was, she was certain of it, her heart belonged to Ben—then she must prepare her father. He would not take her decision well.

However, seeing him in such weakened state . . .

Baynton was present in the room. He'd come to the door of the library and hung back, respecting this moment with her father.

Ben wouldn't have done that. Ben would have burst in the room and taken charge. Gavin was far more diplomatic, and she appreciated his tact, especially right now, when she was so confused.

Her parents had believed in the prophecy her gypsy great-grandmother had declared over Fyclan when he was born. With all their hearts, in spite of being of modern minds, they were determined that their grandson would be a duke.

Elin wasn't afraid to fly in the face of superstition. She would marry Ben. Her male child would be a simple "Mister," and she would love the baby and his father with all her heart.

However, this was not the time to announce such a decision.

Confident that in no way could she be forced to marry the duke against her will, she smiled at her father. "We shall discuss this later. What is important right now is for you to regain your health." She reached for his cup and saucer of tea. She held the cup up to his lips. "Drink. You always claim a good cup of tea can soothe away anything."

He did as bid, as docile and trusting as one of Heartwood's lambs, and Elin feared her heart would break. Fyclan Morris was a lion, not a lamb. She needed to help restore him to fierceness.

She rose to her feet and turned to Baynton, who still stood by the door, his expression solemn and solicitous at the same time. She did not doubt that he empathized with her.

Years ago, when *his* father died, she remembered he had been distraught, if such a thing could be applied to men. Her father had spent a good deal of time by his side, counseling him and helping him pick up the reins of responsibility required of a duke.

"Thank you, Your Grace, for bringing me home." His eyes were blue, the blue of stained-glass windows, a dramatic blue. The blue in Ben's eyes seemed almost washed out in comparison.

He took a step toward her and spoke, his voice low, "Gavin. My name to you is Gavin. I'm not a duke with you, Elin. I'm a man . . . and I know this has not been the easiest time for you. This may also not be the correct moment to speak, but I believe I must say something. I'm here for you. Whatever you need, for your father or for yourself, tell Henry, and he will contact me immediately. I mean this, Elin. I know that perhaps I have not been as attentive as I could be, but I will change. You have my protection. And," he said, almost as if tacking on an afterthought, "my trust."

Elin did not want to hear this. "Thank you," she managed.

It seemed an inadequate response after his uncharacteristic forthrightness. But he acted as if she had said exactly the right thing.

He smiled, a smile that had charmed many. "You must be exhausted. Henry has sent your sister-in-marriage's maid home. There is nothing for you to worry over."

"Except my father."

"Yes," he quickly agreed. "What I meant is that you are safe now." He glanced at Fyclan, who sat quiet, still. That was more of a concern to Elin than anything else.

"Has Father asked about Madame Odette?" She paused and confided, "She might have been his mistress."

"Fyclan? With a mistress?" Gavin almost laughed, and then, seeing that she didn't find the idea amusing said, "Your father doesn't have a mistress, Elin. He's not that sort of man."

Furthermore, her father, as he appeared now, was not interested in mistresses. She felt foolish for even having the thought. Although when she had confronted Madame, a look had crossed the woman's face, a mixture of superiority and disdain. Certainly she had thought Elin provincial and silly . . . but there had been something more in that expression as well . . .

A footstep in the hall alerted them to a new guest before Theresa, Robbie Morris's wife, burst in the room with a resounding, "*Elin*, I'm so happy to see you safe."

Theresa was a few inches taller than Elin and fifteen years older. She and Robbie had four daughters. Each birth had marked her figure, so she now had an ample bosom that was always threatening to overflow her bodice and a pronounced belly. Jenny Morris once observed to Elin that it was too bad Theresa was too vain to let her dressmaker use more material in her skirts.

Of course, none of that mattered. Robbie was devoted to his wife. She had been the daughter of one of his favorite tutors from university. Theirs was a love match.

A love match . . . exactly what Elin wanted for herself—and what she was determined to have.

"Thank you, Theresa," Elin murmured, as the two of them shared sisterly kisses on the cheek. "And thank you for sending your maid."

"That was nothing," Theresa said, waving the glove she'd pulled off her hand. She looked to the duke. "Your Grace, we are all pleased you found her. *Thank* you. Thank *you*."

Elin's smile felt stretched at this effusive sentiment. She was beginning to remember what she truly felt about Theresa, who could be a bit over-bearing.

Over her cousin's wife's head, Gavin met her eye, and he smiled as he said, "You are welcome," in a perfunctory manner, but Elin understood. He found Theresa as exaggerated as she did. He knew she could be a handful. She supposed he dealt with insincerity all the time. Another reason she needed to be honest with him.

He excused himself from Theresa and crossed over to the chair by the fire. "Fyclan, I'm leaving now."

Elin's father reached for his hand. "Thank you." His words were heartfelt.

"Please do what my mother's doctor asks you to do," Gavin said.

Her father waved away his request. However, Elin took it to heart. "He will," she said firmly. "And please thank Her Grace for sending him."

"Your family is very dear to mine." Gavin bowed over her hand and did something he'd not done before. His kissed it. His breath was warm against her skin.

Elin was so shocked by his gesture, she couldn't speak.

Not waiting for an answer, he nodded to Fyclan and left the room

Theresa broke the silence. "Oh. My."

Her declaration reminded Elin to breathe. She looked down at her hand and realized that while Gavin's kiss was a gallant gesture, it shocked her more than pleased her. The sooner she spoke to him, the better.

She turned and realized that her father had been watching her closely. She smiled. He regarded her with solemn concern.

Again, it was Theresa who spoke. "Mr. Bartland, the duchess's physician should arrive momentarily."

"Good," Elin said. "I am interested in what he has to say."

"I am also," Theresa said.

"You?" Elin questioned.

Her cousin's wife had the good grace to blush. "That didn't sound the thing, did it? Very domineering of me. Robbie asked me to be here. He would be here himself except for going with the duke to find you." She moved past Elin to sit on the footstool close to Fyclan. "He'll be here later today with a full report. He said you will find it interesting."

"I believe I shall find the report interesting as well. What time is Mr. Bartland to arrive?"

"At eleven."

Elin glanced at the clock on the mantel. It was

nine. "I have time to freshen up. Will you stay with Father until I return?"

"Of course, I will," Theresa said.

Fyclan raised a hand. "It isn't necessary."

"I would not think of leaving you alone," Theresa said. She'd been carrying a cloth bag and held it up. "I brought my handwork. Or I'll read to you."

"I want more tea," her father said. "I felt better with the tea."

"I'll have some made," Theresa said, her disposition cheerful.

"I shall return shortly, Papa," Elin said, and hurried off.

She found Mrs. Elliott the housekeeper in the breakfast room. Requesting a bath be prepared, Elin hurried upstairs to her room, suddenly in need of privacy.

It had been almost a year since she'd stepped into the room. Memories threatened to overwhelm her. She and her mother had picked out the carpet. Her mother had been the one to insist on the gilt carvings on the four-poster bed. Elin had other ideas for the color of the draperies. However, when they were hung, they were the color her mother had chosen.

Elin had been nine when that happened. She'd appealed to her father, who had patted her on the head, and said, "Whatever your mother decides is right."

She'd learned then that it was useless to challenge her parents. No wonder she'd valued her freedom at Heartwood.

Walking into the room, she noticed that the wardrobe door wasn't closed completely. She walked over to it, wondering what clothing she had left here last time she could change into. To her surprise, the closet was full.

All the dresses Madame Odette had supervised being fitted for her were here. Elin had forgotten that the wagon carrying them had left the day before.

Such beautiful clothes. Clothes she hadn't wanted. Clothes she'd argued over with the dressmaker because Elin had not wanted to return to London.

She looked down at the hand Gavin had kissed. She did not want to marry him, but how could she sway her father, especially as ill as he was?

In her mind's eye, she recalled the shootings. The memory always hovered close.

Here among the dresses fabricated out of beautiful materials, Elin remembered the Frenchwoman's death.

"No," she had said. "This was not to be."

"It was. He just didn't tell you."

Slowly, she sank to the thick carpet, a fear stealing over her. "He" was still out there.

He might try again. From the pocket of her cloak, she pulled out the small pistol, happy to have it.

Gavin was pleased with himself.

Elin had not expected that last little gallantry. Kissing her hand had been the wise thing to do. He smiled at his driver. "I'll walk to Menheim."

"Yes, Your Grace."

The coach rocked as it rolled off. Gavin found himself missing Elin. He'd slept a bit over their night of travel, but he'd also spent a good deal of time just watching her.

He'd not really looked at her before.

Yes, of course, he'd known she was an attractive woman. His father would not have expected Gavin to marry anything less.

However, last night, he'd had the chance to study this woman who would be his wife, and he was very pleased. *Truly*, very pleased. There were women more beautiful, but Elin had a unique vibrancy. She was completely herself. He could never imagine her following the crowd. She was a force in and of herself. He admired her curls, her smooth complexion, and curves that a man could only imagine until he claimed his wife.

He hadn't believed any time could be more

difficult than that first year after his father died. Although his father had preached excellence and demanded it, Gavin had been surprised to discover that the family wealth was not what it had been purported to be. The old duke had squandered a good deal of money on less-than-stalwart investments, and it had taken a mad scramble to recoup his losses.

Thankfully, Fyclan Morris had been there to guide Gavin. The Baynton fortune wasn't as much as it had been, but it was now substantial.

And Gavin was ready to marry. In fact, as he'd watched Elin, he'd become aware of a deep hunger for a companion, someone who would let him be a man and not a duke. Someone he could trust with his thoughts and his doubts.

Someone whose touch would be soft.

Even with his mother, there were expectations. He had enemies, men who wanted power more than seeing to the good of the country. Gavin wasn't afraid of responsibility. He was also certain of his capability to solve all problems. He'd been groomed to do so.

But there hadn't been time for female companionship, not in the way he wanted it. Oh, he could have gone to brothels. Most of his peers did. Many had mistresses.

But Gavin longed for something deeper, and he'd been willing to wait for it. His friends would have mocked him mercilessly if they knew he'd not yet bedded a woman at his age. He thought it only fair that if he expected his wife to be a virgin, he should be unsullied as well. He wanted that moment of joining to be memorable and carry the full weight of its meaning.

In truth, he'd always admired what Fyclan and his wife seemed to share, and he prayed Elin was of the same mind.

They would marry soon. The plans were already in motion. The attack on her coach was unfortunate, and Gavin was deeply grateful to the Almighty that Elin had survived. He needed her. He wanted her.

Gavin marched into Menheim. He was ready for a good meal, a bath, and perhaps a quick nap. He didn't know exactly what was on his schedule, but he was certain Talbert, his secretary, would tell him.

Sawyer, his butler, took his hat and nodded in greeting. Talbert had heard the coach and came running down the hall from the library where his small office was located.

"Your Grace, how good to have you back. Whitehall has been sending messages—"

"I'm not discussing anything yet. Sawyer, have the cook prepare a beefsteak, rare but hot, the way I like it. Have it sent to my room. Oh, and those potatoes. Cook knows what I want."

"Yes, Your Grace."

With Sawyer's help, Gavin shrugged out of his greatcoat. He marched up the stairs to his suite of rooms. His valet, Michael, met him in the hall.

"A bath, Michael," Gavin ordered, moving toward his bedroom door at the end of the hall. His rooms consisted of a sitting room between two bedrooms—one was his and one was for the wife he would soon have.

"Yes, Your Grace," Michael answered, and would have gone hurrying off to heat water except a new thought struck Gavin.

He went back to the stairs. *"Talbert."*

His man came running and with good cause. Gavin rarely raised his voice with the people who worked for him.

"Yes, Your Grace?" Talbert said from the foot of the steps.

"I wish to have flowers sent to Miss Morris. I want a huge bouquet of the most exotic, glorious flowers imaginable."

"Yes, Your Grace. Do you want anything addressed on the card."

Gavin laughed with delight at the thought of Elin's receiving an incredible bouquet . . . but he was no poet. "Just my card. Sign it. You know how."

"Yes, Your Grace."

Pleased with himself, Gavin turned back toward his door, his booted heels heavy on the hall's polished wood. Michael gave him a nod as he hurried down the back stairs. Gavin reached his door handle and gave it a turn. He walked into his room.

His bedroom was the one place Gavin was allowed his personal tastes. Everyplace else in the house was filled with ancestral furnishings that had been handed down from one generation to another—except for this room.

He preferred simple, masculine lines. The bed was oversized and the headboard polished ebony. The floors were bare and the walls white. The drapes were a heavy burgundy color that could shut out the light and allow him to catch a nap to meet the needs of his demanding schedule. A merry fire burned in the hearth, warming the room against the October chill. Two huge, high-backed leather chairs were turned toward it, with tables and reading lamps beside them.

He began pulling at the knot in his neckcloth, anxious to have it undone and to pull off his boots. In a few weeks, he and Elin would be sitting in front of the fire. He and Elin would be in the bed together.

The thought stopped him in his tracks. All of a sudden he stared at the white, clean coverlet and imagined her glorious curls across his pillow.

God help him, he didn't know if he could wait until the wedding—

"It is about time you returned," a male voice said. Ben rose from one of the chairs in front of the fire. The high back had blocked him from Gavin's view. "Hello, Brother," he said amiably. The spark of anger in his eye belied any pleasantry as did the silk in his tone. "Surprised to see me? It is time we have a little discussion."

Gavin could step back out into the hall. He could call for help.

Instead, he shut the door behind him.

Chapter Sixteen

"You look like a rat catcher," Gavin observed as if he was leveling the worst sort of insult against Ben.

Ben could have laughed. "Displeased that Perkins couldn't keep me at bay?"

Gavin pulled off his neckcloth that he had untied. "He did well enough."

A knock sounded on the door. Since he was standing right there, Gavin opened it.

"I have your bath, Your Grace." Ben recognized the valet's voice.

"He's not ready to bathe, Michael," Ben called, earning another scowl from his brother.

However, Gavin echoed his words, adding, "I shall let you know when I wish to be disturbed."

"Is that Lord Ben, Your Grace? Should I tell Mrs. McAuliffe that a room needs to be prepared?"

"You should *not*," Ben answered as bold as one pleased. He'd not spend another night in this house.

"There is your answer," Gavin said in his well-modulated voice. "And see that we are not disturbed."

"No matter what," Ben agreed, moving away from the chair.

"Yes, Your Grace."

Gavin shut the door. He spread his arms. "Well?" he challenged. "We are alone—"

"As alone as anyone can be in a house with fifty servants."

"Would you like to go out into the street? Would that be more private?"

Ben shook his head. "This is fine."

"Then say what you've been waiting to say," Gavin answered, as if certain of what was on Ben's mind—and perhaps he was. The fact that Gavin had suggested Perkins and his men keep Ben from following his coach suggested as much.

So, Ben spoke his truth. "I love Elin."

Gavin did not act surprised, which surprised Ben. After a moment's consideration, he replied simply, "She's mine.

"Are you certain? She has her own will, her own desires. We live in a different world than our parents did, Gavin. Women can and do make their own choices."

"Not in our class."

"Yes, things change even here, Brother."

Gavin frowned as if that was the most preposterous idea he'd ever heard, and perhaps it was. His will ruled in this house and just about everywhere else he went.

But he didn't rule Ben . . . or Elin.

And his brother must have realized some of this because he moderated his approach. "What do you have to offer her? Do you even own a horse? Have a living?"

That was the *wrong* approach, even though Ben had thought it himself. His temper ignited. "I did have a living until you took it from me."

Gavin held up a hand. "Don't go on about the military again. That topic is done."

Ben almost shot across the room. "That topic is *never* done."

"It is with me." He spoke with finality, with superiority, with bloody condescension.

And then Gavin did something that was of even greater insult. He turned his back on Ben, a sign that in his mind the conversation was finished.

The tenuous hold Ben had over his temper, the one he'd struggled with since he and Perkins had begun their cat-and-mouse chase all the way to London, snapped.

In three steps, he was able to grab his older

brother's shoulder, whip him around, and plant his fist in Gavin's mouth. He'd used enough force that Gavin stumbled backward. His legs hit the side of the bed, forcing him off balance, and he sat on the mattress, dazed for a second.

Ben shook his hand. His brother had a hard jaw. "That felt good."

And it did.

"For years," Ben said, practically through clenched teeth, "I've been wanting to do that. I've kept it pent up inside. The military relieved a good amount of that pressure, but you had to take that away from me."

Gavin shrugged off his jacket and bought his hand to his lips, which had been cut open from the blow. He looked at the blood on it.

Ben smiled, pleased.

He also thought they were done. He'd shown his "mighty" older brother what he thought of him. He'd let Gavin know that he wasn't going to be shoved around to his ducal will.

What he wasn't expecting was for his brother to launch himself from the bed, right at Ben.

In truth, if he'd thought of Gavin fighting at all, Ben would have assumed that his brother would be a student of those boxing academies favored by gentlemen. The sort of place a man learned to use his fists by rules.

The force of Gavin's body propelled Ben across

the room, where he ran into one of the upholstered chairs. Then Gavin made a mistake.

He let go.

Ben swung hard, aiming for his brother's jaw.

Gavin blocked him with his arm and took his swing. It connected with Ben's jaw.

For a second, Ben's ears rang.

Who would have thought Gavin had it in him?

As if reading Ben's mind, Gavin explained, "I was a twin. Jack and I went at each other more than a few times."

"I'm impressed," Ben said, before bringing his fist up and into Gavin's stomach. His hand bounced off hard muscles, and it became a set-to.

Brother against brother. Fists flew. Furniture was knocked over. There was nothing pretty or well behaved about this fight. They were angry and each determined the other wouldn't win.

They both landed on the bed and wrestled across the mattress. Ben would land a good blow, then Gavin would, then back and forth again.

Gavin was the one who fell off the bed. Ben dove on top of him, the weight of his body forcing the breath out of his older brother. Ben struck out for the kill, ready to give better than he received—

Strong hands grabbed his arms and shoulders. Ben was yanked up and off and dragged away. Not only were the servants in the room, but so was his mother. She was shouting at them to stop.

Apparently, she had been issuing this order repeatedly for some time, but Ben had not heard her.

Gavin, either.

Indeed, he still hadn't registered that they were no longer alone but leaped to his feet and went after Ben who, being held by three stalwart footmen, was in no position to protect himself.

Fortunately, there were an equal number of footmen to grab Gavin. He pressed against them, the bloodlust still upon him, as it still was with Ben.

In fact, this was the most human Ben had ever seen his brother. He rather liked him for it.

Their mother stepped between them. "*Stop this*, both of you. *Now*."

Gavin stared at her as if she were a rare bird and began to recover himself.

She knew she had him. "You forget yourself, Baynton."

With those cutting words, his brother changed. The emotion that had driven him vanished. His face became impassive, somber even, his bearing erect. He actually appeared to age and become the very semblance of their father.

Ben was stunned—not only by the transition in his brother but also by how he had misjudged him. Ben had assumed that the duke was his brother. It wasn't. It was a role, a mantle he cast over himself day in and day out.

"Don't," Ben heard himself say, surprised he spoke his thoughts aloud. And once spoken, he must explain. "Gavin, don't back away from me. Let us fight it out."

Gavin shook his head. The footmen immediately released their hold. He walked to the window and stood, his back to the room, his silence a statement.

But Ben was not giving up. This glimpse of his brother, the one that at one time had wrestled with his twin, fascinated him. "No, I'm not letting you hide behind the title. Speak to me, Gavin. Shout at me, rail at me—throw another fist at me. Live, man. *Live.*"

In response, his brother looked at him, his eyes hard shards. "She's mine."

Those were fighting words. Ben's hand curled into fists, but he couldn't shake the hands that held him back. "It doesn't work that way," he threw at his brother. "You are not 'duke of everything.'"

Gavin stared at him, the mask carefully in place.

Marcella took charge. "That is quite enough. Take Lord Benedict to my room."

Ben dug in his heels. "I'm not ready to go. Gavin and I have unfinished business."

But what he wanted to do or didn't want to do held little weight. The footmen bodily lifted him. He was swept out of the room, marched to his mother's suite at the other end of the hall, and unceremoniously dumped onto the floor.

In this way, Menheim's servants let him know whom they favored.

The footmen did not wait for orders but silently tromped out the door. Ben sat on the carpet, his legs in front of him, a bit nonplussed by what had just happened.

In truth, he'd always thought of himself as the rebel, the hero in the household. He didn't expect his mother or brother to see him in such a role, but the servants, who had always acted as if they liked him, should have appreciated him. Or perhaps their view of his brother was not as negative?

The door behind him opened and closed. He heard the swish of skirts and caught the scent of his mother's violet perfume before she came to stand beside him. Ben looked up. Marcella was an attractive woman who had always worn her title well, especially in these later years.

She was also a distant figure in his life, especially after Jack disappeared and his parents had left him at Trenton, the family's country estate next to the Morris property. One would think that a mother would hold on to her remaining sons as tightly as she could.

His mother was more complicated.

"I'm disappointed in you, Benedict. You and

your brother are grown men. Why are you behaving like louts?"

Ben frowned, studied the pattern on the India carpet, and then shrugged. "My argument is with Gavin, and it is personal."

"He said the same. What do you believe you are doing?"

"Standing up for myself." His jaw tensed just at the thought.

He was surprised when she stooped down and took his face in her hands, forcing him to look at her. "My youngest son, what has happened to you?"

"In what sense, Mother? Am I a disappointment? Not following the family dictates?"

She leaned back as if he had struck out at her. He didn't care but forged on, "I will not be forced to do my brother's bidding." *Especially when it came to Elin.* "He thinks he has an iron will? Well, mine is stronger. I am not his lackey."

"Why do you believe you are?" Her confusion sounded genuine, almost hesitant.

"He has taken everything that meant something to me away. Well, he won't have Elin. I won't give her up."

The dowager sank to the floor beside him. "Elin?"

He met his mother's eye. "She's *mine.* I love her. I've always loved her." There, he'd gone against his own good intention of only seconds ago. If she wanted to interfere, then let her chew on this.

Instead of the recriminations he anticipated, she reached for his hand, her brows gathering in concern. "You and Elin." She shook her head.

"What?"

She released a shaky breath. "It was always there, wasn't it?" Her hand around his felt warm. There was no anger in her touch.

"Always," he answered.

"I knew she was at the heart of your argument when Baynton said, 'She's mine.' I knew. She's always been a wedge between you as brothers, hasn't she? I didn't wish to believe it true. Your father warned me, but I knew how lonely you were. Holding you back, keeping you at Trenton was unnatural. I didn't realize it until the night you and Elin disappeared."

"There was a storm," he offered . . . the old story, the one that appeased.

Her look told him she was wiser than that.

He shut up.

For a moment, they sat silent. Time to think. To consider.

It was needed.

She spoke, "I was not happy when your father sent you to the military."

"I wasn't either—at first."

"You have a forceful personality, my son. You remind me very much of my own father. You've never been able to pretend." She pulled her hand away from his and stretched out her legs, heedless of her skirts around her ankles. She was facing him as if they were two children clambering around in play. His amazement at her uncharacteristic and decidedly undignified way of sitting made her laugh. "I've surprised you."

"You have."

"Well, the time has come to clear the air. Perhaps that is what is needed in this family. Actually, it was needed long ago. Maybe then, I wouldn't have lost Jack."

Ben had rarely heard his mother speak of Jack since his disappearance. Even his father had stopped talking of him. But now, in the space of an hour, Gavin had referenced his twin, and their mother had said his name out loud—and he realized, in truth, his missing brother presumed dead was never far from anyone's mind . . . and never would be until they'd learned what happened.

"Is Jack involved in this?" Ben wondered.

"In some ways." The confidence she had been showing wavered, giving him a glimpse of a mother's grief.

But she had aroused Ben's curiosity. "Why did he leave?"

"Ah, there is the question. I shall ask him when

I see once more." She paused. "*If* I see him again. I pray I do."

She drew a breath and released it before saying, "His disappearance kept the gossips and papers busy. It was a trying time for all of us, but especially your father. He was a proud man. He didn't appreciate the world's wondering why his son would run away, if that is what happened."

"You believe it is so."

"Perkins . . . he is a man you father used—"

"I've met him," Ben replied grimly. Perkins was not his favorite person right now.

"—Well, he mounted a search. He found no trace of Jack. It had rained the night he disappeared, and there weren't even footprints or a scent for the dogs. So, when your bit of scandal came about—"

"It wasn't a scandal. We were young, but I would have done what was honorable if I'd been given a chance. I loved Elin even then."

"Or so you believe. But do you really know, Ben? Oh, I grant that you were passionate about her, but who knows the direction young love takes? When your father went against my wishes and suggested the military, you didn't kick up a fuss. He said you were defiant after the thrashing he gave you, but you walked on your own to the waiting coach."

"I was overwhelmed." And humiliated. He'd

also been overwhelmed by the disaster of what had happened between him and Elin. He was sure it was of his making. His father had claimed he had hurt her, a devastating charge to Ben at the time.

"Your father said you were a pup who needed direction," his mother was saying. "He regretted that in his pain of losing Jack, he'd not sent you away to school, and that was mostly *my* doing. I convinced him to keep you close with the best tutors we could find. Later, he wished he had at least sent you to Harrow. He was so angry at Eton for losing Jack."

"I did well in the military." He also realized time had given him perspective. Over a year ago, he'd been furious with Gavin for having his commission revoked. However, if that had not happened, Ben would not have been reunited with Elin.

Funny the twists life took.

"I have a confession to make."

Her words grabbed his attention.

"You blame Gavin for ordering your dismissal from the military."

"Are you saying he didn't? Because I saw his signature on the orders."

"He did it at my request. He warned me you would not be happy."

Ben leaned back. "Why, Mother? Why would

you not have written me and told me of your concerns? Why take my life from me?"

"Because I didn't believe you would listen to me. I've lost a child and a husband, and everyone was talking about General Wellesley and how he would engage the French. They talked about battles and I realized I could lose you as well. So I made Baynton's life miserable until he agreed to do as I asked."

"Gavin didn't say you were involved."

"He wouldn't."

Ben felt all the anger he'd harbored against his brother well up inside. "Why would he not tell *me* the truth?"

"Your brother was protecting me. You were very angry when you first returned to London. That anger continued unabated."

That was correct. Nor, at this moment, was Ben proud of the way he'd acted. He wasn't certain when the shift had happened, but he found himself uncomfortable thinking about his past behavior.

"I suppose I can be headstrong." The words came out small and hesitant from Ben's mouth. He didn't want to see Gavin as nobler than he— and yet he knew his attitude toward his brother was changing.

Rediscovering Elin, falling in love with her all over again, had softened his stance toward many things, including his family—to a point.

"I love Elin, Mother. She loves me. I'll challenge Baynton for her, and I shall win."

He had expected his mother to be repelled by the idea. She surprised him. Calmly she answered, "If you do battle for her, understand you will be making a mockery of your brother. Everyone knows that Elin Morris has been promised to the Duke of Baynton for decades. Your brother has enemies, and he has pride. He will not want to be the talk of the Town. Or the center of any jests. Certainly you can agree that Gavin is too good a man to be subjected to such treatment."

"So, Elin and I are to be miserable for the rest of our lives so that Gavin isn't gossiped about? Is that what you are saying?"

"Ben—"

"*No.*" He rose to his feet and offered his hand to her, which she gracefully accepted. She was still lovely and in possession of her full senses . . . but, as he lifted her weight up, he realized she was growing older, frailer.

He forced himself to take the heat out of his words. "I will not give up Elin just so Gavin can appear ducal. He doesn't love her. He doesn't know her."

"Baynton will in time."

"Or he will be so wrapped in his own importance, he won't notice her. He won't appreciate or listen to her, or marvel at her slightest movement, or try to make her life meaningful. He'll expect a child of her, but he won't be her friend. My brother doesn't know how to think of anything other than his own responsibilities."

"Perhaps she will teach him—?"

"*Perhaps?* Possibly? Maybe? Mother, Elin deserves better. Every woman deserves better."

His plea moved her. She walked a few steps away from him, her mind busy, and Ben found himself holding his breath. His father had been a forceful, ofttimes difficult man. It was easy to rage against such a person, even a sire, and willingly reject him if necessary.

But his mother was different. He wanted to trust her.

"I am having your rooms prepared for you," she said.

This information was not what he'd been expecting her to say. When he started to protest that he wasn't about to stay under Gavin's roof, she held up a hand.

"Enough of this, Ben. It is indulgent and childish. You were once a leader, and from all that I've heard, men respected you. Then you return home and you have done—what? *Nothing*, save live an undirected life. Well, Fate keeps putting Elin into your hands. I'm not a superstitious woman, and

I won't pretend to know what that means. If Elin cries off and jilts Gavin for his brother, well, it is just *not* done."

"It *has* been done."

"Not by people of our class."

"Oh, yes, the upper cream—"

"*Stop this.*" She spoke in a tone he'd immediately obeyed since he was a child.

"What I'm saying is that the issue of which one of you Elin chooses is between you and your brother. I've interfered enough in your life. But understand, your brother is a very good man. It is not easy to be the duke, to balance his responsibilities to the estates and our people along with the intrigues and needs of this country, but Gavin does it very well. He is far better at wielding his power than my own husband was. A woman would be lucky to have him."

She let her last statement linger in the moment before she asked, "What do you offer Elin, Ben? And don't play the poet and say something ridiculous like 'your heart.' She is an intelligent young woman. One I shall be glad to call daughter. You say she deserves more than what Gavin can give her. I say she is worthy of more than a man who pouts."

That was a facer.

Ben needed to find his voice. "*I* just saved her life."

"So I've heard. That is a start, Ben. Or are you

proposing that you marry her and the two of you happily spend your time carousing in the taverns and gaming halls that you have been frequenting over the past year?" She took a step toward him, a martial light in her eye. "If you want her, my son, what are you going to change to win her? Because, she may return your love, but Fyclan Morris is no fool. He wants only the best for his daughter. Are you the best you can be, Benedict?"

Her words were tiny darts to his conscience.

At last, he recognized what a dunderhead he'd been. He saw himself as Elin must have seen him when she came upon him rolling dice at The Oak. He had not appeared to be a man who wanted something meaningful from his life. Instead, he'd been playing at being common.

Pride was a hard thing to swallow.

Instead of answering, Ben left the room. A part of him wanted to march down the stairs and out the front door.

Love made him realize he must change.

Elin would defy her father for Ben, but not without a painful cost. He could run that gauntlet of society's opinion. However, his mother was right, what did he have to offer? Everyone he knew would believe Elin a fool to reject the Duke of Baynton for Benedict Whitridge.

So, instead of leaving, Ben found himself going to his old set of rooms. All was almost as he'd left it except that the bed had been replaced with one that was bigger, and there was a sizeable new wardrobe in the room. The walls were green, a color he had once appreciated. Now he realized he'd had terrible taste.

A fire burned in the hearth. His mother had been confident.

But as Ben stood in the doorway, he found himself longing for Trenton, his family's seat next to the Morris estate.

A footstep sounded behind him. Ben turned to meet a man of medium height with brown hair and graying temples, conservative dress, and a freshly pressed coat draped over his arm.

"Lord Benedict?" he said pleasantly.

"Lord Ben, they call me."

The man nodded. "I didn't want to seem presumptuous, my lord."

"And you are?"

"George. Her Grace asked me to attend you."

Ben had to laugh. His mother was *very* sure of herself.

"Did Her Grace tell you, George, that I would be quite a project?"

The valet swallowed a smile. "She hinted that you might be a challenge. But I enjoy a challenge, my lord."

"So do I, George," Ben confessed. "Let us set to work. I have a woman to win."

Chapter Seventeen

*G*eorge was a miracle worker.

Ben had not realized how rough he had become. Mirrors had been in scarce supply where he'd been over the past twelve months or so. One glance in the mirror confirmed that Gavin was right. Ben did look like a rat catcher, or worse.

He'd always been a proponent of daily bathing. He just felt better when he was clean, and he'd maintained the habit as best he could while traveling with Hooknosed and the others. They mocked him, but Ben didn't care.

However, running through the woods with Elin had taken a toll. No wonder he'd been so angry at Gavin's words.

Soon George had Ben sitting in a steaming bath. Most bathing tubs were too small for Ben. His legs always hung out or were folded so that his knees almost hit his chin. This was a leg-hanging venture.

George poured buckets of water over Ben's head. The water splashed everywhere. George didn't care.

"Don't worry about the floor, my lord. I'll see that mopped up." He picked up a stiff brush and a bar of sandalwood-scented soap and set to scrubbing Ben's feet.

"*Hey,*" Ben said in surprise, his toes curling in reaction to the bristles against his feet. He yanked his foot back, but George had a firm grip.

"Ticklish, my lord?"

"Damned right, and I want my foot back. I don't need *that* much personal attention."

"You have been traveling for a long time, my lord," George intoned. "A man needs this from time to time." He obeyed Ben's order to return his foot, but went after the other with equal vigor.

And it all became a penance of sorts. As George snipped hair, polished nails, and shaved off a ghastly stubble, Ben accepted that this was a part of the price he needed to pay to become worthy of Elin.

His wardrobe held the clothes he'd left behind when he'd stormed out of Menheim after his last argument with Gavin with only the clothes on his back. His brother had wanted Ben to accept a position with the Home Office under the Home

Secretary Richard Ryder. Since such an endeavor would further burnish Gavin's political influence, Ben had been set against the appointment.

Now, he was reconsidering. A post with the government had once seemed deadly boring. However, after a year traveling around at loose ends, it now stuck him as productive.

And it would give him time with Elin.

Elin. When she jilted Gavin, the scandal *could* rob Ben of any opportunities. They would leave the country in that situation, he decided. They would do what they must to be together, and he hoped she agreed with him.

After almost three hours of scrubbing and pruning, George presented to Ben a new man in his mirror. He wore a jacket of darkest blue over a golden-patterned waistcoat and buff-colored breeches. His hair had been trimmed to above his ears and styled *à la Brutus*, a favorite with all the dandies, including his brother. Of course, Ben's hair lacked an abundance of curls unless he was caught in the rain, so this style appeared as one of his own. He was pleased.

"Impressive, George," Ben admitted. "I've never seen a shirt this white or crisp." He straightened the knot George had tied in his neckcloth. "Nor a shine this gleaming to my boots. Not even my batman could do as well," he said, referring to the soldier who had served as his personal servant.

"Champagne blacking, my lord. All the boots in the house are polished with it."

"Amazing." In the face of his transformation, Ben's argument with his brother a year ago seemed trivial. His pride had not served him well.

Or had he been mourning? Grieving the loss of not only a career he'd enjoyed but also Elin's friendship? He valued her friendship almost as much as he treasured the growing love between them.

Now, studying the figure he cut in the looking glass, he felt himself a very lucky man. He knew Elin would be pleased.

"I do wish you'd let me do something with your eyebrows, my lord. They are very distinctive but not at all the style. They should be thinner and more arched—"

"Don't touch my eyebrows." Just the thought of what George might have in mind made him shudder. "They are as God made them."

"Yes, my lord."

"My coat and my hat, George. I'm going out." The hour was half past four, a good time for paying a call.

George dutifully took from the wardrobe a greatcoat. It was of dark gray wool. Ben didn't remember it from a year ago, but it fit well. The hat was a curled brim beaver. George handed him gloves. Pulling them on, Ben almost felt a man of means.

An idea was beginning to form in his head, a thought for his future. He was anxious to discuss the matter with Elin.

"Thank you, George," he threw over his shoulder as he left the room.

There was no sound or sight of his mother or brother in the house. Ben wasn't disturbed by this. He was a man on a mission. He was calling on the lady he loved.

The sky was clear, the air brisk—the sort of day it felt good to be alive. Ben walked with purpose.

A few feet from the Morris front door, a carriage rolled past. Ben glanced at it, and his step slowed. Baynton was riding in the open vehicle, with Fyclan Morris and his daughter.

When the carriage stopped, Baynton jumped out and held the door open for Elin and her father. Elin laughed at something Gavin had said. She'd not noticed Ben. She hadn't even glanced in his direction.

Perhaps she hadn't recognized him.

Jealousy was an ugly emotion. Ben knew because his body was rife with it.

The front door to the house opened. Elin went inside. Gavin, ever the diplomat said something to Fyclan who still sat in the vehicle. He waved the duke on into the house. Ben couldn't hear what he said, but Gavin walked into the house after Elin.

Now, Ben moved forward. He wasn't about to

let his brother have any more time with Elin than necessary.

However, Fyclan climbed out of the carriage, leaning heavily on his walking stick and confronted Ben on the walk before he reached the door. "I thought that was you." There was no welcome in his tone.

Ben decided to ignore his coldness. He wanted Fyclan's approval. Her father's opinion was important to Elin. "How are you, sir?"

"Very good," Fyclan answered, holding up his walking stick as if to bar Ben's passage to the door. "And now, I shall say that you are not welcome under my roof."

"I love your daughter."

"Love? You almost destroyed her."

Ben frowned. "Did she tell you about the men trying to murder her? That I helped her escape and protected her from them?"

"And compromised her while you did it." Fyclan had lowered his voice on that one. His eyes were alive with a father's outrage.

"She told you I 'compromised' her?" A heaviness grew in Ben's chest. This was very much like the conversation he'd had with his father and this man years ago.

"Not this time. She's being very coy. But a father knows. You plan to take her for everything she is worth."

"And you want only what is best for her, regardless of her feelings or what she desires?"

If he had popped Fyclan in the nose, the man could not be more insulted. "You can't understand how much I detest you. You won't know until you have a daughter and some callow lad tries to rob her of her future with talk of love while he ruins her. Jenny and I waited and prayed for Elin. She is a gift."

"That she is," Ben quickly agreed.

"And you *sullied* her. She was barely a child."

"We were both young," Ben started, "but what we felt for each other was very real. It *is* real, even now."

Fyclan pounded his cane on the walk, punctuating his words as he said, "And you can't have her. I won't let you."

"Why? My feelings for her are true. Everyone knows that you and your wife were a love match. Why can't you allow Elin to make up her own mind?"

"Because she is to be a duchess."

"That can change—" Ben started.

"It cannot. It *will* not."

"Is this about that prophecy or whatever?" Ben demanded, his temper growing to match Fyclan's. "This belief that you and your wife had that your grandson would be a duke. It's ridiculous. Nonsense."

"Nonsense? In two weeks' time, Elin will marry your brother, and it will come true. She deserves to a duchess."

"You would put something some fortune-teller—"

"My grandmother made the prediction. She had the gift."

"Very well, something 'your grandmother' claimed over your daughter's happiness? Mr. Morris, if Elin told me that she never wanted to see me again, then I would comply. I love her that much. But she hasn't said those words. I would know. My heart would shatter from the sound of them."

"You are not good enough for my daughter."

And there it was.

"True," Ben agreed. "But I will change. I can change."

Fyclan's response was to turn and walk away.

His driver and the butler who had opened the door stood watching the exchange. As Fyclan reached his front step, he said to the butler, "Don't let that man enter this house, Henry. I will have nothing to do with him. Gordon," he addressed the driver, "bring the town coach at seven. Caldwells' house." The driver nodded. Fyclan went inside.

The butler lingered, giving Ben a hard look before he closed the door firmly.

The driver waited on the walk for Ben to leave, his arms crossed, a bull of a man ready for a fight.

Ben was not going to battle on Elin's doorstep. It would create too great of a scene in this fashionable neighborhood.

Furthermore, every wise military officer knows there are times retreat is the best option.

He returned to his brother's house. As he walked in, his mother came rushing down the hall, then stopped when she saw Ben.

"Why, you are quite handsome, my son," she said approvingly.

"Thank you."

"You went out?"

Ben knew her tone. She fished for information. She probably knew where he'd gone but wondered.

"I needed fresh air," he said.

She smiled, noncommittal. Did she know Gavin was paying a call on Elin? Possibly.

"What are the plans for dinner tonight?" Ben asked.

"Oh, well, we are to dine with Lord and Lady Caldwell. They are having their annual ball. Lord Caldwell has been working on a new farm bill with Baynton. I expect to be bored over dinner and anxious for the evening ahead."

Ben waited, wondering if she would include him.

She didn't.

"It is a pity you can't join us. The event will be a crush, and I know that one more guest, no matter how handsome"—she smiled as if paying him a great compliment—"can't be included. Actually, I should start dressing. Tell Mrs. McAuliffe what you wish for your supper." She went up the stairs.

A second later, the front door opened, and Gavin walked in.

He was back to being "the duke." He had that air of superiority that rubbed Ben the wrong way, the one that brought out the worst in him.

They took each other's measure. His brother was stiff, unyielding. Ben could hate him for spending the past hour with Elin. Hate him for having a life where everything was clear-cut and all fell into his lap . . . and then something inside Ben shifted, just as it had that day in the woods.

He realized Gavin wasn't his enemy.

Yes, Gavin was an easy target to rail against. Gavin did have what Ben wanted, specifically Elin—and perhaps the respect of their father and everyone else within a thousand mile radius. It had been so easy for his oldest brother whereas Ben and, yes, Jack had been merely necessary protection against Gavin's death for the sake of the "title."

Perhaps their father hadn't really seen Gavin as a whole person any more than his oldest brother saw Ben as something more than a human standby in case of the unthinkable happening. In truth, their father had behaved as if Gavin were nothing more than an extension of his own wants and expectations.

"I'm sorry," Ben heard himself say, the sincere words flowing out of him. "I shouldn't have attacked you earlier."

"Perhaps you just desired to be taught a lesson," Gavin answered, sounding slightly bored.

Ben forced himself to smile. "I was angry that you had ordered your man Perkins to keep me away from the coach."

"I was thinking of Elin and her reputation. How odd would it be for us all to come rolling into Town, especially after your spending so much time with her."

"Time? You mean when I was keeping her alive—?" Ben caught himself. "Wait, this is not how I want it to be between us—"

"It is how it has always been."

That was true. Even when they were younger, Ben had keenly resented that Gavin was more important in their father's eyes than he was.

But was that sort of resentment something Ben wanted to continue to carry?

"Then," Ben answered thoughtfully, "perhaps the time has come to change."

Baynton was unyielding. "Is that possible?"

"I don't know." Ben took a step toward him. "I love her, Gavin. Love *her*. With that between us, I don't know what is realistic, but I don't want a quarrel with you. What is between Elin and me started long ago."

"It shouldn't have started at all."

He could be right. Ben had no answer.

Gavin shifted his weight. He appeared ready to say something, thought differently, and started up the stairs, but then he came back down.

His voice low he said, "I understand why you love her, Ben. She is all that is gracious. But we are trapped. There are expectations. Appearances."

"To the devil with all that, Gavin. Those things are unimportant."

"Not in my world."

His words hung in the air between them, then Gavin went upstairs.

Ben had a strong desire to plow his fist in a wall . . . but that had been the way he'd handled matters in the past.

What are you going to change to win her?

His mother's words echoed in his ears. He found in himself a desire to be more than what he had been.

Speaking to Gavin had been a good step. Before, the two of them would have brooded over the matter and let it fester.

However, Ben was not about to give in. He went to his room.

George had tidied it up nicely while Ben was gone. The valet was humming to himself as he closed the wardrobe doors. He started when Ben entered the room as if he hadn't expected him.

"My lord, you are returned early."

"Is that a surprise, George?"

The servant appeared discomforted before admitting, "They told me you were one for late nights. That I should not be alarmed if you don't return for days."

"That might have been true," Ben conceded. "But it is no longer. My evening clothes, George. I'm going out."

"To anywhere of importance, my lord?"

"I understand Lord Caldwell is having a ball."

George had the audacity to blink. "I did not know you were included on the invitation, my lord, or had planned to go. I would have laid out your evening dress."

Ben remembered when Gavin had literally ordered him to have evening clothes made. It had been a huge row between them. One of many in those days.

"I'm not invited, George. I doubt if Lord and Lady Caldwell know I'm in Town."

"So you will be going with His Grace and Her Grace?"

Ben laughed. "No, I make my own plans."

Elin had not wanted to go to dinner with Lord and Lady Caldwell this evening.

Her father had insisted. She knew what he was doing. He wanted her to be seen in Baynton's company as much as possible.

That Ben had saved her life didn't matter to him.

He'd even insisted, when Baynton politely came to call to see how Elin was faring, that they take a ride through the park in the open landau. He wanted anyone who was in town this time of year to see her with the duke. Thankfully, the day had not been too cold.

The duke and his mother rode with them in the Morris coach to Lord and Lady Caldwell's.

To her surprise, Gavin sensed her unhappiness. He didn't say anything, but he didn't press her either with references to the wedding as he'd done earlier that afternoon.

And she didn't find herself in his company a great deal. At the Caldwells', the duke's attention was quickly claimed by many among their company who wished to discuss politics. Her father fell in with that group as well.

The women at the table were all Marcella's

age. They doted on Elin as a soon-to-be bride, but there their interests ended. They had their own social set, and Elin was not part of it. She contributed where she could to be polite but was vastly relieved when the ball started.

Lady Caldwell insisted that the duke and Elin lead the dancing. The role took Elin back to that fateful night when her mother died. She tried not to think of it.

At the end of the set, Gavin bowed over her hand. "Thank you, Miss Morris." She could feel the warmth of his body even through his gloves and knew every eye in the overcrowded ballroom was on them. Fans fluttered as ladies murmured their approval to each other, or their jealousy.

Elin could only nod. She had a strong desire to run for the doorway and never stop until she reached Heartwood. As she smiled and pretended to be serene, she feared this was her life—constant formalities while waiting for her husband. She would die of boredom. She'd wither.

Her father had to see reason. He must.

"Keep a brave face," Gavin whispered in her ear as he led her back to where his mother sat with her father. "Don't think about the last time we danced together."

Ah, so he had realized . . . and yet, his considerate comment left her dissatisfied, and she couldn't quite decide exactly why. Perhaps because Gavin was always too considerate.

People milled around them, fawning over both the duke and her father. Fyclan was in his element. He was pale but appeared to be enjoying himself and Marcella, the Dowager, had a great deal to do with that.

"They seem to enjoy each other's company," Gavin observed.

"Yes," Elin had to agree. "Have they been like this before?"

"They have always been good friends, but I sense tonight there is a spark of something perhaps more familiar. Do you mind?"

"Mind?" The question caught her off guard, then she realized, she wasn't bothered that something more than friendship might be growing between her father and the Dowager, or indeed, any other woman.

She didn't understand why . . . until she remembered the dream with her mother bathed in gold. Here in the middle of the glittering company her mother had so adored, Elin could sense her presence and her approval.

"Of course, I don't mind," Elin said. "It might ease his—" She broke off, realizing she was speaking to the air. A group of men had claimed Baynton's attention. They'd just stepped right between her and the duke, and something said was so interesting to Gavin that his attention was immediately caught by it.

Theresa and Robbie had joined their group, and her cousin's wife quickly included Elin with her friends. They were closer to Elin's age but young matrons with children. Theresa complained of having nothing but daughters. Her oldest was seventeen.

"I'm doing what I must to see she is launched properly, but her ideas and mine are very different," Theresa said. Her friends immediately commiserated. They offered suggestions of how to bring daughters out properly, especially when one must economize.

Or, at least, that is what Elin gleaned from Theresa's complaints. She knew that both Robbie and his wife could be spendthrifts. She'd overheard her father offering Robbie advice on the subject of curbing his loose ways with money more than once.

Several gentlemen asked her to dance.

However, their true goal was to gain admittance to the group of powerful, important men gathered around Gavin. Elin found herself on guard against saying anything she shouldn't.

And in the back of her mind, she remembered Ben's warnings. He had predicted that life as a duchess would be a lonely one.

She was lonely already . . . but lonely for him.

With a smile that was beginning to feel plastered to her face, she excused herself to no one who was paying attention to her and went in search of the Necessary Room set aside for the ladies. She knew few of the women whose paths she crossed. London had never held any attraction for her.

Inside the room for the ladies, a woman with a bright yellow feathers in her hair and green dress caught Elin in passing and carried on for a good ten minutes about what a good friend she'd been of her mother. Elin nodded, kept her smile, and couldn't recall her mother *ever* speaking this lady's name. As soon as Elin could, she escaped, but she didn't return to the ballroom.

No, she wandered down the hall, enjoying a moment to think, to breathe . . . to miss Ben—

A footstep sounded behind her. The hair on the nape of her neck tickled with awareness. She knew who was behind her even before Ben whispered, "Elin."

Joy surged through her soul.

Yes, *he* was what she'd been looking for, why she was wandering aimlessly, not just in this hall but all evening.

All day.

Ben took her arm. He opened the nearest door. The room was dark. There was not even a fire in the hearth.

They didn't need one.

She threw her arms around his neck, pressed her body close, and kissed him with the promise that she would never let him go.

Ben closed the door.

Chapter Eighteen

𝒩othing had ever felt so reassuring to Elin as Ben's presence. She was stunned by how much she needed him. The very fiber of her being wanted to hold him and never let him go . . . while other parts of her, those demanding, delicate, sensitive places he had so recently woken, sprang to life.

His hand was at her waist. It slid down to cup her buttock while she let her hand smooth over the fine weave of his jacket to slip between the line of his breeches and his shirt. She could feel him, insistent, bold, hungry.

Deep inside her was a need that only Ben knew how to appease. She was certain of that fact.

They shared the same soul.

And the same desire.

He broke the kiss. His lips brushed her ear. "You'll unman me, Elin."

"It is the man in you I want," she answered, her own voice breathless. She went for his lips, but he pulled back.

"If we keep this up, I'll take you against the wall."

"Would you?"

His answer was to brace his arms on either side of her head, his body leaning in to her. She caressed his hardness beneath the material of his breeches.

He breathed as if she challenged him in ways he'd not known. She liked feeling as if she had a bit of power over him. He certainly held power over her—

Ben kissed her again. His kiss demanded everything of her, and of him. When he could speak, he whispered hoarsely, "We mustn't do this here. Someone could walk in—"

"And then everyone would know I love you," she replied, hooking her hand in his arm and pulling it down. She pressed his gloved hand against her breast. His touch felt good. Her breasts were full and tight against his palm. "I want them to know," she said. "I want the world to know."

"You say that, but you didn't recognize me earlier on the street—"

"I did," she answered, her lips so close to his she could almost taste them. "I saw you walking. I'd know your swagger anywhere, and you looked so handsome, so completely fashionable that I wanted to laugh."

"But you walked by me."

"I had talked to Father earlier. He is unreasonable. I told him I love you."

"He is set against me."

"Is that what he was saying to you? I don't know if Baynton realized it was you, but Father seemed to sense your presence at the same time I did."

He started to move his hand from her breast. She caught it, held it in place.

"I want to do this right, Elin. So far, we've only done it wrong."

"Make love to me," she whispered. "Right here. Anywhere. I miss having your arms around me. I miss laughing with you and arguing with you and having you inside me."

His response was a low, deep groan. She had him. He wanted her as much as she ached for him. The longing, the need, it threatened to consume her.

"Elin—" he said, attempting to protest again, but she silenced him with a kiss as insistent as the one he'd just given her. She wasn't about to let him leave, not yet. He pulled off his gloves, letting them drop to the floor.

His hands began lifting her skirts. She smiled

against his lips in anticipation. His hand touched her intimately.

She started to reach for the buttons of his breeches, to free him so that he could give her what she sought. Instead, he surprised her. He grabbed her wandering hand and pinned it to the wall. "Let me," he growled against her mouth.

A jolt of lightning could not have had a stronger effect than when his finger slipped inside her. Her whole being centered on his delicious play.

Elin came undone. Her legs opened to him. Out in the hall, she heard voices. Whoever they were, they could have walked through the doorway, and she wouldn't have cared. She wouldn't have moved, either.

The sleeve of her finely woven gauze dress slipped down her shoulder. Or had Ben pushed it? Because her breast seemed to easily pop out of her bodice—and then his lips were on it. The wet heat of his mouth combined with the magic of his touch overwhelmed. He knew what she liked. He'd learned about her during their sojourn in the forest, just as she had so ardently studied him.

Elin wanted to cry out. She wanted to laugh with joy. Ben was doing the most marvelous things, and part of the delight was in knowing they must be quiet. *Don't draw attention.*

He knew when she'd had too much, when she

was ready. He gave one hard pull on her breast, then quickly covered her mouth so that her cry of completion wouldn't sound an alarm.

Her legs no longer supported her. His strength did. And then he held her as if he'd never let her go.

Finally, she was able to lift her arms, to wrap them around him. "That was the most astonishing thing that's ever happened to me in my life," she said into his neck. He smelled good. Ben had always smelled good to her, but she liked the clean scent of sandalwood.

Standing over her, he chuckled his answer, very pleased with himself. Her skirts were caught between them. She shifted, and they fell to the floor. Ben picked his gloves off the floor.

"I can't go back out there," she said. "Everyone will know what has happened."

"No one will know. This will be our secret."

She placed her hand against his face. His skin felt good beneath her palm. "I can't decide if I like you clean-shaven. I'd grown accustomed to your whiskers."

He pressed his lips against her forehead, his clever, clever hands at her waist. "You must return."

"I don't know why. No one notices me. They are more interested in pleasing Baynton, as you predicted. And he easily becomes completely entrapped in duties and responsibilities—not to say his work is unimportant."

"I know."

"But I want to be important to the man I marry." Something her father had thrown at her when she'd tried to talk to him about Ben haunted her. "Or do you want marriage?"

"I want you for my wife, for my lover, and to be my helpmate and the mother of my children. Your father has warned me to stay away from you. I don't wish his animosity, Elin. I know how important he is to you."

"You may never win him over. He is set on his belief that his grandson will be a duke. It all sounds so silly now. He was deaf to my explanations about how, if it hadn't been for you, I would be dead. Ben, let us not wait. Let us run away." She gripped the lapel of his coat. "Please. There is nothing wrong with your brother—"

"He is a good man."

"But I love *you*. I can never be the wife he deserves. And if I have to spend every evening of my life at affairs like this, talking circles around politics, I shall die of boredom. Or worse, return to Heartwood and live apart from my husband. That is not the married life I want."

"Will you trust me, Elin?"

"Of course."

"This may take time."

She didn't like the sound of that. "What do you mean?"

"I told you I want to do this right. I didn't garner goodwill when I was last in London. I need to make some amends, but I hope to change that. I don't want us to be a scandal. I love you too much to let you be food for the gossips. I want our love for each other to be noted and praised."

"I want you to make love to me again," Elin answered candidly. "This is all your fault. You've turned me into a wanton woman. Ben, I miss you."

His answer was a kiss, one that framed better than words his devotion to her.

"Don't take too long saving us," she said, leaning into the haven of his arms. "Please, don't take too long."

"I won't. I promise."

"And you will tell me what you are doing? My curiosity can only be held at bay for so long."

"I will. I'll send a note or something." He took her face in his hands. "However, trust that I'll never be far from you, Elin. I want to keep you safe."

"Father is convinced that Darby and his men really wanted to kidnap me for ransom."

Ben was quiet a moment, then he said, "Tell me again what the Frenchwoman said to Darby?"

"That he was not supposed to approach the coach until it reached a certain place."

"And what else? What did Darby say before he shot her?"

"That 'he' had told Darby to kill Madame Odette. I suppose to not have any connections leading to him."

"Possibly." He gave Elin a quick kiss. "Come, you need to return."

She groaned. "I'm really not ready."

"I'm not either." He gave her a kiss. "But you've been gone for some time."

"I wonder if anyone will notice?"

"Your father might."

His words reminded Elin of something that should interest him. "My father is flirting with your mother."

"*What?*"

Elin stifled a laugh and nodded. "Do you mind?"

Ben released his breath. "I suppose not. Has Gavin noticed?"

"Actually, yes."

"Mother," Ben said under his breath as if she exasperated and pleased him at the same time. "You need to go. One moment." He opened the door a crack and checked the hallway. "It is clear. Go. I'll see you as soon as I can."

"Don't make it too long," she whispered, gave him another quick kiss, and slipped out the door.

New people were gathered at the hall near the ballroom, but they were involved in their own flirtations. No one paid attention to Elin.

She had been gone close to an hour. She hoped

that what she'd been doing didn't show on her face. She was glad Ben had been clean-shaven.

More guests must have arrived because the ballroom was an absolute crush. Elin made her way over to her father. Theresa and Robbie were still talking to their friends. Baynton was standing even farther away, and there was a heated discussion taking place with him in the center. Elin recognized the prime minister and several prominent leaders gathered there. Her father was also in their midst.

Gavin caught sight of her and smiled. In that moment, he appeared charmingly boyish. He was a handsome man. Uncommonly so.

But her heart belonged to his unruly brother.

And then she was dismissed from Gavin's thoughts as a gentleman must have said something so audacious, he had to be challenged. The politicians were a nucleus of opinion and argument in the middle of guests sharing gossip and stories of their children, and flirtations, and the swirling of dancers—and Elin felt quite apart from it all, even as she stood in their number. This was not where she belonged.

"Did you see Benedict?"

Marcella's question startled Elin. She glanced to her left, where the Dowager had slipped beside her. Elin tried to be calm. "Is Lord Ben here?"

The duchess's expression said she was not fooled. "Be careful, my girl. Be very careful." Not waiting for a protestation or an answer, she walked over to the politicians, pulled Elin's father from their group, and the two of them walked toward the supper room.

And Elin was alone.

Ben stole a look into the ballroom. He couldn't help himself. He saw Elin standing by herself, vibrant, unique, and ignored.

He longed to cross the room to her, to take her hand, and lead her onto the dance floor. He'd never been much of a dancer, but he would do anything to be close to her.

Instead, he backed away from the guests. He didn't recognize anyone, and few knew him—

A man pushed his way through the guests and walked past Ben. He moved gingerly and groaned with every other step, the sound like the lowing of a bull. That is when Ben recognized him. He followed.

"Roger? Roger Cooper?"

The man stopped, shifting his weight from the ball of one foot to the other and peered through thick spectacles to see who was speaking. "Whitridge?"

"It is I," Ben said, genuinely happy to see Roger.

Coop had been one of his first friends in the military. They'd been ensigns together. Coop was one of the worst soldiers imaginable. He was portly in size and abhorred giving orders. Many a time, Ben had either backed him up or taken the task over for him.

In truth, Ben admired the talents Coop did have. Not only did he have a brilliant mind, he also had the ability to locate and procure needed supplies everyone thought impossible to find.

He was also a cousin of the Duke of Marlborough. A heady connection.

"It is good to see you, Whit," Roger said, taking Ben's offered hand. "Especially on an evening like this."

"You don't want to be here?" Ben asked innocently, knowing full well the answer. Coop was a notorious hermit. He could have happily lived out his life in a library.

"Dancing is not one of my passions. However, I have a wife now. Demanding creatures. When I received the invitation, there was nothing for it save we come. She has talked about this one evening for weeks. And she will probably go on about it for weeks after. Here, follow me." Without waiting for Ben's agreement, he hastily went on his way, again with the strange mincing step as if his shoes were too small.

He pushed open the door to the room set aside for the gentlemen. Ben followed. The room was empty save for a footman there to service any needs.

Coop threw his considerable bulk onto a tufted settee and pulled off his shoes. He began scratching his feet, sighing happily as he did so.

"That is such a relief. The itch was about to drive me half-mad."

"So, what are you doing nowadays?" Ben asked. The footman had poured fresh water in the bowl of one of two washbasins, and Ben took advantage of it. Lord Caldwell had set out a lemon-scented soap. Ben rather liked the fragrance. He must tell George to purchase some.

"Working in the War Office." Coop stopped his furious itching. "They have me responsible for fielding supplies. It is a frustrating business. There isn't a politician worth his salt, save for Liverpool." He spoke of Lord Liverpool, the Minister for the War Office and the man responsible for seeing Wellesley placed in charge of the Peninsula army.

"You like him?"

"I admire him."

"That is high praise from Roger Cooper."

Coop grinned, pleased. And then his expression changed as if he was struck by an idea. "What are you doing?"

Ben leaned a hip against the washbasin. "I'm at loose ends."

"Would you like to do something of service?"

He had Ben's attention. "What do you have in mind?"

"The War Office is understaffed with *knowledgeable* people." Coop padded over in stocking feet to the washbasin next to Ben's. "You can't imagine the silliness of civil servants. Sometimes I think they believe we are planning a picnic instead of trying to defeat the French. Liverpool is frustrated as well. The minister was railing to me just the other day," Roger continued, "about how he needed men who understood the situation in Portugal working for him. I tell you, Whit, it is dire, dire indeed." He took the linen towel offered by the footman and dried his hands before saying, "If you were of a mind to, we could use someone with your knowledge. Would you be interested?"

Would he be interested? It took everything Ben had to not leap into his friend's arms and kiss him for the opportunity.

Instead, Ben replied soberly, "I could be convinced."

Coop's face came alive in delight. "That would be capital." He took Ben's hand and shook it vigorously. "We need you, Whitridge. We *need* you. Come to my office tomorrow. Liverpool was here tonight, but he's left. I'll speak to him in the morning, and I'm certain he will want you on the staff. However—" Coop paused as if measuring his words. "—You may not want to say anything to your brother about this opportunity. Baynton and Liverpool are at cross-purposes right now."

"I won't whisper a word."

"Good. *Good*. Tomorrow then." Coop then groaned as rubbed a stockinged foot furiously against the calf of his other leg. "Damn it all," he muttered.

"My man might have something that could help you with that," Ben offered helpfully.

"Truly?"

"I believe so. He's quite focused on feet. He says a good washing with a stiff brush will do the trick."

"Stiff brush," Coop repeated as if wanting to log the information into his memory.

"He may have other tricks," Ben said. "I'll have George talk to your man."

"Thank you, Whitridge. Thank you, thank you."

Ben said his good-byes then. He left Coop scratching away. He then took his leave of the Caldwells' house. He'd wanted to find Elin and share the news of his interview; however, it would not be wise. Not yet. The next time he ran the chance of meeting Fyclan Morris, Ben wanted it to be on *his* terms.

George did have some ideas to share about Coop's itch. The valet chattered happily away on the subject and remedies he had discovered until Ben ordered him out of the room. The next day, Ben was up early, too excited to sleep.

He didn't share his plans for the day with his mother, and his path did not cross his brother's.

At half past ten, he presented himself to Cooper's office. Lord Liverpool was there as well. After a good two hours of meaningful discussion, Ben was proud to join the War Office as one of Liverpool's personal aides.

Had the fact Ben was Baynton's brother played a part? Liverpool did not mention the Duke of Baynton, but Gavin's political presence was in the room.

For once, Ben didn't mind. That he was related to the powerful Duke of Baynton was a reality. However, the cabinet minister spoke as if he wanted to know Ben's mind and not his brother's.

"I'd thought you hotheaded," Lord Liverpool said. "However, right now, I need a man who understands the war. Your presence is fortuitous. Wellesley asked about you in one of his dispatches last week. He believes you are a good man. Prove him right."

"I intend to, my lord," Ben answered. With that, Ben was given instructions on reporting to Lord

Liverpool's office the following week, followed by a handshake.

"We shall do great things together, Whitridge," His Lordship said, and left the room.

Coop was happy. "I don't believe I've ever witnessed him taking two hours with anyone. He likes you. You will do well here, Ben. Very well."

"I plan to do so."

"Now," Coop said, leaning on his desk, "have you told your man to be in touch with my man? My feet, Ben. My feet."

"Have no fear," Ben said, "George promised he has a few cures and should be in contact with your man even as we speak."

"Bless you."

Ben laughed and took his leave, deciding the time had come to turn his attention to solving the mystery of who had wanted to murder Elin.

Her father and his brother acted as if the attempt was of no consequence. Ben thought differently. Perhaps it all had ended with Darby's death. Maybe she was safe. He needed to be certain.

Mulling over the matter, Ben decided to start with the dressmaker, Madame Odette.

Leaving Whitehall, he made his way to Bond Street, home of many fashionable shops, and, after a few discreet inquiries, discovered the location of Madame Odette's. Her establishment was on a side street off of St. James's, of all places. St. James's was a busy thoroughfare but known more for gentlemen's clubs than dressmakers.

Ben found her choice for the location of her shop curious. However, he did learn that she had been building a strong reputation and had several patronesses who were the wives of ambitious young men.

Ben could believe that having an account like Fyclan Morris's would be a boon to her business as well as to her pocketbook. He wondered how Fyclan had chosen the woman's services. Who had recommended her?

The mystery deepened when Ben found her shop and discovered it closed.

He peered into the dark shop windows. The place was deserted. There was furniture inside, but all was dark and, from what he could see, dusty. She'd been closed for some time.

Ben walked to the alleyway behind the dressmaker's building. There was a sturdy wooden door and no window.

The door was not a problem. Glancing over his shoulder and seeing no one in sight, Ben gave a strong shove of his shoulder. The lock broke.

He slipped inside. The back room was a thin darkness. He let his eyes adjust. There were curtains with feminine stripes that separated this room from another. Long tables had been set up as workspace. Chairs were shoved to one corner. He could see signs that there had been sewing activity recently, but most of the dresses, material, scissors, and other sewing supplies were gone. What was abandoned was broken or useless. Certainly, he could see no sign of a thriving business.

Ben moved into the room beyond the curtains and looked into each of the dressing rooms. Again, there was nothing of interest.

He poked his head into the shop itself. The only item left was a small, dainty bell on a painted desk. It would have been used to ring for service. He could imagine how this shop must have looked with ribbons and fabrics on display. All was gone. There wasn't even a ledger for him to explore in the desk's drawer.

Either someone had thoroughly cleaned out the establishment, or Madame Odette had done it herself . . . which would make sense only if she wasn't expecting to return.

Ben suspected the latter.

He walked toward the back of the shop, flicking aside the curtain out of frustration over the lack of clues.

Then again, the absence of any professional or personal belongings indicated the attack on Elin's coach had been planned well in advance.

But where could Ben go from here?

Just as he was reaching for the door handle, he heard voices outside. He stepped back, listening— and recognized Gavin's deep rumble.

The Duke of Baynton was right outside.

Chapter Nineteen

What the deuce was his brother doing here?

The Duke of Baynton rarely did anything himself. He had servants and men like Perkins to carry out his wishes. Or was there a whole army waiting on the other side of the door for Ben? His brother was talking to someone. Ben couldn't distinguish the words of their conversation. They were moving toward the door.

They were about to enter the shop.

Ben stepped back and leaned against the wall, letting the door shield him from view.

"Damn it all," a male exclaimed. "Pardon me, Your Grace, for my temper, but the lock is broken."

"So it is," Gavin answered.

The door swung open. Gavin stepped into the room first. He paused and looked around, cautious. Ben could have reached out and tapped his brother's shoulder if he so desired. Instead, he held still.

A narrow man with the air of business walked in behind him. "Whoever broke in was disappointed. Sally didn't leave anything of value when she left. She was a wise one, she was. Always feathering her own nest."

"Sally?" Gavin said, asking the question Ben wondered.

"You don't think she was truly French, do you? I mean, she sounded the part and looked it. However, when she first rented from me three years ago, she was Sally Mays. She was· from Devonshire. She did well for herself. Pretty girl with a skill for the needle. Hated me every time I called her Sally. She always corrected me, and I kinda liked it."

The man was the landlord. Ben saw no sense in hiding. Besides, he would be discovered soon, so he shut the door.

Gavin did not act surprised to see him. "Here is your culprit, Monroe. My brother."

"Your brother, Your Grace?" Monroe gave Ben a critical eye. "I see a resemblance, but why did he break into my building?"

"That is a good question," Gavin answered. "Tell us, Ben, why break the lock when you could have knocked on Monroe's door as I did and ask for his assistance?"

Ben had no answer for that, save to say, "I took matters in my own hands."

"Send the bill for the lock to me, Monroe," Gavin said in that tone that conveyed the burdens of a duke were many, a tone Ben detested.

"No, Monroe, send it to me and accept my apologies. If I had known you were such a splendid gentleman, I would not have damaged your lock."

Monroe looked from one to the other as if he were trapped between two lions. "It will take nothing to fix. Why don't I leave you both alone while I fetch a hammer. Do you mind?"

"Of course not," Gavin said at the same time Ben said, "Capital idea."

The landlord ran.

"You frightened him," Ben commented.

Gavin's response was a ducal scowl. "What the bloody hell are you doing here?"

"That is the question I have for you."

"Your answer first."

Ben struggled with the childish desire to argue the point, then he thought of Elin. Jousting with his brother was not finding the murderer.

"I came to discover what I could of Madame Odette . . . or as we now know, Sally. And you?"

"The same thing."

"And you came *yourself*?" Ben said before he questioned the wisdom of speaking his wonder aloud.

"What is that supposed to mean?" Gavin threw out as he turned and marched through the curtains the way Ben had.

"Just commenting. After all, don't you usually employ Perkins or a half a dozen other men like father did to ferret out information for you?"

Gavin practically flew back through the curtains. "Stop this nonsense, Ben. I'm not Father. I use Perkins because he is effective. He can discover more in an hour than I could over days of sleuthing."

"Then why didn't you send him?"

"Always challenging, aren't you?"

"I'm my father's son as well."

Gavin swore under his breath, and it was at that moment, that Ben had a moment of recognition. Sniping at Gavin was not what he wanted. He held up a hand. "Listen, I'm sorry. My attitude is uncalled for."

Gavin raised his eyebrows in disbelief. "What game is this now, Ben?"

"I'm being sincere."

"Pardon me if I doubt your sincerity." He charged back through the curtains.

"You won't find anything," Ben called out. "Sally was thorough, just as Monroe said."

His brother didn't answer but began opening and closing the dressing-room doors.

"I don't blame you for distrusting me," Ben

continued, speaking to his brother through the curtain. "We haven't been good friends."

There was no response.

Ben plowed on, "We could probably solve the mystery of the attack on Elin if we work together." He listened. Gavin was in the shop. "By-the-by, I have a position. I don't know if you will be surprised or not, but *I* am going to be part of *Liverpool's* staff."

"Yes, I know," came the bored reply. Gavin walked through the curtains, flipping them out of the way with the annoyance Ben had shown. "Liverpool told me."

Anger surged through Ben. He tamped it down. He was to be a diplomat, and apparently must start by being diplomatic with his brother. "Is there anything you *don't* know?"

The words still sounded biting, and they, of course, struck Gavin wrong. "No, that is my task in life, to know what my family members will not tell me."

"Is there a reason you *must* know everything?" Ben asked, completely out of curiosity.

"I am the head of this family," his brother stated as if that should say everything . . . and perhaps in his mind it did.

"Father indoctrinated you very well."

"He *schooled* me in what I should know. Which,

if I may remind you, is one of the reasons I had for ordering you back to London."

"That and wanting to please Mother."

"She likes you."

"You sound as if you can't fathom why."

Gavin's answer was a thin smile. He walked out the door. Ben followed.

Monroe was approaching with a hammer. He took one look at the two brothers and pivoted around toward the building he had just exited.

"We make him nervous," Ben observed.

The duke shrugged.

Ben faced him. "Say it. Don't hold in whatever is eating at your gut. I've been a bit of a bastard. I admit it. I've been headstrong and disobedient."

"That is a good start." There was no humor in Gavin's voice.

"I've also been true to myself," Ben continued. "And brutally honest. Can you say the same?"

"*There it is*," Gavin said. "Always the criticism. Always the undermining—"

"I have never undermined you—"

"You always do. You wanted to surprise me with your news of Liverpool without understanding he would have come to me directly *before* he interviewed you. That's the way matters work, Ben. I didn't create the world. I just happen to be very good at operating in it."

And he was right.

There was nothing Ben could say. He stood a moment, letting the tide of Gavin's anger ebb a bit. Finally, he said, "I don't want to be at cross-purposes with you."

Gavin glared as if he spoke gibberish, then the wind went out of his sails as well. "I need a brother. I miss my twin. We were close although since he ran off, everyone supposes that we were at odds. Do you know how many times Father demanded to know what I'd said to Jack to make him want to leave?"

"Father would have been wiser to have looked in a mirror."

For the briefest second, Gavin's eyes looked watery, but he blinked any emotion back. After all, he was Baynton. "It is of no matter now."

Ben held out his hand. "Brother?"

The air seemed to still between them.

Gavin frowned at the offered hand . . . then he accepted it. "Brother."

"I shall need some practice," Ben warned him. "We were never a close family. Even the concern from mother astonishes me."

"Father was a tartar."

Ben couldn't stop a smile. "He was, may his soul rest in peace. But let's not make the mistakes he did, Gavin."

"An admirable suggestion . . . save for Elin between us. You saw her last night, didn't you?"

"Was Perkins watching me?"

"No, I was." He shrugged and amended his statement. "Elin disappeared for quite some time."

"Did she say where?" Ben asked carefully.

"I didn't ask. But you were there, weren't you? You saw her."

Ben didn't answer. He didn't need to.

"Elin probably believes I am oblivious to her. I'm not, Ben. I know what a remarkable woman she is."

"That is the crux, isn't it, Gavin? We want the same woman. You have her, and I love her."

"I love her as well," Gavin answered, but he spoke quickly and without conviction.

Do you even know what love is? Ben wanted to fire back, but that would upset the fragile alliance between them. "Actually, she could use both of us," Ben heard himself say. "Someone attempted to murder her."

"I've had Perkins on it."

"Has he learned anything?"

"Nothing. He has been here as well." Gavin nodded toward the open shop door. "He told me the place was vacant, but I had to try. He also combed the wharves last night for word of—what was his name? The leader?"

"Darby."

"Yes, Darby. Again, no information. The man

hadn't been seen with anyone other than his usual mates."

Ben swore under his breath, then he remembered something. "I asked Elin who stood to gain in case of her death."

"What did she say?"

"She was tired. We were on the move trying to avoid Darby and his ilk. At the time, she said she couldn't think of anyone. If she was married, we would look at the husband."

"Aye, because with her death, he would be a wealthy man."

"So we know it isn't you because you would be foolish to kill her before the marriage."

"Thank you."

"Anytime, Brother." Ben took a few steps away, working the puzzle in his head, then said, "Robbie. Her cousin."

"Robbie? He would only gain if Fyclan and Elin died."

"Fyclan hasn't been looking well."

"No, his wife's death almost destroyed him. Watching him has given me an appreciation for Mother's strength. She carried on smartly after Father died."

"Mother's physician is attending him. What does he say?"

"He can find no cause other than deep grief.

Frankly, he has been worried. He warned me that many men do not survive the death of a beloved spouse. However, last night, Fyclan appeared in better spirits."

"Mother may have had something to do with that."

Gavin chuckled. "She may have. She's always been fond of him. It would make sense if a tendre sprang between her and Fyclan."

"Why, Gavin, you are a romantic."

His brother shook his head to deny it, but he was comical in his embarrassment.

"Don't worry," Ben told him. "Your secret is safe with me."

"I don't have a secret."

Ben laughed, then stopped abruptly. "What if whoever attacked Elin was expecting Fyclan to die soon? Perhaps even be pushed in that direction by the murder of his daughter?"

"The man is only in his sixties."

"Indulge me," Ben said to his brother. "If we remove both Elin and Fyclan, then who gains?"

"Robbie. He is Fyclan's only relative and, I assume, would be heir to his fortune."

"*If* Elin died without a husband."

Gavin frowned. "Here is my problem with your theory. Fyclan raised Robbie as if he were his own. He educated him. I've worked with him. I can't see the man I know arranging for the murder of that many people. And why? He has been at Fy-clan's side all these years. Fyclan made him a rich man." He paused, then added thoughtfully, "Of course, that might just be an impression. Every-one believed Father was wealthy as well."

"He wasn't?"

"He made bad investments. I didn't know how disastrous the family books were until I inherited. Furthermore, Father spent money like a madman. Building the garden park at Trenton cost a king's ransom. I had my hands full trying to right what he'd undone. Of course, Fyclan helped me."

This was stunning news to Ben. He'd assumed everything his brother had inherited had been right and in order. "Had Fyclan suggested the bad investments to Father?"

"He knew nothing about them. However, some-one must have talked to Father. He wasn't one for dirtying his hands over such matters."

The door to the building next to the dress shop opened, and Mr. Monroe, with a beleaguered expression on his face, came out followed by a well-endowed woman in a lace mobcap and fichu over her shoulders. The landlord still carried the hammer he was planning to use to fix the lock on the door.

"Your Grace," he started, pulling his hat off his head in the manner of a supplicant, while the woman stood back, trembling with excitement, "this is my wife, Dotty. She has heard much about you, Your Grace, and I hope don't mind, but she would like to pay her respects." He lowered his voice, and said, "Please, Your Grace, help me. She can be as insistent when she wants something."

Sounding confused, Gavin said, "Of course."

He'd barely had the words out before Dotty came mincing forward. She curtsied and Ben was certain a finer curtsy had never been made. The woman almost brought her head to the ground and stayed there.

Embarrassed, Gavin said, "Please come up, Mrs. Monroe." When she had difficulty, he did the gentlemanly thing and helped her.

Quivering, rapid breaths came from Dotty. She gazed at Gavin with nothing short of complete, loving admiration. "You are as handsome as they say, Your Grace. More so."

"Thank you," Gavin murmured, inching away from her.

"There now, Dotty," Monroe said, "go on. I did what you wanted; now see to my supper."

"Oh, but doesn't His Grace want to ask me questions about the dressmaker? Isn't that why you said he was here? Sally and I became friends of sorts for a while."

Now she had both Ben's and Gavin's attention. "Close friends?" Ben asked.

"For a while," she answered.

"What came between you?" Ben wondered.

"Oh, she took on airs. Dressmaking wasn't her true business—"

"Dotty," her husband said in a warning voice. "His Grace doesn't want to hear gossip. Besides, I've already told him that."

"But I'm always willing to hear more," Gavin answered. "Tell me everything you know about Sally."

"Well, I know she'd found a benefactor and wasn't planning on dressmaking any longer."

"Really?" Gavin said. "Do you know who her benefactor was?"

"I only saw him once. They would have lovers' meetings away from here. After being with him for a while, Your Grace, she felt she was too good for me and everyone else."

"But you set eyes on her lover?" Ben prodded.

"Once. He was a good-looking man even though he was only a bit taller than me. He had sandy colored hair, although it was red around the ears, and a strong nose."

Her description matched many men. It also matched Robbie Morris.

"Did she ever speak a name?" Gavin asked.

"No, Your Grace. She was very secretive about him. Not like she'd been with the others she entertained. Very full of herself. I believe she expected him to marry her, but he was already married. I told her not to be a fool, but she said I didn't know a thing, and now I learn she is dead. A sad tale."

"And you can't recall her ever using this man's name?" Gavin pressed.

"I'm so sorry, Your Grace. She was careful about him."

"Thank you, Mrs. Monroe." Gavin took her hand and bowed over it. "We appreciate your sharing your knowledge.

The woman almost swooned while tossing an I-told-you-so glance at her husband.

"Enough, Dotty," Monroe said. "Upstairs now. You've had what you wanted."

She nodded happily and did as bid, backing up so that her adoring gaze never left Gavin's face.

"I'm sorry, Your Grace, but once my wife knew you were out here, well, she was like a cat begging for a taste of cod. Pestering me and pestering me. Of course," he confided, "she'll now be very nice to me, if'n you know what I mean, Your Grace."

Gavin appeared speechless. Ben took pity on him. "He knows, Monroe, he knows. Come, brother," he said, tugging on Gavin's sleeve. "Let us leave the good Monroe to his supper *and* his wife."

"Yes," Gavin agreed with great relief, and strode purposefully from the alley.

Once they were out of sight of Monroe, Ben doubled over laughing.

"It isn't that funny," Gavin muttered.

Ben's answer was to open his eyes wide, mimicking Dotty's, and gazing at Gavin in such a way, his brother gave him a shove on the arm.

"I can't help it if I am better-looking than you," Gavin said.

"A freak of nature," Ben agreed amiably, and that startled a laugh out of Gavin, who tried to recover himself and couldn't. Indeed, he laughed as hard as Ben did.

All of the resentment and grievances Ben had harbored against his brother fell away. He saw Gavin not as a rival—indeed, not even as a competitor for Elin—but as someone trying to do his best against impossible expectations.

Of course, Gavin couldn't ever relax completely. He was Baynton. If the House of Lords didn't have demands of him, the Fashionable World and Dotty did. Ben could feel a bit sorry for him. Ben preferred his freedom.

"Let's talk to Robbie Morris," Gavin suggested. "If nothing more, I'd like to hear what he has to say. My vehicle is around the next corner," Gavin said. "My tiger is walking the horses."

"You brought the phaeton?"

"Of course I did. I don't have opportunity enough to drive it."

"If you call what you do driving," Ben had to say. In truth, Gavin was a notable whip—but a brother had to tease a brother.

"Scoundrel," Gavin replied without heat.

"Cod," Ben returned, and they both laughed at the name.

They set off to pay a call on Robbie Morris who generally could be found at this hour of the day with Fyclan.

Elin could think of nothing save Ben.

A little over two years ago, she had sat at this dressing table in her bedroom, looking into this mirror, and had asked her mother how could she be dishonest with Baynton?

Back then, her question had been asked about a youthful indiscretion . . . something she now realized had not been a mistake. No matter what her parents had told her, she'd belonged to Ben, even back then. When she was apart from him, she felt as if she was missing a necessary half of her being.

And when she was with him, the world felt right.

Elin had to cry off. It was easier for a woman to cry off than it was a gentleman although jilting an important person like the duke, especially for his brother, would cause talk.

But Elin was discovering it no longer mattered if people talked or not. She and Ben could live at

Heartwood, and if her father would not let her live under his roof, then they would return to the forest.

Elin rose from the dressing table. She was dressed in a blue day gown trimmed with tiny ribbon flowers. Her maid, a girl assigned from the staff, had piled her curls high on her head.

The time had come to be honest with her father.

She went downstairs. The house was very quiet. She soon learned why. Her father was not in his office. Henry told her that her father had left with Robbie for the Exchange.

"Did you need something, Miss Elin?"

"I wanted to speak to him. I'll wait in the library."

"Is anything wrong?" Henry asked.

The butler knew her so well. All of the servants had taken good care of her over the years. She had an urge to tell Henry her decision and swallowed it. She needed to speak to her father first, then Baynton, and by that time, the servants would know. They always knew everything.

"All is good," she informed the butler. He nodded, but his glance said he thought better.

"I need to tell you, Miss Elin, that I shall be going out. Mr. Robbie sent a note requesting I bring a certain book to the Exchange for Mr. Morris. Since this is the afternoon when most of the servants are allowed personal time, I shall make the trip myself."

"Which book is that?"

"A ledger on the right-hand side of the desk."

The request was easy to fulfill. Elin helped Henry find the book. After the butler left the house, she settled into the library, choosing her father's chair in front of the dying fire.

Her parents had designed the library themselves. They shared a passion for books, for knowledge. Her mother had adored telling the story of how they'd first met at a private lending library.

The air in the room was cooling. She pulled a lap blanket around her and tried to read but started dozing off, which was not surprising since she'd slept so little the night before. However, now that she was taking decisive action, she was at ease.

The sound of the library door's opening disturbed her. She was so comfortable and drowsy, she didn't want to wake.

But then Robbie was beside her. "Elin, thank God I found you here. I've been looking everywhere. Something has happened to your father. You must come."

She came alert instantly. "What is it?"

"There isn't time to explain. Where is your coat? Never mind, use mine." Robbie helped her up and threw his greatcoat around her shoulders.

"My hat," she murmured, then said, "it is unimportant. Please, take me to Father."

He led her out of the house. A footman was not in attendance at the door. Preparations were being made for dinner, and there were tasks to be seen to by the household servants who had not gone out for the afternoon. Usually, Henry would have this station, but he was with her father.

A hired hack waited outside. Robbie hustled her into it and told the driver to go.

Elin sat back against the hard seat. "Can't he go faster?" She turned to Robbie. "Now tell me, what has happened to Father?"

"He's not well," Robbie answered.

"In *what way* is he not well?" Elin demanded. Her cousin was annoying her.

"You'll see when we get there."

"The Exchange?"

"Yes," Robbie said, sounding distracted. He glanced out the window and swore. "What is Baynton doing out and about?"

Elin looked past her cousin and saw the duke with Ben on the seat beside him turn onto the street. They rode in a flashy rig with big yellow wheels and pulled by a matched pair of blood bays.

Her heart leaped not only at the sight of Ben but also at the knowledge that whatever was happening with her father, she would have Ben by her side. She reached across Robbie toward the window ready to wave down the brothers. "We need to stop them. They can help us with Father—"

Robbie jerked her back. He threw her to the floor, his knee on her chest, his gloved hand practically smothering her.

She closed her eyes and in her mind shouted, "*Ben.*"

Chapter Twenty

A hired hack around St. James's Square was not in and of itself unusual.

What caught Ben was a sudden sense as the vehicle passed that something was wrong with Elin. He could feel her distress. It was immediate and deep in his soul—and it had to do with the hack.

He knew when to trust his instincts.

Grabbing Gavin's arm, he said, "Turn around. Follow that hack."

"What?"

"*Do it.*"

For once, his brother listened to him. Ben knew he sounded like a madman. But he couldn't shake the sense something was wrong, and what he was feeling convinced Gavin to turn the phaeton in the middle of the road and follow the hack.

"Drive up on it," Ben said. "And hurry before it

reaches Pall Mall." If his suspicions were correct, the hack could escape them in the traffic of the busy thoroughfare.

"What do you have in mind?"

"I'm going to stop that vehicle."

"Do you know why?"

"Elin is in trouble. I believe she is in the hack."

"How do you know?"

"I *know*," Ben answered, not taking his eye off the vehicle ahead of them.

With a flick of the reins, Gavin set the horses prancing.

The hack driver glanced in their direction, and Ben could almost see the world-weary sigh. Gavin was not the first whip who had passed him, and he wasn't happy about it. He knew there was little he could do save slow down and let them have their way

However, he was not pleased when Gavin pulled ahead and turned his animals to block the hack's passage, placing both vehicles halfway into the intersection of Pall Mall.

Now it wasn't only the hack driver who was upset but a number of drivers from coaches, drays, and even a dog cart were understandably livid when they found the road blocked. They did what every good Londoner did when needing to be on one's way, they started shouting.

Ben ignored them as he jumped to the ground.

Gavin set the brake and ordered his tiger into the seat.

"Sir, what do you think you are doing?" the hack driver demanded of Gavin.

"Stopping you," he answered, unperturbed, as Ben yanked open the hack's door.

Elin *was* inside. Thank God.

However, Robbie Morris held her in front of him, a knife at her throat.

"Leave us be," Morris said. "Or I shall kill her."

Ben held up his hands to let Morris know he would try no tricks. As he did so, Gavin opened the door on the other side of the hack. Robbie was surrounded.

"Let her go," Ben said. "There are two of us. You can't expect to escape."

"I can," Morris answered. "You'll let me go to protect her. Tell Fyclan, I want twenty-five thousand pounds, and I'll give him back his daughter. I'll send a note telling him where to send the money."

Ben's eye met Gavin's. His brother didn't believe Morris's promise not to hurt Elin any more than Ben did.

"Why?" Ben asked. "I understand your trying to have her murdered on the road. Fyclan hasn't been well, and you would inherit provided she didn't have a husband. It makes sense," he agreed conversationally. "But what is this now? We have no evidence you have been involved in anything. Why are you being so desperate?"

"Do you think I'm a fool?" Morris pressed the knife closer to Elin's throat, the edge forming a line against her skin. "I saw Baynton's phaeton by Odette's shop today."

"Wishing to pay your respects to the lover you had murdered?" Gavin asked.

Morris frowned at him with complete disdain. "We weren't lovers."

"That isn't what Mrs. Monroe thought."

"She's a busybody." Robbie spit the words out with distaste. "Forms her own conclusions, and since she thought Odette and I were friends, we saw no need to let her believe different. No, Odette wanted the money I was paying her, plain and simple."

"And you had her killed for it?" Ben suggested. "Not the best way to treat a partner."

"A partner?" Robbie shook his head. "I knew what she was about. She'd blackmail me forever."

"No honor among thieves," Gavin agreed.

Several of the drivers, pedestrians, and the curious around them had drawn close. Someone had been able to glance inside the hack and had noticed the knife being held against Elin. Word traveled through the crowd. Necks craned in interest. Many had already recognized the duke, and London came to a standstill.

"I didn't want to murder anyone." For a second, Morris appeared remorseful. "I had no choice."

"Why not?" Ben asked.

"I have four daughters and a wife who spends and spends."

"But you are related to Fyclan," Gavin said. "Ask him for help."

"I did. Several times. He used to be quite good to me. However, after his wife died, he changed. He was no longer generous. He didn't care about anything but his grief."

"And you noticed he was failing," Ben suggested. Elin's face was pale, but she was listening. Her gaze never wavered from his face. She trusted him to rescue her . . . and he was frightfully conscious of how all Morris had to do was put pressure on that blade, and no one could save her.

"I did notice," Robbie said. "So did my wife. She's the one who said it was a shame that here I was so close to Fyclan, had done so much for him, yet everything would go to the man his daughter married."

"But if she was gone before she married, then you inherited, correct?"

"Yes." Morris didn't even blush as he spoke. "It would all be mine."

Ben leaned against the hack. "So where are we now, Morris?"

"You will let me go with Elin. You will tell

Fyclan my demands and wait for me to send word where the money should be delivered."

"What if he says no?" Ben asked.

Morris made a sound as if that was impossible. "He won't say no. He wants her to give him a grandson who will become a duke, haven't you heard? Fyclan lives for the fulfilling of some gypsy's prophecy. All he has built has been for that child."

"Do you blame him?" Ben asked, keeping his voice casual. "You have children, don't you?"

"Daughters. Four daughters. Was there ever a man so cursed?" Morris raised aggrieved eyes to the duke. "You know how expensive it is to see them off right. My wife is adamant they should have the best. They are lovely girls. They could marry well . . ."

"But it is expensive," Gavin agreed.

"Theresa doesn't accept that. I made some poor choices. Fyclan says that building wealth takes time. He is conservative in his decisions. I don't have 'time.' I tried doing what he had done. You know, advising those with money. I wasn't afraid of risks the way Fyclan was."

"My father agreed with you," Gavin said. "He gave you some money. Quite a bit, actually."

Morris didn't deny the connection. "With luck, we could have tripled our fortunes. I lost money as well, Your Grace. I know your father was disappointed. We purchased two ships together. You can't imagine how quickly a man can go from being wealthy to afraid for his future."

Gavin asked, "Fyclan knows what you did, right?"

"Once he discovered what I had done, he has persistently refused to advance funds. The old duke was his closest friend. He felt I went around his back. He said he would have given me the sack except I was a relative." A storm cloud seemed to cross his face. "I've come to hate the man."

"And you could even the score by taking his daughter?" Gavin suggested.

"I could," Morris said quietly, his attention on Gavin. "But I need the money. I need to leave the country."

And Ben doubted if Elin would be handed over alive after the ransom had been paid.

He was also learning that his trust in his brother was well placed. Gavin was keeping Morris occupied. The man seemed to appreciate having the great Duke of Baynton commiserate with him.

In a soothing voice that had calmed many an irate politician, Gavin said, "I understand. I can appreciate your position."

"I don't mean to hurt her," Morris said. "Elin should understand, this isn't personal."

"Of course not," Gavin agreed.

"I'm going to tell the driver to go on now. You

gentlemen leave me." As Robbie spoke, he gave Ben the opportunity he'd been waiting for. Morris forgot himself. He gestured with the knife since his other arm and hand were around Elin.

The movement was not large. But in that moment, the blade was not tight against Elin's throat.

Ben struck out, his fist as hard as a rock. He rammed it into the side of Morris's head.

At the same second, Elin, bless her, went limp and slid out from under Morris's arm to the floor.

Once she was safe, that was all Ben needed.

With a fury he didn't know he possessed, he grabbed Morris and dragged him out of the hack. He held him up with one hand, his fist doubling—

Morris raised his arms and cried out in alarm. "Don't hurt me. Don't hurt me."

The crowd gathered around the vehicles begged to differ. They had been enjoying the show, and a good beating would make a fitting end.

Gavin came around the hack. "Ben, don't. He deserves a throttling and anything more you have in mind, but let us turn him over to the courts for justice."

"Just one blow, brother. Just one."

"Give it to 'em," an ostler shouted.

"Please don't," Morris begged. He was visibly shaking. A coward to the end.

Ben let go.

The man dropped to the cobbled street like a wheel of cheese. He would have crawled off, but Gavin grabbed his coat collar, set him on his feet, and took control of the situation.

Ben didn't care. Elin had climbed up on the seat. She leaned out of the doorway, her glorious curls undone from the pins that held them, her eyes wide and luminous with unshed tears. Ben didn't think; he reacted.

He opened his arms and she leaped into them. Their lips met. Hot tears of relief rolled down her cheeks. He could taste the salt of them in her kiss and tightened his hold.

The world fell away. He didn't care who was watching. All that was important was that Elin was safe.

The kiss broke.

"I was afraid," she whispered.

"I was as well," he agreed.

Her hands at his shoulders curled up tightly, clutching the material of his jacket. "I didn't think you saw me. I wanted to call your name, but he covered my mouth."

"I heard you in my heart." Ben kissed her again. This time, lingering over her, worshipping her. How had he ever found life worthwhile without her—?

Gavin cleared this throat. "We should move out of the street."

Elin appeared stupefied to see the crowd openly gawking at them, as did Ben. Having her safe and in his arms had robbed him of all sense of time and place.

And then the audience began clapping.

Ben felt himself blush. He'd been holding Elin so that her feet didn't touch the ground and he wasn't ready to give her up.

His brother understood his predicament. "Take her home. I'll see to Morris. Use the hack."

Gavin didn't meet Ben's eye as he spoke. He appeared completely divorced from the unseemly display save for one tight muscle that worked in his jaw. Ben understood. He had the same character trait, and his jaw muscle tightened when he was angry . . . or uncertain.

Ben would have to talk to his brother about this unseemly display of affection later. But for right now, he was overwhelmed with joy and thankful Elin was alive.

He did as his brother suggested.

The hack driver was happy for the coins the Duke of Baynton gave him and even more anxious to remove himself from such a scene. Elin and Ben could not release their hold on each other. They sat on the hack's hard leather seats, shoulder to shoulder, thigh to thigh, hand in hand.

"Now what?" Elin whispered.

"Now I speak to your father."

"He will not give us his blessing."

Ben looked at her. "Will you come with me?"

"I will go anywhere with you."

The Morris household was very quiet. Elin took Ben into her father's library to wait upon Fyclan.

They did not have long to cool their heels.

The front door opened and shut. Elin reached for Ben's hand. They laced their fingers together.

Ben didn't think he had been this nervous since he'd been a boy.

There was the sound of voices. "Henry is with him," Elin murmured as if to reassure Ben.

He nodded.

Footsteps on the hall tiles told him Fyclan was walking heavily on his cane. Ben wondered what he'd heard already and how to start explaining that the nephew one had embraced had attempted to murder the daughter. It was outlandish, actually. But then, murder rarely made sense, especially performed with cold reason.

Fyclan came to the doorway. He stood there a second, studying them. He did not appear surprised to see them together.

The clock on the mantel seemed to stop, then Elin spoke. "He has saved my life twice, Father. Do you know what happened?"

Her father nodded, his dark, somber eyes the very reflection of Elin's. "I came across Baynton. He told me all."

Suddenly, Ben didn't care about Morris or murder plots. His concern was Elin. "I want to marry your daughter. I know I have broken all rules of good conduct for her. If I were her father, I'd want me flayed alive. Please understand, I meant no disrespect. But we must be together."

Fyclan walked into the room. He stumbled over the carpet and almost knocked over a table.

Elin let go of Ben's hand and would have gone to him, but her father raised his hand, warning her back. He sat heavily in the chair by his desk.

And then he spoke. "I am stunned by Robbie's actions. I didn't want to believe them, but Baynton and I went over to his house. Theresa and the girls are gone. Packed up. They'll show up sooner or later. Baynton has a man looking into it."

"Perkins will find them," Ben said.

"Yes, Perkins . . . that's the name." He raised his gaze to his daughter. Ben fought the urge to step in front of her and protect her from the obvious disappointment of a parent . . . but what Fyclan said next surprised both him and Elin.

"I'm sorry, daughter. So sorry."

"Robbie's doings are not your fault," she said.

"I'm not talking about him. I admit the betrayal is stunning. I treated him like a son."

"You did," she agreed.

"And like a son, I indulged him. He hoodwinked your father, Whitridge. Plain and simple. Your father never let me know what had happened. He was a proud man."

Ben nodded agreement. Pride was a Whitridge trait.

"I didn't know of your father's losses until your brother came to me after his death. Of course, Robbie paid a price as well for his foolishness. I lectured him. I never asked if he'd misled others. I suppose I didn't want to know. I helped Robbie repair his losses, but he never learned. He just kept spending."

Fyclan drew a deep breath and released it, studying the floor as if wrestling with a demon only he could see, then he addressed Elin, "Your mother and I only sought what was best for you. We wanted you to marry Baynton because you would be safe."

"And there was my grandmother's prophecy," she reminded him.

He waved that away. "Vanity. *My* vanity. Sounds silly now."

"Mother believed it."

A smile came to his face. "She did. The things a man will say to win the heart of the woman he loves. I needed to pump up my own consequence to open her eyes to me."

"Are you saying there was no prophecy?" Elin asked surprised.

"There was. Is." Fyclan mugged a face and shrugged his shoulders. "It is true that on the day I was born, my gypsy grandmother predicted that I would be a great man and my child's children would be dukes and princes. As a child, I believed. Later, after her death, people claimed she spouted all sorts of things. Mostly nonsense. However, I did trust her gift. Of course, when Baynton came to me with the idea of promising our children to each other, well, what man wouldn't want to believe he had guidance from beyond to create an empire?"

Elin started laughing. "That is such a relief. I don't want to disappoint you, but I don't want to be part of an empire."

"But look how far it has taken you. I've done well for my family with that belief." Fyclan shifted his gaze to Ben. "I wanted a duke for her."

"I could someday be a duke," Ben answered. "However that could only happen if Baynton dies, and I prefer my brother alive and well, thank you."

Fyclan acknowledged that sentiment with a nod, but then the question every father wondered. "Can you keep her?"

Before Ben could answer that he now had a position of trust and respect, a new voice joined the conversation. "He has no choice, Fyclan. He must keep her," the Duke of Baynton said from the doorway.

Gavin walked into the room, accompanied by his mother. Marcella rushed to Elin and threw her arms around her. "You poor child. What a horrible ordeal. Fyclan, we are so lucky my sons could save her."

"We are," he agreed. "And thank you, Your Grace, for the part you played in rescuing my daughter."

"Actually, if it had been up to me," Gavin said, "Elin would have been kidnapped, and you would be reading a ransom note at his moment for twenty-five thousand pounds and the sure knowledge that Morris had no intention of setting her free. Ben is the reason she is hale and hearty."

"You were there," Ben said, wanting to give his brother credit.

"I would have driven past the hack without a second glance," Gavin answered. "And it is for that reason I finally understood."

"Understood what?" their mother asked.

Instead of answering her, Gavin crossed to Elin. "Miss Morris, I apologize in advance for choosing a less private moment to discuss this matter, but I find I must cry off."

Elin gave a sound that was part relief and part gasp for joy.

"You see," Gavin continued, "I will never love

you as fully as my brother does. He knew you were in that hack and in trouble. It is as if he could feel your spirit. Furthermore, there isn't a man, woman, or child on Pall Mall today who couldn't see the deep affection the two of you feel for each other. And I found myself thinking, I want that. I want a woman who would kiss me with such un-restrained passion. I want a woman who would defy her parent and society for me. So, for those reasons, I cannot marry you, Miss Morris. We are not suitable. Fyclan, I pray you accept my broth-er's suit for your daughter's hand. He can be a pain in my backside, but he is also one of the most remarkable men I know."

Ben reached out and took his brother's hand. But that was not enough. An arm reached out, then another, and, for the first time in their lives, they shared a brotherly hug.

Their mother beamed her approval, then she said to Elin, "My dear girl, you've been jilted."

Elin laughed her response.

"There will be talk," Fyclan predicted.

"Elin and I don't mind what anyone says," Ben assured him as he placed his arm around her.

Fyclan noticed the familiar arm. With a fatherly wag of his finger, he silently ordered a bit of dis-tance, and Ben happily complied—although he did take Elin's hand.

"There is always talk," Gavin said. "If anything,

I don't believe I'll mind being called a scoundrel a time or two. Might be a novel idea. In the past, Ben has been the one having all the fun."

"However, if *you* feel right about it," their mother said to Gavin, "and Elin and Ben have no complaints, and Fyclan and I seem happy—which we are, aren't we, Fyclan?"

"I will live with it," he answered, but his smile said he was not displeased.

"Well then, why should we give a care what the world thinks?" Marcella finished.

She held out her hand to Fyclan. He rose and joined their circle—and in that moment, Ben discovered true happiness.

He had his family. He had the respect of his brother, and, in return, he trusted Gavin.

Best of all, he had Elin. Vibrant Elin. His love.

Had she once wondered at the purpose of life? Well, he could tell her the answer now. The sole purpose to a meaningful life was to love and to be loved.

That was what made living good.

Very good indeed.

Marcella,
Dowager Duchess of Baynton

Announces that the

wedding breakfast

celebrating the marriage of

Miss Elin Tarleton Morris

to

Gavin Thornhill Alexander
Whitridge, Duke of Baynton

has been canceled.

Kindly disregard your invitation.

**Lord Benedict Dunston
James Whitridge**

will marry

Miss Elin Tarleton Morris

Tuesday, 12 November, 1811.

**The Dowager Duchess of Baynton
and Mr. Fyclan Morris**

request the honor of your presence

at the wedding breakfast at 2 p.m.

R.S.V.P. Menheim House

Epilogue

$\mathcal{O}$f course, the sending of both announcements simultaneously was unconventional.

Gavin found he rather enjoyed the moment they were delivered as busy noses raced around London wanting to know all the details. The men in their club rooms were worse than the women.

All parties involved, Ben and Elin, Fyclan, Marcella, and Gavin made a point of being seen together on the day of delivery. They dined at a popular hotel and attended several soirees afterward.

Ben and Elin married by special license a week after the date Gavin was to have married her.

As a sacrament, the ceremony was strictly for family. The wedding breakfast would be a celebration for guests. His mother used the same list she'd planned for Gavin's along with several of Ben's military friends. No one sent their regrets.

What had once been hailed as the Match of the Century—the joining of a wealthy dukedom to an even wealthier estate—had now become the Wedding of the Century because there was so much speculation over it. Many who had already sojourned to their country estates for the winter holidays returned to town just for the occasion.

To further confuse Society, Gavin served as a witness to the marriage. Gavin knew there were whispers but not the sort damning him, which he had anticipated. The tittle-tattlers were shocked but not because they had heard Gavin had jilted Elin.

No, they were astounded that Elin preferred Ben over a duke.

Gavin found the gossips puzzling.

Any other gentleman would have been branded a scoundrel for reneging on his promise to a lady. When Gavin did it, Society appeared to rejoice. He was actually congratulated.

He said as much to his mother who answered, "Oh, Gavin, you have given a brigade of mothers new hope. They are all telling their daughters to set their caps for you. And while they may shake their heads and say 'Poor, Elin,' they are happy to have her out of the way. Mark my words for it."

She was right. Over the weeks after the announcement came out, Gavin was deluged with invitations to routs and balls. His peers cornered him in his clubs or while he was walking Westminster's halls to sing the virtues of a daughter, sister, niece, or cousin.

The Duke of Baynton was on the Marriage Market. All of London rejoice! The coming season had never been more promising. Someone *must* bag the Duke of Baynton, and a bevy of women had decided they would be his next duchess.

Gavin began to feel besieged.

However, at the wedding breakfast, where Ben and Elin glowed with their happiness and glittering company happily drank his wine and ate his food, Gavin discovered he was lonely.

This wasn't the first time. The title kept him set apart. Having Ben's friendship helped, but Gavin felt a discontent . . . and it had started when he'd witnessed Elin kiss Ben in the middle of Pall Mall.

No one had ever kissed him, period. Nor had he felt great passion for any woman before.

Gavin had only let himself think of Elin, and his thoughts hadn't been particularly passionate, he realized. She'd always been in the background of his life, one of many expectations. He'd admired her, hungered for female companionship as much as he could let his guard down on that account, but he had never had strong feelings for her. Furthermore, his admiration was a thin shadow of emotion compared to the one on display every time Ben looked at her.

There again, unlike so many of his contemporaries who patronized brothels or kept mistresses, Gavin had not yet been initiated into the rites of Venus. His father had kept him busy and always under his control. The old duke had been strict, puritanical almost. Gavin had never been given the opportunity for a licentious adventure and, in truth, it had seemed meaningless because he was to have married Elin years ago.

So Gavin had staved off charged, discomforting feelings with work or any of a number of physical pursuits, such as boxing or fencing.

But observing the kiss she and Ben had shared had brought those feelings roaring to the forefront, and he knew he'd best marry soon, or he might tempted to do the sort of thing his father had always warned him against—appear vulnerable.

"Gavin?" His mother's voice intruded upon his doubts.

He put a smile on his face. "Yes, Mother?"

She stood with Dame Imogen, his great-aunt. The dame was a diminutive woman dressed in purple from her shoes to her turban, which sported a jewel the size of pigeon egg holding a curling feather in place.

"Is the wine not to your liking?" his mother asked.

"What?" he said, confused.

"You've been standing here holding the glass without touching it. I didn't know if it displeased you."

"No, it is fine." Gavin took a sip to demonstrate.

She smiled, then raised the subject that was her true reason for speaking to him. "Your aunt and I have been talking. We are going to find you a wife. A wonderful wife."

"Yes, one with lineage," Dame Imogen said with a sniff. She was the sort who would always see Fyclan Morris as an interloper. She rarely praised anyone whose ancestry didn't stretch back to the Conqueror.

"We are going to open the coming season with a ball," Marcella announced. "One that every marriageable young woman will want to attend."

"I'll vet the young debutantes for you," Aunt Imogen assured him. "We'll catch you the best of the lot."

Gavin's first reaction was to demur. He wasn't certain he wanted this much attention paid to his search for a wife.

But as he shifted his weight, he felt the weight of the pearls he'd once put around Elin's neck in his pocket. They had been his gift to her the night of their betrothal ball.

Right before saying her vows to Ben, she'd given them back to Gavin before meeting Ben.

Those pearls now deserved a home. A beautiful home.

"And exactly what will you be looking for in my wife?" Gavin asked the women.

"*Breeding.*" Imogen spit out the word.

"And manners," his mother agreed. "But also, a woman who is lovely and strong and will give you sons and daughters, a healthy family."

Children. Gavin wanted them. He had a responsibility to his title to procreate. Many of his friends his age already had several.

His eye fell on Ben and Elin.

They stood off to the side and were kissing again. In truth, Ben struggled to keep his hands off of his new bride.

She acted eager as well. If they kept going the way they were, they would have a gaggle of children before Gavin had even started.

The old competitive feelings with his brother returned.

Gavin looked to his mother. "Kissable," he said. "My bride should be kissable."

"Kissable?" Dame Imogen frowned as if he was stating the obvious. "Of course. We want babies from this marriage."

And so did Gavin.

"Very well," he said. "I approve the plan. Let us

throw a ball the likes of which London has never seen."

"And may the best woman become your duchess," his mother chimed in.

Gavin raised his glass. "As long as she is kissable."

Don't miss the next novel in
New York Times bestselling author
CATHY MAXWELL's
Marrying the Duke series

The Fairest of Them All

Coming May 2016!
Read on for a sneak peek . . .

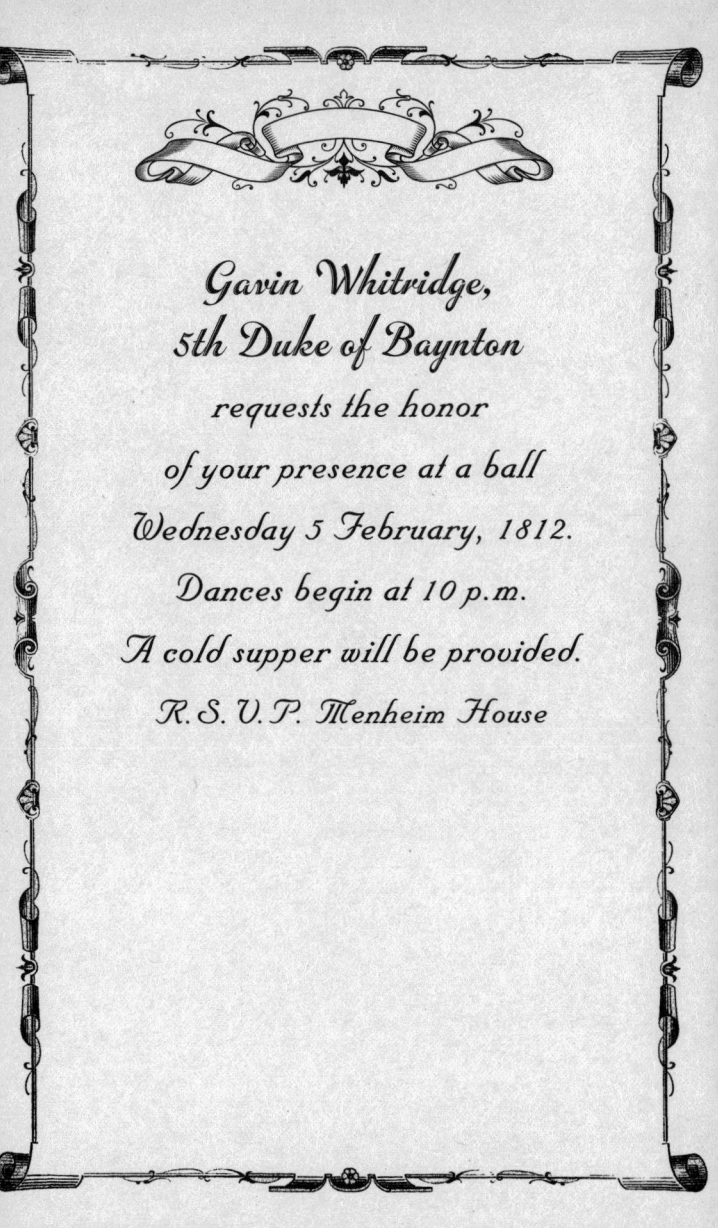

Gavin Whitridge,
5th Duke of Baynton

requests the honor

of your presence at a ball

Wednesday 5 February, 1812.

Dances begin at 10 p.m.

A cold supper will be provided.

R.S.V.P. Menheim House

What the devil had Gavin put himself into . . .

"Wellbourne," his great-aunt Imogen whispered, her voice still crisp in spite of quiet speaking. She referred to the tall, long faced man coming in the door with his wife and daughter to take his place in the receiving line. "Lady Amanda is the earl's only child—wrong politics, but loyal and well connected. A possibility."

Gavin had long respected Wellbourne's loyalty to his ideals, although he thought him deluded. Could he tolerate being related to the Opposition by marriage?

"Granted she is horse-faced like her sire," Imogen continued as if he could not see the obvious, "but her breeding is impeccable and she comes with an income of five thousand."

Not for the first time this evening was Gavin uncomfortable with his aunt's bluntness. Hopefully, the musicians in the ballroom covered his aunt's more acerbic comments, like the horse-facedness. Intent on finding Gavin a wife who met her high expectations, she'd maintained her cataloguing all evening as one proud family after another presented their daughters, nieces, even sisters and second cousins for Gavin's consideration.

And the line was endless. Gavin understood that it would be a fine thing to be a duchess, but this gambit to find him a wife was turning ridiculous. He felt as if he'd been standing there for hours. His mother, who had organized this ball, stood on Gavin's other side, her smile growing as strained as his own. As his hostess, he didn't believe she had *ever* invited so many people to an event at Menheim. Peers of the realm, his friends, and many mere acquaintances, all dressed in their finest, poured through his front door. Each touted a flower of English womanhood for Gavin's perusal before happily tottering off to drink his punch and devour his food. These weren't guests. They were locusts.

Of course, the idea for a ball was not an unsound one. Gavin was a busy man. There were affairs of state that needed his immediate attention. Britain was at war with France, a conflict that extended to almost every corner of the world. Meanwhile, domestic issues threatened to erupt into violence if not finessed soon. And as if Gavin didn't have enough concerns, the Prime Minister insisted on his guidance with an American delegation that had been expected months ago and had yet to show.

Gawd, the Americans. The damn upstarts thought to bully Britain out of her holdings. They wanted all of North America and would settle for nothing less. They said one thing out of the left side of their mouths and something completely different out of the right.

Still, Gavin needed a wife. It was time. He was thirty-two years of age. He was ready.

In fact, *past* ready. While other men had indulged themselves in wildly wicked ways, Gavin had been the dutiful heir to a dukedom. He'd not wenched. He had morals. He was known for his character. No bastards would muddy his line for the simple reason that he had yet to give in to base impulses and "know" a woman, as the theologians were wont to say.

But he wanted to. He wanted to very much.

However first, he must survive this travesty and Imogen's strong opinions.

If a young woman had the right connections and bloodlines, Imogen might dismiss her for what he believed were flimsy reasons.

"Unsuitable," Imogen asserted in Gavin's ear when Miss Vivian Dorchester was presented to him.

"Because she is petite?"

"Because you are tall."

"But the last one was tall and you rejected her."

"*Too* tall," Imogen argued. "The portraits of you together will look odd."

"I'm choosing my wife for how she will look in portraits?" Gavin replied in disbelief, annoyed beyond reason.

His aunt smiled her complete conviction. "The portraits will outlast both of your lives. Do you wish future generations to find you fodder for jests? To mock your images?"

To worry about what his descendents thought long after he was gone sounded outlandish to Gavin, until he remembered the numerous quips and jibes he and his brothers had made about the ancestors already hanging on the Menheim's walls.

"You definitely," his aunt continued, "don't want a petite wife. Yes, they are attractive bits, but you run a danger of breeding runts. And is that what you want in your son?"

Gavin could have replied he just wanted to breed . . . but in truth, he was as picky as his aunt, well, when it came to looks or figure. Imogen was more a stickler for the family bloodlines. The duke of Marlborough's niece was not good enough for her. However, the Most Reverend Berk's family could be traced back to the Conqueror so his oldest daughter had possibilities in Imogen's eyes. Gavin tried not to stare at her mustache.

Money was also of little consequence to either of them. Gavin was a very wealthy man.

Of course, if he could have his choice . . .

Gavin's jealous gaze drifted down this interminable receiving line where his brother Ben stood with his new wife Elin. They were very happy in their love. Elin was to have been Gavin's, even though they hadn't really known each other. The betrothal had been arranged by their parents more than two decades ago.

However, Elin had wanted more. She'd wanted a man who loved her with Ben's devotion and Gavin had reluctantly let her go.

Now, he found himself on the hunt for—what? Love? What the devil was that?

His fate was to marry out of obligation and duty, hence Aunt Imogen's whispered cataloguing of each young woman's assets without respect to their, hmmmm, well, what Gavin and any other male in the room would consider *assets*.

At the same time, Gavin had a sense he, like Elin, wanted more. The word *kissable* came to mind as did the thought of companionship. He longed for a helpmate. Ducal responsibilities wore a man down. Gavin could only bear so much alone—

A prickling of awareness tickled the hairs at the nape of his neck. He looked to the door and his gaze honed in upon a young woman waiting her turn in the receiving line. Woman? Goddess was a better description.

She was not too tall and not too petite but exactly right.

Her eyes were a sparkling blue, as clear as pieces of cut glass. Her hair was so blonde it was close to white, speaking to some Viking forbearer and her brows were dark, expressive. They added character to a face that would have been otherwise bland in its perfection. Her gown was layers of sheer white gauze trimmed in sky blue ribbons that emphasized the womanly curve of some of the best *assets* Gavin had ever seen.

She was undeniably kissable. Her lips were full and pink and, he was certain, very sweet.

Gavin's mouth went dry. His knees turned weak. For the first time in his life, he had the urge to toss aside all veneer of civilization, throw this woman over his shoulder, and carry her off to his bed.

Aunt Imogen noticed the direction of his interest. Her voice purred with satisfaction as she confided, "This is one I wanted you to particularly meet. The late Lord Dearne's only child, Lady Charlene."

"Dearne? The profligate?"

"And buried years ago for his sins. He left his wife and daughter destitute. However, their bloodlines are the purest in the realm. Their stock is hardy. Look at the hips on that child. She will bear many sons."

Gavin couldn't stop staring at her hips or any other part of her. "And the portraits?"

"Will be spectacular," Imogen promised.

And then Lady Charlene stood in front of him.

His aunt introduced them as if he wasn't ready to fall into her arms and beg her to kiss him. The tops of breasts swelled against her bodice with the graceful movement of her curtsey and Gavin could barely stifle the rush of desire.

He barely heard his aunt introduce him to Lady Charlene's chaperone. He wasn't interested in her. His focus was on the beauty before him.

Lady Charlene—even her name was lush and full. He took her gloved hand and helped her rise.

She appraised him frankly and with the promise of a good intelligence and he realized she was waiting for him to speak. Everyone was waiting for him.

On the morrow, he was certain the papers and

anyone witnessing this meeting between them would claim he'd been smitten—and they would be right.

"Welcome to my home," he managed to say.

"Thank you, Your Grace. It is an honor."

Her voice surprised him. There was a huskiness to it, a unique, melodic timbre.

Out of the corner of his eye, he caught his aunt exchange a knowing glance with his mother. They approved. *He* approved.

He was cognizant that they were holding up the receiving line. He didn't care. In fact, he was done with this nonsense. He'd found *his* woman. Let the dancing begin and let him stake his claim by leading her first onto the dance floor.

Gavin looked for Henry to signal the receiving line was officially at an end. The waiting guests could meander their own way in. However, the always present butler was missing from his post by the door. Instead, there was the sound of stern words and indications by the number of footmen moving toward the door that there was a disturbance.

Gavin stepped forward, placing himself between the door and the ladies even as Henry burst through the knot of footmen and waiting guests. He strode to Gavin's side. "Your Grace, there is a difficulty."

"With whom?"

"The American delegation has arrived and wishes to present himself to you."

"I have no time for thorny Americans." For the first time in Gavin's life, he was done with duty and obligation. He desired to spend an evening basking in the company of a woman. He did not want to discuss negotiations, or business, or favors. "Tell them to present themselves to my secretary on the morrow. He will schedule a meeting."

But Henry didn't bow and obey. He leaned close to Gavin. "With all due respect Your Grace, you may wish to meet this man."

"Not tonight," Gavin repeated, his tone alone making it clear he was in no mood for argument.

He turned to Lady Charlene who had not stayed safely behind him but had moved to his side, obviously curious about the disruption. "My lady, would you honor me with this first dance?"

But before she could answer, the American literally muscled his way through the door, several footmen gingerly holding on to his arms as if both determined and uncertain about holding him back—and in the blink of an eye, Gavin understood why.

Of course this man would not wait in any line, any more than Gavin himself would.

Lady Charlene vanished from Gavin's mind.

The spectators in the crowded front hall all faded from his view as did the humming of voices in the ballroom and the strains of music.

The "American" was tall and dressed in plain clothing. His jacket was one that had been worn many times before but he filled it well. His overlong dark hair touched his collar in contrary to any style on either side of the Atlantic.

He gave the impression of being headstrong and proud, something Gavin knew to be true because he understood this man well. He even knew his name before it could be announced

Gavin and Jack were not identical twins, but enough alike in appearance that people would immediately recognize them as brothers—even now, over fifteen years after Jack had vanished without fanfare from his bed at school.

His disappearance had been the great mystery of that year. Their father had hired men to search for him and they'd found not a trace of his whereabouts or even a clue as to why he would go off in the middle of the night.

Bones had been found during that time in a shallow grave not far from the school. Some believed they were Jack's. Experts their father had hired to evaluate them could not reach a consensus.

But Gavin had known. In his heart of hearts, he'd always believed his twin was alive. No one knew Jack better than Gavin. They had shared the same womb, the same mother's beating heart. In their childhood, there had always been just the two of them, in spite of their brother Ben's birth eight years later.

And now here they were, face-to-face.

At last.

There were no hello's, no outstretched hands, or brotherly hugs. Instead, they squared off, stoic men, men much like their sire.

In a voice as familiar to Gavin as his own, Jack said what Gavin and all who had been listening already knew, "I'm the American delegation."

Their mother swooned.

_G_ive in to your Impulses!

These unforgettable stories only take a second to buy and give you hours of reading pleasure!

Go to _www.AvonImpulse.com_ and see what we have to offer.

Available wherever e-books are sold.

AVONIM